Dr. Poggioli:
CRIMINOLOGIST

Dr. Poggioli: CRIMINOLOGIST

T.S. STRIBLING

Edited by
Arthur Vidro

Crippen & Landru Publishers
Norfolk, Virginia
2004

Copyright © 2004 by Kathryn Gaddes, Amelia Hughes, Dorothy Myhr, and Theodore J. Warken

Lost Classics cover and jacket design by Deborah Miller

Cover painting by Barbara Mitchell

Crippen & Landru logo by Eric D. Greene

We are very grateful to Joseph Wrzos for locating, and sending to us, the previously unrecorded Poggioli story, "The Newspaper." His generosity has contributed greatly to this book.

ISBN: 1-932009-24-8 (cloth edition)
ISBN: 1-932009-25-6 (trade softcover edition)

FIRST EDITION

Crippen & Landru Publishers
P. O. Box 9315
Norfolk, VA 23505
USA

E-mail: info@crippenlandru.com
Web: www.crippenlandru.com

Contents

Introduction by Arthur Vidro	7
A Pearl at Pampatar	17
Shadowed	30
The Resurrection of Chin Lee	85
Bullets	101
The Cablegram	114
The Pink Colonnade	128
Private Jungle	146
The Shadow	163
The Newspaper	177
A Poggioli Bibliography	193

INTRODUCTION

Poggioli's Origins

It all started with a Camay soap salesman.

But I get ahead of myself.

Thomas Sigismund Stribling is chiefly remembered today for two reasons. He won a Pulitzer Prize in 1933 for his novel of the previous year, *The Store*. And he won critical acclaim for his 1929 short-story collection, *Clues of the Caribbees*, quirky mysteries starring one Henry Poggioli.

If Stribling hadn't won the Pulitzer, it is doubtful that libraries today would still stock any of his books. Even with the Pulitzer, he is largely forgotten, even among collectors of 20th century literature.

But the mystery world will never fully forget him. *Clues of the Caribbees* was recommended in the two most important guides to collecting detective fiction: "The Haycraft-Queen Definitive Library of Detective-Crime-Mystery Fiction" (compiled by Howard Haycraft and Ellery Queen) and (Ellery) "Queen's Quorum," the latter honoring the best short-story collections in the detection field. A book included on either of those influential lists will always be sought after by collectors.

Additional praise came from critic Anthony Boucher, who included *Clues of the Caribbees* in his "Silver 13" list of the 13 best detective short-story collections published between 1920 and 1945; and from James Sandoe, who included it in his "Reader's Guide to Crime."

Though critically acclaimed, the book did not sell well. As Stribling explained in his autobiography: "I have at home a row of detective anthologies, each collection containing one of these [*Caribbees*] stories. They were never popular on their own as a single book, but they were quite popular torn all to pieces. Just what one would make out of that, I don't know; are they the flavoring in the cake, or the drop of deplorably scented ambergris in the perfume vials?"

In 1965, the year of his death (at age 84), Stribling stated: "I had a funny series of detective stories about one Henry Poggioli, Ph.D., LLD, Doctor of Criminology, and Professor of Criminology in the Ohio State University. The reason I made him from Ohio State was to prevent him being from Harvard, Yale, or Princeton, not to mention the fact that I rescued him from the still greater dangers of Oxford, Cambridge, and the Sorbonne."

Now we come to the Camay soap salesman.

Still in 1965, Stribling stated: "The actual reason why I ever started Dr. Henry Poggioli on his career of illustrious obtuseness was quite personal. A boy had come down to Clifton [Tennessee, Stribling's hometown] from the North to visit my girl. When he was gone, I used the name Poggioli, which vaguely resembled that of the interloper, wrote these stories of dumbness, and read them to Louella. They amused her very much and we got married."

The interloper from the North was a traveling salesman who peddled Camay soap.

The Original Five Stories

Perhaps Stribling exaggerated. Or he repeated a legend that had evolved away from accuracy. For although the very first Poggioli story does indeed contain an unlikeable soap salesman, it isn't Poggioli.

The five stories in *Clues of the Caribbees* were first published in *Adventure* magazine in 1925 and 1926, and collected in book form by Doubleday, Doran in 1929. The stories, often with exotic elements, each take place on a different Caribbean island. The islands are brought to life by Stribling, who had visited South America earlier in the decade.

The humor of the Poggioli series is evidenced on the first page of the debut story, "The Refugees": "Deposed presidents flying out of Venezuela are a fairly ordinary phenomenon in the West Indies."

Set on the island of Curacao, "The Refugees" concerns a death by poison at the Hotel Saragossa, whose international guests include two Americans; one, a traveling soap salesman, upon hearing of the death, says: "It's a shame we can't go in and look at the body. I paid my three bucks a day here, and they told me it included everything." The unnamed salesman later offers to defend the murder suspect, Pompalone, a deposed Venezuelan dictator. Upon learning the salesman's business, Pompalone says: "I am afraid you lack the reasoning faculty if you are trying to sell soap in the West Indies. Is there anyone else?" That's when Poggioli offers his assistance, and we get our first glimpse of him, as "a smallish dark-eyed gentleman of a certain academic appearance." Poggioli is an instructor in psychology on sabbatical from Ohio State University.

The soap salesman's arrogance to the native employees and offensiveness to the hotel's management position him to become poison victim number two, but Poggioli saves his life just in time.

During the investigation, Poggioli proves himself open-minded: "Not that I agree with Senor Pompalone, but I recognize his hypothesis as tenable." Poggioli is thorough: "In solving a problem, it is our duty to pursue every line of evidence."

But Poggioli is not a patient man. As Stribling says: "The psychologist's patience was of academic brevity."

Poggioli's deductions, often brilliant, are not always correct; and even when correct don't always lead to success. In "The Refugees," after Poggioli solves the case and correctly proves Pompalone innocent, Pompalone commits murder and escapes the island.

Poggioli then goes to Haiti in "The Governor of Cap Haitien." To gain Poggioli safe admittance to the anti-government forces, the governor dubs Poggioli "the great American voodoo inspector" and sends him to the enemy's camp. The explanation given to, and accepted by, the awe-struck populace is: "You know the Americans inspect everything." In that tale, more novelette than short story, Poggioli shows an anti-imperialistic view, which he expresses to a man named Clay who represents the foreign interests on the island: "Had it ever struck you, Mr. Clay, that fifty or a hundred thousand [native] persons ought to be allowed to run their own country in their own way and not be forced to arrange their political life for the convenience of two dozen foreigners?" Once again Poggioli solves the crime but the case ends far from successfully; nobody but Mr. Clay gets what they want.

Poggioli goes to Martinique, and after several mistakes neatly solves "The Prints of Hantoun," featuring a Golden Age-style puzzle: how was it possible for the bank thief to have worn gloves and yet to have left fingerprints? During the case, Poggioli muses: "Who has investigated the influence of music on crime? It is quite possible that some tunes incite robbery, some murder, others assault. If we could learn this we might formulate laws forbidding certain airs and thus protect the morals of the people." Three generations later, the U.S. Congress, to protect the morals of the people, would consider laws regulating the music industry because of crime-encouraging musical lyrics. Also in this tale, Poggioli confesses that he is a better crime solver when the guilty are rich: "I don't know the psychology of the miserable. I am an American."

Poggioli goes to Barbados in "Cricket" and fails miserably at solving a murder; but it does get solved. In the next day's newspaper, each person who contributed to the solution attributes their detections to Poggioli, who, ego overflowing, mistakenly believes he had brilliantly solved another.

Poggioli goes to Trinidad in "A Passage to Benares" and ends up the chief suspect in the murder of a child bride. After being arrested and jailed, Poggioli solves this extremely suspenseful tale, in which his initial investigations turned up more and more evidence against himself, tightening the noose around his own neck. It shows Stribling and Poggioli at their finest; it was adapted for radio and broadcast as an episode of "Suspense" (on September 23, 1942). The third-from-last paragraph has Poggioli asking: "What did you mean, keeping me locked up here when you knew I was an innocent man?" The answer is as chilling as any ending in detective fiction history.

In these five cases, Poggioli was a brilliant but fallible sleuth whose failures formed an ironic commentary not only on the standard deductive detective story but also on the limits of human reason. And, whatever else might be read into Poggioli's failures, it was clear that "A Passage to Benares" allowed no room for further cases.

The Second Cycle of Poggioli Stories

From 1929 through 1935, nevertheless, Stribling published nine more Poggioli stories, which have all been gathered into the book you now hold. It is only the third Stribling short-story collection, ever.

The new series began in 1929 when *Adventure* asked their most popular authors to contribute stories for its anniversary, and Stribling responded with a Poggioli tale, "A Pearl at Pampatar," still set in the Caribbean and perhaps taking place before "A Passage to Benares." This time Poggioli deduces the whereabouts of a stolen pearl on an island named Margarita, while trying in vain to persuade Mrs. Gelleman that it takes more than dreaming and wishful thinking to change an imitation pearl into a real one. For the rest of his recorded career, Poggioli would stay away from the Caribbean islands.

Like their predecessors, the eight 1930s Poggioli stories are laced with humor and permeated with psychological insights and philosophical musings. But the 1930s stories are less exotic, less adventurous, less panoramic. Poggioli no longer runs around foreign lands. Only once do we see him at Ohio State. He stays where Stribling stayed. Stribling lived in Tennessee and Florida and occasionally visited New York or Mexico. Poggioli's post-*Caribbees* cases take place in Tennessee and Florida, with an occasional trip to New York or Mexico. The 1930s tales are confined, neat, narrow in scope though deep in story, character, and psychology.

The post-Caribbean stories begin with "Shadowed," which in dealing with the survival of the soul may have been Stribling's way of bringing Poggioli back after the devastating conclusion of "A Passage to Benares," but, with its mystical elements, "Shadowed" defies simple explanation or straightforward summary. Here's what little I dare tell you: it is set in Columbus, Ohio, and is the only story where Poggioli can be found working at Ohio State University; it is the tale that prompted Ohio State and Poggioli to part ways; it has a different voice than the earlier tales, for instead of third-person omniscience we are given Stribling as the chronicler of events based upon his examination of the written record of the case (but not as someone who participated in or witnessed the events, nor even as someone who necessarily knows Poggioli firsthand). In "Shadowed" the impossible happens with great regularity and without neat resolution; Poggioli makes physical and psychological deductions galore; he pithily waxes philosophic ("Cynicism is a shield, not a sword."); but in the end the case defies credible solution, so Poggioli gives us an incredible solution. "Shadowed" is the most ambitious (though not the most satisfying) of the Poggioli tales; it is simultaneously Poggioli's strangest case, his greatest case, and his fall from grace.

The remaining stories follow the model of fictional detection more closely. "The Shadow" is tightly written. It contains only two characters—Poggioli and a bank clerk, plus a cameo appearance by a process server. Poggioli rattles off psychological deduction after psychological deduction. Some seem far-fetched. But the pace is fast, just about every sentence is in dialogue, and the clues are all psychological, never physical.

Not so with "Bullets," which touches upon the then-relatively-new science of ballistics. But, as ever, psychological deductions carry the day; such as how fear of being accused of theft would influence the behavior of an innocent Negro in a white man's store in the deep South. Indeed, as I shall point out shortly, this powerful story depends on Stribling's knowledge of racism.

"The Cablegram" is the most taut Poggioli story I have read. It is extremely confined and would require hardly any effort to be turned into an effective one-act play. The cast includes Poggioli, a Miami customs official named Slidenberry, and our old friend Pompalone—the exiled dictator cleared of murder by Poggioli a decade earlier in "The Refugees." This time the suspected crime is smuggling. The tale is brilliantly constructed. The culprit outwits Poggioli, who reaches the true solution too late.

Sequels, though common enough in novels, are rare in short stories. But Stribling twice penned sequels to his Poggioli tales. The first sequel, "The Newspaper," picks up where "The Cablegram" leaves off, with Poggioli and team continuing their pursuit of the smuggler and eventually cracking a dope ring. (His second sequel would appear eleven years later, when "A Note to Count Jalacki" followed the superb "Count Jalacki Goes Fishing.")

"Private Jungle," gloriously illustrated by John F. Clymer in its original *Blue Book* appearance, shows Poggioli in sharp form, saving a life, preventing an act of vengeance, and possibly ending a feud. This time our sleuth deftly fuses clues both psychological and physical. There is a funny misunderstanding between Poggioli and Jim R., who believes a criminologist is someone who helps people commit crimes.

The humor in the Poggioli tales is character-driven and has aged well. In "The Resurrection of Chin Lee" Poggioli's host asks him to keep private whatever murder solution he might arrive at, because it would be bad publicity for the community—unless the killer or victim was very rich, in which case a lot of tourists would pop in for the trial. Humor also reigns when Poggioli asks the night watchman if he heard the shot; the watchman explains that when he's on duty it takes more than a pistol shot to wake him up. This tale contains a rare example of a Golden Age detective (Poggioli) making reference to the Great Depression going on around them.

The Depression rears its head more prominently in "The Pink Colonnade," in which Poggioli investigates the psychologically strange disappearance of a man who once was worth ten million dollars but who can no longer afford gasoline for his speedboat. This tale suggests Poggioli regards himself more as a criminologist and a psychologist than as a detective.

The Final Stories

The autumn of 1941 marked the debut issue of *Ellery Queen's Mystery Magazine*, the first issue of which reprinted "The Cablegram." Its editor, Frederic Dannay (one-half of the Ellery Queen writing team and a huge fan of Poggioli), requested that Stribling begin a new series of Poggioli tales. Stribling undertook the challenge and in 1945, after a ten-year hiatus, new Poggioli stories began to appear. Amazingly, Stribling's only published pieces of new fiction from 1940 onward were the 23 Poggioli short stories that appeared from 1945 to 1957. Although Stribling continued to write fiction for the rest of his life and completed several more novels, those novels were never published.

Stribling got along well with Dannay, a hands-on editor, and allowed him considerable leeway in shaping the final versions of the Poggioli stories. As a result, Poggioli himself developed. In the words of Stribling biographer Kenneth W. Vickers:

"Under the tutelage of Fred Dannay, the erstwhile bumbling former professor of psychology and amateur criminologist became a sleuth of near superhuman ability. . . . Poggioli's brilliance reached the level that he read the morning papers looking for clues to crimes, solved the mystery, and then waited for one of the principals in the case to come to him for help."

Stribling himself commented on the evolution of Poggioli: "All the other detectives were so brilliant I thought a dunce would be a relief to thousands of earnest who-dun-it readers. Now a mystery writer may start out with the most honorable intentions of making his protagonist a punk, but the first thing he knows practice will make his hero grow brighter and brighter until in no time at all he knows far more than his author does. That is what happened to me and Poggioli. I now stand in awe of him. I shudder to offer him the semblance of a clew for I know that he will unravel my whole mystery in the twinkling of a ballerina's toe; then I—I—will have to construct more mystery to make the story long enough to sell. It's a dog's life catering to such a genius."

The final 23 stories differ greatly in one way from all the previous Poggioli tales: instead of the standard third-person narration that was used to follow Poggioli through the 1920s and 1930s (with a slight variation for "Shadowed"), Stribling now inserted himself into the tales as Poggioli's friend, companion, and chronicler, telling the tales from the point of view of a secondary character. In effect, Stribling becomes Watson to Poggioli's Holmes. Given the characters' personalities, a better comparison would be Stribling becomes Captain Hastings to Poggioli's Poirot. The unnamed Stribling character in these tales, though an accomplished writer, is even more a simpleton than Hastings. Witness this exchange from "The Mystery of the Chief of Police":

Poggioli: Miss Eliot lost new fresh bills. The police department returned dirty bills. What caused that?

Stribling: Mm—mm . . . well . . . the thief got her bills dirty.

In "A Note to Count Jalacki" the Stribling character is referred to by the others as "a man of no talent whatever."

The observations of the Stribling character, and the interplay between him and Poggioli, give these tales an extra appeal; we get closer to Poggioli by seeing how he treats (or mistreats) his friend; and having a slow-to-comprehend sidekick gives Poggioli more reason to vocalize his deductions.

Fifteen of those later tales were collected into one volume in 1975 by Dover Publications, but several remain uncollected. I heartily recommend three of those later tales as prime examples of vintage Poggioli—"The Mystery of the Chief of Police," "Count Jalacki Goes Fishing," and "The Mystery of Andorous Enterprises." In each, Poggioli takes disparate elements with no conceivable connection and shows how truly interwoven they are. Along with the much earlier "A Passage to Benares," these are stories that ought never to go out of print (but, alas, already have).

The weaving together of disparate elements is Stribling's modus operandi. In his autobiography, *Laughing Stock*, Stribling commented on his short, unhappy, unsuccessful foray into journalism: "I had no interest in news. Single isolated happenings did not attract my attention; to command my pen they had to be a series of closely connected events that led up to a situation." Likewise was Stribling's approach to the Poggioli tales.

What Makes Poggioli Tick

Ellery Queen once wrote: "Poggioli's trial-and-error deductions are unorthodox and humorous, but successful." He described Poggioli as having "an impersonal attitude towards his clients" and judged the author's style as "cunning—factual, conversational, and yet he shows a complete grasp of Southern character, builds up an authentic atmosphere."

Two other elements make the Poggioli series special. One is Stribling's mastery of social observation. He can, for instance, paint a scene where people of different nationalities dine at the same table; describe in detail the dining methods peculiar to each land; and then show how each diner is repulsed by the habits of the others. Or he might quietly point out that wares in the market on a particular island are sold by the pile, without regard to weight or measure.

The second special element lies within Poggioli himself. We tend to see him as a detective, a professor, a psychologist; but equally valid is Poggioli as a philosopher. In any story Poggioli can start philosophizing, as he did this way in "The Refugees": "What we call our reason is never the fatally sure, mathematical progression we fancy it is. If you will examine reason in the making you will find it a very cloudy process, a kind of blind jumping among hypotheses. When it finally hits the right one, it then proceeds to build a logical bridge from its point of departure to its goal, and it imagines it has crossed on that bridge, but it has not. The bridge was flung out afterward." Those who enjoy such speculations will surely enjoy Poggioli.

Race, Dialect, and "Nigger"

It is hard to read some of these stories without stirring a certain race-consciousness. The author asserts that whites and blacks differ in ways unrelated to skin pigment—such as the sound of their laughter.

Nevertheless, Stribling was ahead of his time in depicting race relations, especially in his breakthrough novel, *Birthright* (The Century Co., 1922). Edward Piacentino, a modern scholar in southern literature, wrote about *Birthright*: "Stribling dared to portray the black man and his plight sympathetically, emphatically showing him to be a helpless object of hatred and oppression, an individual denied political and social equality . . . Stribling in *Birthright* sharply disparages all his white characters, making it emphatically clear that they are responsible for the black man's dehumanizing existence."

Birthright is the story of Peter Siner, a Harvard-educated young black man who encounters great difficulties after returning to his small Southern hometown to build a school for blacks. Although Siner, a black, speaks with intelligence and dignity, his black neighbors, uneducated and untraveled, often speak in dialect, as do some of the black and oriental and other characters in the Poggioli stories. For instance, the mother of the accused killer in "Bullets," rooting for the pending ballistics results to help her son Slewfoot's defense, prays: "Oh, Lawd, let dem bullets be jes' alike an' save po' Slewfoot." Yet the power of "Bullets" as a detective story and as a story of human conflict is based on Stribling's knowledge of race relations in Florida during the 1930s. We learn that a black man "done what he was told—he was a nigger." But Poggioli remains above the racism and the racial epithets, while knowing their effects. "Negroes," he explains, "don't walk behind white men's counters. They have been accused of stealing too many times when they were innocent for them to take a chance of being seen behind a white man's counter." "Bullets" is an uncomfortable story on several levels, and I think that Stribling hoped for that response from readers.

Stribling rendered accurately the speech patterns of all those around him, from the educated to those ethnic social groups who have been marginalized by society. It is not strictly the blacks but all poor people—white, brown, or yellow—whose speech is rendered phonetically. But no matter how much the dialect may reflect the reality of the time period, some readers will be offended.

Certain words that give offense today were standard in the early part of Poggioli's career. Although Stribling let his non-recurring characters speak the word "nigger," neither he himself nor Poggioli comes across as racist.

On the race question, Poggioli can speak for himself. In "The Governor of Cap Haitien" he is asked: "You don't believe a nigger is the equal of a white man, do you?" After giving the matter a moment's thought, Poggioli replies with a question of his own: "Do you believe the leopard is the equal of the polar bear, or the dodo the equal of the wallaby?" He is saying that, like peaches and carrots, the races are far too dissimilar for either to claim superiority—and this is where Stribling differed from his own time (he did not believe in the inferiority of blacks) and from our time (he did believe that the races are fundamentally different).

Stribling showed a strong social conscience. "Judge Lynch," a powerful short story without Poggioli, tackles the question of lynching—and this was in the 1930s South, before lynching had become quite so rare. The point is driven home that yes, maybe you can make a plausible case for lynching a black man suspected of a crime, but only if you were to lynch a white man just as eagerly and unhesitatingly when he is suspected of the same crime. Whatever the punishment should be for a particular crime, the skin color of the perpetrator should have nothing to do with the punishment imposed.

Final Point

One final point. Throughout his career, Poggioli was referred to as "Mr. Poggioli," "Dr. Poggioli," and "Professor Poggioli," all with roughly equal frequency. None of the appelations is wrong; it's personal preference. To me he will always be

Professor Poggioli. But on this question, too, Poggioli can speak for himself. In "A Passage to Benares" he says, "I am not a professor, I am simply a docent."

Hence this collection of *Doctor* Poggioli tales.

As for Stribling, who is buried in Clifton, Tennessee, the final word comes from his tombstone: "Through this dust these hills once spoke."

Arthur Vidro
April 2004

A Pearl at Pampatar

THE hot wind that blew across the town of Pampatar in the island of Margarita kept Mr. Henry Poggioli more or less marooned in the lobby of El Grand Hotel Rey Phillipe Segunda de Espagñe, and reduced him to conversation with Mrs. Gelleman. It was either that or read the paper backed Spanish novels which lay about on the tables; and, as the insides of the novels were as torrid as the outside of the hotel, Mr. Poggioli talked to Mrs. Gelleman.

On this particular morning she was saying:

"I had the oddest dream last night. I couldn't wait to tell you about it. I dreamed Mr. Gelleman gave me a large pearl. Does that mean he is really going to give me one, or do dreams go by contraries?"

"I daresay it doesn't mean much of anything."

Mrs. Gelleman lifted a penciled brow.

"I thought you were a psychologist?"

"That is my profession."

"And you don't know whether dreams go by contraries or not?"

"Dreams don't really 'go' at all. They are supposed to be more a reproduction of one's wishes and desires than a prophecy of the future."

The lady made a *moue* with her small buttonhole mouth.

"Good gracious, there's no use in dreaming; you already know what you want."

"No, I don't suppose dreaming could be listed as one of the gainful occupations."

The matron sat with disappointment on her round face because she had thus casually lost a pearl.

"Have I ever shown you my pearls, Mr. Poggioli?" Without waiting for an answer, she called aloud, "Chrysomallina! Oh Chrysomallina, bring my jewel case, will you? I'm down here in the lobby."

She looked with distaste at the dust blowing past the doors of the hotel.

"The only reason I keep Mr. Gelleman here in Margarita is to collect a necklace of real pearls for myself. Mr. Gelleman works for the pearl company, you know. My mother told me once that when I was born she had wanted a pearl necklace, very bad, she said, very bad . . . Do you believe I inherited that desire?"

"Probably not, a momentary desire like that."

"Doesn't psychology teach that whatever an expectant mother desires, her child will get?"

"That's a folk belief, but science has not adduced any proof—"

"Huh! It seems to me psychology misses out on everything a person is interested in."

The topic was dropped through the advent of Chrysomallina at the head of the staircase. She was one of those black West Indian Junos whose physical perfections are entirely overlooked because there are so many of them. As she glided down the steps with the carved jewel case in her ebony upspread hands she had a heraldic quality which her white overlords entirely neglected to observe.

As Mrs. Gelleman reached for the chest she moistened the small circle of her red lips with her tongue.

"Some of these pearls are real and some imitations. I try to think the imitations into real ones. The harder I keep my mind on making them real the sooner I'll get them. Doesn't psychology teach that?"

Mr. Poggioli pondered a moment just what Mrs. Gelleman meant, then answered with a grave face—

"So far as science has investigated, Mrs. Gelleman, no tendency has been detected in real pearls to substitute themselves for imitation pearls through the process of their owner's thinking."

"A Hindu mystic told me that, Mr. Poggioli," interrupted the lady tartly. "He said when I concentrated on an imitation pearl it helped my atman mold a real pearl and then—"

In the midst of this explanation the door was flung open and a black boy was blown in by the wind. He was out of breath.

"I was lookin'—for the Americano—who works voodoo—on t'ieves."

"You mean the psychologist," ejaculated Mrs. Gelleman in sympathetic excitement. "What sort of thieves?"

"Some black boy stole Mr. Gelleman's pearl."

"Oh goodness, what a shame! You know I despise a thief more than a snake . . . to take something that doesn't belong to . . . this is the man, he's the psychologist. Here, Chrysomallina, take my chest back to my room and lock it in my trunk!"

The black boy looked at Poggioli.

"He don't seem much like a voodoo doctor."

"American voodoo doctors never do, Taprobane," hurried Mrs. Gelleman. "Now direct Mr. Poggioli to my husband's office."

The jet Taprobane watched the retreating form of Chrysomallina.

"*Si, señora*; at the second turn let him take the third door on the left. Chrysomallina, where do you feel like you is goin'?" He made rather a graceful bow with his peaked head, at the same time keeping a respectful mien toward the whites.

"I feel like you is goin' back to the playa and show Señor Poggioli where Señor Gelleman's office is located," rebuked the black girl pointedly.

"Now, Chrysomallina, the gentleman is forced to know the pearl office is the third door on the second turn." He moved after the girl with a sidelong movement which kept him virtually attentive to the whites until distance should remove him from their influence.

Mrs. Gelleman walked to the door with the psychologist.

"To steal a pearl," she bewailed. "I think that's the worst sin . . . I hope you'll find it, Mr. Poggioli; anybody who would steal a pure, innocent pearl . . . I wonder if this has anything to do with my dream?"

"I shouldn't think so," said the psychologist, and he passed through the door.

IN THE gale outside Poggioli caught the faint scent of decaying oyster meats which taint the air of Pampatar. It had not occurred to the psychologist when he sailed for Pampatar that pearl fisheries were smelly. One somehow does not connect pearls with malodors.

In the Gelleman office Mr. Gelleman was walking nervously up and down in front of his desk. He was a small dried up little man, and when the scientist entered he turned to him in a sort of tentative relief.

"Awfully good of you to come, Mr. Poggioli." He drew around a chair and stood tapping his fingers on its back. "Did Taprobane tell you what I wanted?"

"He said you had a pearl stolen."

"Yes, taken from the box before it started from the boiling vat for this office."

"How do you know just where it was taken?" inquired the psychologist.

"Because Taprobane brought them in, and I asked how many he had. He said six. I thought he meant six carats, and when I looked into the package I said, 'I don't believe there are six here.' Then he looked in and gasped out, '*Dios mio*, I meant six pearls; the big one's gone!' I said, 'For heaven's sake, go back and check it up!' He ran back and when he returned he was all shaking. He said, 'Señor Gelleman, there was a five grain pearl in the package!' 'Who do you suppose took it?' I asked. But there was no way to tell. You know how clannish the blacks are, Mr. Poggioli. Not one will breathe a word against another one, not if he hangs for it. Well, we stood there all torn up; then I thought of you and sent Taprobane up for you."

The psychologist observed the pearl factor's chest rising and falling.

"You're all torn up about this, Mr. Gelleman?"

"Yes, my firm is already—well they are naturally careful, so many gems passing through my hands."

"Of course, and just what did you expect me to do for you, Mr. Gelleman?"

"Well, you know the negroes are all alike. Any one of them might have done it."

"M-m. Yes?"

"So I thought I might get the pearl divers before you and you could pick out the thief: some sort of scientific test, you know; hypnotism, I didn't know what."

"I might devise a word reaction test, something of that sort."

"Do you think you could spot the man and get the pearl back in two days?"

"Why precisely two days?"

"You see the Trinidad steamer is due here two days from now and I think—I'm afraid she will have a—" the little man moistened his lips nervously—"an auditor from my company aboard."

"Oh, I see."

"Yes. So of course I want everything straight. To have a five grain pearl missing, and the auditor expected—" The agent's face wrinkled in misery.

"Sure, I see." Poggioli was moved. "Where are the boys you want me to test?"

"Up at the pearl beds now. We can walk up there right now. If they get wind of what we're up to, they'll be off."

"I believe I can disguise my tests so they won't know what it's all about," suggested the psychologist.

Mr. Gelleman hoped this could be done, and the two men started out for the pearl beds. Out in the street they angled into the wind along an old stone flagged walk until they reached the beach which they followed up to the pearl fisheries.

The sea was too rough for diving. The men were ashore, and Poggioli could see them far down the strand, boiling their oyster shells in a cauldron. The smoke whipped down the beach bearing the smell of dead oyster meats.

As the two white men hurried forward a disconcerting thing happened. Of a sudden all the black men rushed to their boats, hoisted their scraps of sails and the whole tiny fleet went bobbing out to sea.

Mr. Gelleman stopped in his tracks.

"Isn't that the devil?" he cried in frustration. "They caught on to us somehow. I don't know how. You never know how, but invariably these damned nigger divers find out any—"

"Why are they all running? They didn't all steal one pearl."

"Because they think you are a voodoo doctor; and every man-jack has done something he doesn't want you to find out—the beggars!"

THE TWO men stood and watched the boats disappearing and reappearing, sails and all, amid the marching waves.

"Where are they going?" asked the scientist.

"They will probably sail around to Porlamar and hide there until they think the hunt is over."

Poggioli watched the diminishing boats with the feeling of a duck hunter who has flushed his game before he gets a shot.

"It's gone," bewailed the little man, "a fine pearl gone and the auditor coming in two days—" His complaint was cut short as he stared off across the foam spangled sea; his eyes widened, his mouth dropped open and he blurted out, "Oh, my Lord, I have no time at all. He—he's right on me!"

The psychologist looked at his companion.

"What do you mean, Mr. Gelleman?"

"Why, look yonder." He pointed.

Poggioli looked and saw a faint feather of smoke lying flat on the horizon.

"Well, what do you make of that?"

"The Trinidad steamer—two days before her schedule. It's this damned wind!" he reasoned bitterly. "A howling stern wind all the way; no wonder she—"

"See here!" cried Poggioli. "Don't be so upset. Thefts occur everywhere. If this were the first crime of the sort in the world a fellow might take it hard, but—"

"Say," ejaculated the little man, his eyes coming back to the tiny sail boats. "Those niggers are not running away."

"No?"

"No, they're going to meet that steamer and dive for pennies. Every time a steamer enters this port, it's a holiday for my divers, always has been."

"M-mm, then I wonder if it would be possible—"

"It certainly would!" declared the little man with renewed hope. "We can row out to the steamer and have the boys come aboard one at a time." He clutched Poggioli's arm in excitement. "It'll be handy. Why, it's the very thing. Come on; let's get back to town!"

And the two set off back down the beach as hard as they could leg it.

When they reached the quay they obtained a dory from the end of an old wooden pier where the waves were not yet pulverized into a white roaring surf. The doryman they chose was old and made microscopic progress against the curling sea horses. Over the bay Poggioli could see the jack boats of the pearl fishers careering toward the steamer like a swarm of little brown winged butterflies. By the time the dory was in hailing distance of the *Reina Isabella*, the divers were already in the water and groups of passengers on deck were flinging them coins. The dory weaved its way up and down among these black mermen and finally Poggioli and Gelleman hooked on to the ship's ladder and skedaddled up it as hard as they could climb so as not to be caught by a wave.

Mr. Gelleman's face wore the light of hope until he clattered over the rail, then it lengthened again.

"There he is," he grumbled *sotto voce* to the psychologist, "throwing pennies to the niggers to pretend he's charitable. But there's no charity in him. He's hard as the andirons of Hades."

"Which one is the auditor?" inquired Poggioli.

"That one with the black eyes, keen nose and spats. Lord! I wish I hadn't come. I wish I'd stayed in my office and waited till he was ready to come to me."

"Let me make the approach," offered the American. "You just stand here and I'll speak to him. And remember, theft is a habitual thing. It's to be expected, and a company simply has to underwrite it, like insurance."

"Sure they do," nodded Mr. Gelleman with an apprehensive look on his face. "Try to get Señor Gonzalez to see it that way. I don't see what he wants to make such a howl for."

AT THAT moment Señor Gonzalez glanced around from his coin throwing; his face lighted up and he came toward Mr. Gelleman.

"*Bueno, bueno!*" he exclaimed. "Señor Gelleman, surely you didn't come out to meet me through a sea like this?"

"Oh, no, not at all, I just came out—"

"You are not sailing on this boat?"

"No, I'm not sailing. I came out because all our divers were—"

Señor Gonzales glanced at the black boys in the water and raised his brows in Latin interrogation.

Here Mr. Poggioli interposed—

"As a matter of fact, Mr. Gelleman brought me out here to—to—to psycho-analyze his divers."

The auditor stared at his visitors.

"To psycho-analyze what? You don't mean to tell me these negroes are afflicted with neuroses!"

"Oh, no—"

"Who are you, señor?"

Mr. Gelleman jumped at his lapse.

"Excuse me, Mr. Poggioli is an American psychologist traveling through the West Indies studying criminal behavior."

"Criminal behave—what's criminal about our boys?"

Mr. Gelleman moistened his lips.

"To tell you the truth one of our boys has taken a—a—a small pearl."

The Spanish gentleman's face assumed quite a new look.

"How large a pearl?"

"Oh, a small pearl—small—three—four—five—or six grains."

"You don't mean to say we've lost a six-grain pearl?"

"Five grains!" hastened Mr. Gelleman with precision.

The auditor straightened and his black eyes hardened.

"Gelleman, the company will hold you strictly responsible for this."

"I told you so," said Gelleman, looking at Poggioli.

"Why did you come aboard this ship?" asked the auditor of Gelleman.

"I told you once!" cried the pearl factor. "I am trying to find the thief among these negroes. If you hadn't jumped down on me like this two days ahead of schedule—"

"*Ca*, you would have sailed?" suggested the inspector ironically.

"Mr. Gonzalez," interpolated the American stiffly, "I know it is your duty to check these things up, but thefts occur everywhere. For you to be severe with Mr. Gelleman—"

"Listen, Señor Poggioli, you are not in this matter—or are you?" The Spaniard's heavy brows went up suspiciously.

"I'll probably be in it if you get your pearl returned?" suggested Poggioli dryly.

This brought the inspector around; he stood studying the two men.

"If you are *bona fide*, Señor Poggioli—and you appear to be—"

"I am," nodded the American, "and also I am something of a judge of men and their motives. I can assure you Mr. Gelleman here is absolutely innocent. His distress at the loss was quite unfeigned. I am telling you this out of a simple human desire for justice."

"*Sí, sí!* Let's go to my suite and talk this over in private," suggested the auditor.

The three men walked, wide legged, across the heaving deck, entered a companionway and presently were in Señor Gonzalez's cabin. The Spaniard turned to the psychologist.

"Señor Poggioli, you appear to be a dependable man, and I am going to put the situation before you frankly since Señor Gelleman has seen fit to bring you aboard."

"Yes, I wish you would."

"The facts are, Mr. Gelleman is deeply in debt to our company for pearls. The man seems to have an obsession for pearls. The company should not have extended him so much credit. Now for a large pearl that was in his hands to be stolen, knowing as we do his passion, it puts the loss in a very bad light."

The psychologist was quite taken aback.

"I—I would like to say one thing," he suggested in a less assured voice. "The temperament that runs into debt seldom steals outright. Their moral infringements are usually legal, I mean, by contracting debts they know they can not pay."

"That may be true, but as an inspector of accounts, you can't expect me to go into so refined a theory."

The psychologist was casting about for another tack when suddenly Mr. Gelleman cried out:

"Look, there's one of our boys coming aboard now. We can begin on him!"

"ONE of the divers?" inquired Poggioli, turning to stare at the porthole with Mr. Gelleman. "Which one was it?"

"Taprobane."

"I thought I left him at the hotel."

"When a steamer comes in they all know it, and you can't keep them away."

"Very well, let's start with him," agreed Poggioli. "I'll give him a word reaction test."

"It could hardly be Taprobane," said the factor on second thoughts. "He is my bus boy, and besides he is the one who reported the loss."

"All right, call another one; that is if it's agreeable to you, Señor Gonzalez?"

"It's all right with me. I hope from the bottom of my heart we find the gem. Use every method you know, Señor Poggioli."

When the three men stood on the wind swept deck again, Señor Gonzalez glanced around and said:

"Could you have been wrong, Señor Gelleman? I don't see any black aboard."

"No; Taprobane passed the porthole. I saw his face distinctly."

"*Pues*, he would hardly have hid; if he came aboard, why should he have hid?" The auditor glanced around among the lifeboats and coils of rope as if he expected to see Taprobane under one of them.

At that moment Poggioli heard the sloppy voice of a West Indian negro coming out of a cabin door. He moved around and saw Taprobane and a ship's officer inside. The white man was saying—

"You want to ship as a stoker, you'll have to sign these papers."

And Taprobane replied—

"I can't sign my name."

"Then make a cross mark here." The officer touched the paper with his forefinger.

Mr. Gelleman caught Poggioli's arm.

"Thunder and lightning!" he burst out in a whisper, stretching his dried eyes. "It's Taprobane!"

"Of course it's Taprobane; you saw him come aboard yourself."

"I mean he took the pearl," hurried the agent in a shocked tone. "To think, after I trusted him—"

"What makes you think he's the one?"

"The devil, signing on as a stoker! Stoking's work; it's hard work! No Margaritan negro is going to stoke unless he is in a desperate plight and wants to get away from the island quick!"

Poggioli looked at Taprobane again.

"You think this is flight?"

"Couldn't be anything else—shipping as a stoker."

By this time Taprobane had finished the papers and was saying to the ship's officer that he would go ashore for his dunnage.

As the big black man came out on the *Reina Isabella*'s deck Mr. Gelleman snapped—

"Taprobane!"

The negro whirled, then bobbed with widened eyes.

"*Si, señor!*"

"Hold there a minute, Taprobane," and the pearl factor started for him.

At the command the ebony diver made a movement toward the taffrail. Instantly the small man lunged after him. Taprobane leaped backward, but the little tackler caught him around the knee. The diver began backing away, dragging Mr. Gelleman after him with the swiftness of a stag dragging a fice.

The pearl buyer shrieked for help in a high desperate key. Both Poggioli and Gonzalez dashed forward. The Spaniard grabbed an arm while the psychologist caught the other leg. Instantly Poggioli felt himself lifted, swung about, churned. The ship's deck seemed to leap against him. The ocean weaved about him. The psychologist tried holding on with one arm and pounding Taprobane in the belly with the other. It was like hitting rubber. He nearly lost his hold altogether.

In his struggles the negro fell on deck full length. Poggioli's head knocked against the planks. The diver thrust out a long arm and just clutched one of the stanchions of the taffrail. Instantly the whole struggling mass was drawn sharply across the tarry planking. The next moment the black man was kicking and wriggling over the top of the rail trying to fall into the sea.

Poggioli wriggled upward, wrapped his arms around the black waist and clung on for life. In the struggle he got twisted around so his head and chest were under the negro and jammed against the rail. He nearly choked. He could not breathe. It seemed to the psychologist that the other two men were doing nothing. He could feel the powerful muscles of the diver writhing and slipping through his arms. Taprobane was wet with sweat and slippery as an eel. As the taffrail choked Poggioli the black body slid through his arms with slow, greasy certainty.

Tingling sensations went through the American as the man wormed out of his grasp. He wished he had sand, a brake belt, something with traction . . .

At that moment the three captors sent up a unanimous shout for help. Half a dozen Spanish sailors came running out of the forecastle.

"*Ladrone! Ladrone!*" shouted Gonzalez in extreme necessity.

THE SAILORS charged across the deck in a squad, but Taprobane was actually wriggling over the top of the rail. Poggioli felt a tearing in his arms. Taprobane slid with increasing greasiness through his upturned clutch. Then, for one moment the black man was hanging by his ankles in the white man's arms; the next moment the ebony form of the pearl diver fell end over end into the sea. It looked like a deliberate fall, a long deliberate fall into the depth of a wave trough as if he were in no hurry. As a last glimpse the men saw a dark shape slice downward through the clear blue water. Taprobane was gone as irrevocably as a mishandled tarpon.

Poggioli had the mad impulse of a fisherman to fling himself into the water and try to catch his game again. It always seems as if one can do it. The fish seems right there, just at hand—but it is gone.

In the midst of this cruel torture of the 'almost,' Poggioli became aware that he was holding some tattered clothing in his arms. He looked at it and then recalled that Taprobane had fallen into the sea as naked as he was the day he was born. Mr. Gelleman suddenly observed the same thing.

"Mr. Poggioli!" he cried. "The pearl must be in those rags!" He reached for them.

The psychologist handed over part of them and both men began searching the negro's clothes. The auditor watched with his hands spread as if he meant to catch the pearl when it made another attempt to escape.

The search through the pockets produced nothing. Poggioli was about to throw the clothes down when he felt a lump in the seam of the cotton trousers. He picked at the place, then holding a hand toward the crowd in general, cried—

"Gimme a knife!"

A knife was thrust into his hands and in another moment he was carefully cutting at a new delicately sewn bulge in the seam. After a moment his unsteady fingers spread open the little pocket to disclose the serene rondure of a pearl.

The American blew out a long breath of relieved nerves at the outcome. What Gelleman felt Poggioli could not guess. The little man trembled so he had to cup his two palms together to catch the pearl as Poggioli squeezed it out of the seam. The agent then handed it to the auditor, saying—

"There—take it, take it."

Mr. Poggioli tossed Taprobane's clothing over the taffrail.

Even the sailors were relieved. They broke into a rattle of Spanish conversation.

In the meantime Mr. Gonzalez was examining the jewel. He looked at it this way and that and finally burst out—

"*Diablo*, Señor Gelleman, this pearl—this jewel—"

"Yes, what?" The factor's eyes became apprehensive again.

"A thousand devils! It's paste!"

"It's what?"

"Paste! Glass! Look at it! You know an imitation pearl when you see one, Gelleman!"

"But how under heaven could it?"

"That's enough! That's quite enough, Señor Gelleman! To have a black accomplice; to go through all these maneuvers in order to—"

"But how in heaven's name did a glass pearl come out of an oyster!" wailed Gelleman.

"It didn't!" snapped Gonzalez. "Gelleman, I'll give you credit for one of the most elaborate and insane conspiracies to rob my company—"

"Wait! Wait! Wait!" cried the psychologist.

"Wait what for?" demanded the auditor. "Why shouldn't I have this scoundrel arrested?"

"Because he didn't take the final step," cried Poggioli. "If he had dropped the pearl overboard and lost it, that would have been the most perfect crime ever invented by a criminal brain. It would have been amazingly clever."

"He didn't have the nerve to do it," cried Gonzalez.

"It required no nerve, the whole thing was done for him, ready for the finale—no, this was not planned, Señor Gonzalez, or it would have worked beautifully."

"Then what do you make of it?" inquired the Spaniard skeptically.

"Well, I don't know . . ."

The facts of the incident floated through Mr. Poggioli's mind. Then he recalled the delicate sewing of the pearl in the seam and a queer possible solution of the enigma filtered into his head.

"I have a tentative solution," he ventured at last.

"What is it?"

"If you don't mind, I won't say just at this moment, but may I ask you gentlemen to come with me to my hotel."

"On the way up," snapped out Gonzalez, "I'll stop by the magistrate's office and swear out a warrant for Señor Gelleman."

"Don't do that until you come to my hotel."

"Very well, then I'll do it on my way back."

THE THREE men went ashore and, when they approached El Grand Hotel Rey Phillipe Segunda de Espagñe, the trio caught another glimpse of Taprobane. He was clad in a fresh white cotton suit and was signaling excitedly toward the second story window of the hotel. He vanished like a jackrabbit when he saw the men.

"Let's hurry," advised Poggioli.

A little later the three men climbed the stairs to the Gelleman apartment on the second floor.

"I want to speak to your wife," explained the psychologist to the pearl factor.

"Now look here," cried the little man, rebelling at last, "you can't bring Mrs. Gelleman into this affair!"

"Not at all, not at all," Poggioli assured him. "Announce us please."

The factor tapped on his own door.

"Seraphina darling, may I bring in some friends?"

Mrs. Gelleman's voice inside invited them in. She seemed surprised at her guests.

"Mrs. Gelleman," began Poggioli, "your husband and I were telling Señor Gonzalez about your exquisite collection of pearls. Would you mind showing them to us?"

"I will be charmed," cooed the matron, changing her psychology entirely. "I like showing my pearls. Chrysomallina! Oh Chrysomallina, will you bring my jewels, please?"

"I don't believe Chrysomallina will come this time, Mrs. Gelleman," said Poggioli in a low tone.

"Why won't Chrysomallina come?" asked the matron, lifting her brows at this odd turn.

"To tell you the truth, Chrys—"

He was interrupted by the black girl's entrance. Her eyes were very wide and white. She bore the chest with upturned hands in her habitual processional attitude.

The mistress took it.

"I don't see why you imagined Chrysomallina would not come?"

"I will explain," said Poggioli nervously. "The black boy Taprobane is Chrysomallina's sweetheart, isn't he?"

"I suppose so. Taprobane is always hanging around."

"They want to marry and haven't the money?"

"Most young people of both sexes are in that condition, either white or black," said Mrs. Gelleman, smiling.

"They needed the money," went on Mr. Poggioli. "This morning Taprobane stole a pearl. He brought it here and gave it to Chrysomallina to hide for him. She decided to conceal it where pearls were safest from search and suspicion, that is in your own chest there, Mrs. Gelleman."

"My own chest!" ejaculated the matron, looking down at the box in her hands.

"Yes, and in order to keep the number of pearls correct, she took out one of your paste pearls. She gave this to Taprobane to keep until they were ready to sail, then she meant to exchange them again and get away with the real pearl. In the meantime, if a paste pearl were found on Taprobane, they could convict him of nothing."

Mrs. Gelleman looked around at her maid who was standing transfixed, all white eyes.

"Chrysomallina, did you do such a wicked thing?"

"No, no, señora, you know I didn't—you know I didn't."

"I can't believe it myself," cried Mrs. Gelleman, looking first at Chrysomallina and then at her jewel case.

"It's true enough," said Poggioli, quite satisfied. "Just look inside and assure yourself. Mr. Gonzalez there has the paste pearl which your maid took out."

Mrs. Gelleman looked at the chest again, then at the men, then slowly opened the box. All three of the men came closer and looked into it. Poggioli put in a finger and touched a shimmering gem which he had not seen that morning.

"This one, isn't this a new pearl in your collection?"

Mrs. Gelleman ran the tip of her tongue over the small red circle of her babyish lips.

"Why, no—no," she said. "I—I've had that pearl all the time."

"Seraphina," ejaculated the pearl factor, "I never did give you such a pearl as that; I couldn't have afforded it."

"No, you didn't dear—uh—mother gave me this one a long time ago."

"You never showed it to me before!"

"No, no, I never did—but I was talking to Mr. Poggioli this morning about how my mother loved pearls. Don't you remember that, Mr. Poggioli? I was asking you if my desire for pearls wasn't inherited. You remember that, don't you? You said you didn't think it was, and I said I thought it was. We had quite an argument about this pearl—you must remember—No, Chrysomallina wouldn't have done such a thing as that. She has been in my service for—oh, for a long time. You may go now, Chrysomallina. I won't need you any more. I'll lock the pearls in the trunk myself."

And Mrs. Gelleman closed her box.

Shadowed

A Compilation from the Case: Ohio State University vs. Henry Poggioli, Ph.D. As made from the notes of the Rev. Mr. Lemuel Z. Bratton, by T. S. Stribling.

FOREWORD BY THE COMPILER

THE resignation, or to put it baldly, the dismissal of Mr. Henry Poggioli from the docentship of criminal psychology at the Ohio State University, not only caused one of the widest and bitterest newspaper discussions since the Scopes trial, but it was a shocking disappointment to Mr. Poggioli's classmen and friends.

The actual article which Mr. Poggioli wrote for the *American Journal of Psychology* and which led to his academic downfall has been too widely circulated in America, and indeed throughout the civilized world, to need reproduction here.

Mr. Poggioli's trial, which was transferred from Columbus to Dayton, Ohio, in what was perhaps an impossible attempt to obtain a fair and impartial trial, is a *cause célèbre* which will not soon be forgot in educational circles. The formal charge against him, of disrespect for the canons of the university, and scientific heresy, was, as every one knows, soon lost in personal bitterness and recrimination.

Something else also was lost: the strange and abnormal happenings on which Mr. Poggioli based his article and so involved himself in scandal and final dismissal. The educational world was so shocked that a docent in a leading university should be so lost to the conventions of his position as to assert in public print if not an actual belief in, then at least to hypothesize the possibility of the existence of a God; I say the educational world was so shocked that it has completely overlooked the amazing and sinister facts upon which Mr. Poggioli reached so unheard of a conclusion.

These facts it has been the good fortune of the transcriber to reassemble; not with an idea of reviving that bitter and acrimonious controversy, but simply to present the record to that broader court of public opinion before which even the regents assembled in Dayton eventually must bow.

The transcriber obtained these facts from the notes of the Reverend Mr. Lemuel Zimcoe Bratton, a Tennessee revivalist, who was closely associated with

Mr. Poggioli in his defense. It was the Reverend Mr. Bratton, who, in the course of the proceedings, so amusingly wrung from the president of a great American university the admission that though he had heard of the Bible he had never seen a copy.

The facts themselves, upon which Mr. Poggioli sought to base his defense, were ruled out of the evidence by the Dayton court on the ground that they had no bearing on the specific charges against Mr. Poggioli, of disrespect for the canons of the university and of scientific heresy. In this stand, however, even the counsel for the defendant felt the court was justified and made no serious effort to have the actual facts read into the record of the case.

This hiatus in public knowledge, the transcriber undertakes to fill. However, he must hasten to add that he has transposed the Reverend Mr. Bratton's notes both in time and space in order to enhance the dramatic and literary effect of the narrative.

THE GIRL from the office brought a card into the laboratory and, after standing among the cages of white rats for several moments, found a favorable opportunity to hand it to Mr. Poggioli.

The docent in criminal psychology took the card with a touch of protest in his manner.

"I have instructed you, Janet—" he began, then broke off, looking at the name—

CLAYMAN MORDAG

It was somehow a depressing four syllables. Poggioli drew his thumb across the engraving as a kind of test of his visitor's financial and social standing.

"I have told you, Janet," he continued on the sentence he originally had started, "that I don't want to waste time seeing people with cases. I'm not a detective. I'm a psychologist."

"Yes, sir, but—but they know you're a criminologist, too, Mr. Poggioli," ventured the girl.

"Well, what of that?"

"It—it seems to me," hesitated Janet, "that the trouble this Mr. Mordag is in would have something to do with criminology."

"About the same relation that a colicky baby bears to the mortality tables."

"Yes, sir."

"So you can go back to the office and tell him that I can't see him."

"I—didn't leave him in the office," said the girl.

"Where did you leave him?"

"In the cloakroom."

Poggioli came to a pause and looked at the girl.

"Why did you leave him in the cloakroom, Janet?"

"Well—he asked if I would mind if he waited for you in a room without any windows in it."

"And you put him in the cloakroom?"

"Yes, sir."

The docent in criminology glanced at the card again, then started for the front of the building.

"Really—really, Janet, that's the dumbest thing— Why, he won't be there!"

"Why won't he?"

"By now he has run through the pockets of the coats, and gone," forecasted the docent. "Janet, you are the—"

"I'll bet he has," cried the office girl, shocked at her own gullibility.

The two hurried toward the front of the building. As they went the docent ventured—

"It is barely possible the fellow is suffering from agoraphobia—"

Janet made no reply to this. She had developed too much poise to inquire the meaning of a polysyllable in a psychological laboratory.

Poggioli went downstairs and found Mr. Clayman Mordag just inside the cloakroom on the first floor.

"Oh, you did come," ejaculated the visitor in a tone of profound relief. "The girl didn't think you would; I was about to give you up."

Poggioli looked over the stranger's thin face, sandy hair and high, narrow forehead.

"As a matter of fact," said Poggioli, seeing that the coats were safe, "I have just come down to excuse myself, Mr. Mordag."

The visitor became distressed at once.

"You aren't going to take my case?"

"Mr. Mordag, I have five hundred white rats in this laboratory on fifty different diets—"

"Mr. Poggioli!" exclaimed the thin man with a desperate note in his voice. "Isn't a man's life worth more than five hundred white rats?"

"Yes, yes," agreed the psychologist, withdrawing a little from the man's insistence. "But there are professional agencies for the protection of life and property, Mr. Mordag; the police, private detectives—"

The thin man lifted a protesting hand, glanced up and down the corridor.

"Mr. Poggioli, you might as well try to sweep out the air with a broom—a detective—" he shook his head—"I had hoped a psychologist might help me. If a psychologist can't, or won't—" The man spread out his hands and dropped them.

"Are you in personal distress, or danger?" asked the docent, his curiosity aroused by the stranger's extraordinary manner.

"I am; I am indeed, Mr. Poggioli. Only this morning I barely escaped—" He broke off again in his disconnected fashion. "I am followed about all the time—everywhere I go—" He glanced up and down the hallway again and instinctively moved deeper into the doorway of the closet.

"You mean you are shadowed?"

"Yes; oh, yes—all the time."

"You don't mean here—at this moment?"

"Yes; every single moment of the day and—and night, too, I suppose."

Poggioli glanced around and then said in a somewhat different tone—

"Well, at this particular moment you may be sure that nobody is shadowing you."

Mr. Mordag smiled, the faint mirthless smile of utter disbelief.

"In the morning—when I get the note—you'll see."

SO MANY odd revelatory half-phrases cropped out in the visitor's remarks that the psychologist began trying to piece them into something coherent.

"If you would like you can stand completely inside the cloakroom door, Mr. Mordag. Yes, that's all right. Now you were saying something about this morning you barely escaped—escaped what?"

The sandy man was well inside the cloakroom now.

"Being poisoned," he said in a low tone.

"Who tried it?"

"The man who follows me."

"Do you know who he is?"

"Why, Mr. Poggioli, of course I know who my enemy is. His name—his name is—*La Plesse*." This last, the visitor concealed in the cloakroom whispered.

The psychologist pondered a moment or two.

"But he didn't succeed in his purpose?"

"No; he poured a tiny bit in my drinking glass. It just happened that my cat mewed for water while I was still in bed. I got up, took a little in the glass and poured it in the cat's saucer. When I glanced at it again—it was dead."

"Where are you staying?"

"At the Hotel Vendig, on the eighteenth floor."

"I suppose after the death of your pet you had the hotel authorities investigate to see who had been in your apartment?"

Mordag shook his head.

"Why, Mr. Poggioli, there is no more use in placing a guard to keep watch for him than—than to try to control the thoughts that pass through a man's mind."

The psychologist smiled.

"Your similes are expressive enough, Mr. Mordag, but let us hope they exaggerate the facts. Let me see—how long have you been in the Vendig?"

"I came there last night."

"Last night!" ejaculated the docent in surprise.

"Yes, I registered there last night—after midnight. I was traveling to New York on a through ticket. But at some city west of here our train stopped. When

I felt it stop I looked out between the curtains of my berth and I saw him come in the door. By good luck he passed through into the car back of mine. So I dressed as quickly as I could, got my bags and got off here in Columbus."

"Then you believe after this, *he* got off here in Columbus also, followed you to the Vendig, found your room, put a potion in your drinking glass?"

Mr. Mordag stood nodding slowly and watching Poggioli with questioning eyes.

"At least you see why it is no earthly use for me to apply to the police, or the private detectives. When I tell them what happens they simply look at me as you are doing. Sometimes they tell me to call tomorrow; or say they are sorry they can't do anything for me; or that they are very busy."

"And just why did you think a psychologist—" began Poggioli curiously.

"Professor La Plesse is a mind reader," said the sandy man in his monotone.

"Oh, I see," nodded Poggioli, looking carefully at the man.

Clayman Mordag gave another of his wintry smiles.

"No, you don't see—I know what that means, too. Here, would you mind looking at these—"

He ran a hand into his coat pocket and drew out a leather case. He opened this and displayed a collection of newspaper clippings. They were theatrical columns clipped from a score or more of papers throughout the South and West. They began usually, "Professor La Plesse Mystifies Audience," or "Herman La Plesse Finds Long Missing Jewels." They were all of a tenor. Nearly every write-up bore a picture of the thaumaturgist himself, a heavily bodied man with a Van Dyke beard, and the wide face and full eyes of a strongly animal man.

"This—this," said Poggioli, tapping one of the notices, "is all right for a newspaper to run. And believe, too, if one has the taste for that sort of thing. But, Mr. Mordag, this building is the psychological department of the Ohio State University. Not only the instructors, but every undergraduate devotes himself to the best of his ability to strictly scientific material. Now, for you to ask me to investigate the doings of a charlatan—" Poggioli shook his head and handed back the clippings.

The visitor seemed somehow to sink into himself at this ultimatum.

"You mean," he said in a hopeless voice, "that how he got into my room and poisoned my glass isn't scientific material?"

"If he did that—if he could do it—yes. But to go off on a wild goose chase—Now, just for example, Mr. Mordag, suppose the faculty of the Ohio State University should investigate every sea serpent yarn it read in a newspaper . . ."

"I—I can show you the dead cat, Mr. Poggioli," faltered Mordag. "It—it's a Persian cat. It's still up in my apartment."

"I believe you have a dead cat in your room," admitted the docent, "but cats have fits and just die; and you are nervous and expecting—For instance, you are standing here in this cloakroom now because it has no windows."

"Yes, sir."

"You imagine you are being watched here at this moment while we are entirely alone."

"I know I'm being watched," admitted Mordag in a low voice. "My note will prove that in the morning."

"Well, now, that is the reason why I can't spend time investigating the death of your cat. You are not in a mental state to give unbiased evidence; and, moreover—"

AS POGGIOLI uttered this "moreover" he heard a faint step at the top of the stairs. Mordag started painfully and peered up the ascending flight. Poggioli himself was startled. He stepped out into the hall where he commanded a better view of the stairway. Then he called out sharply:

"Confound it, Janet—moving around up there like a ghost . . . Haven't you gone back to the office yet?"

The girl upstairs made no reply, but the two men could hear her walking away.

Poggioli looked at the sandy man's wide eyes.

"You see that's why you aren't reliable; you translate everything into this Professor La Plesse."

"N-n-no; I—I didn't think that," stammered Mordag. "N-nobody thought that b-but you, Mr. Poggioli. I—I knew it wasn't him. T-the noise just made me jump, t-that's all."

"Well, how did you know it wasn't he?" asked Poggioli.

"B-because when I—I see him, he—he don't make any more noise than the sunshine falling on a g-grave."

"I see," nodded Poggioli faintly amused. "It was my mistake."

"Yes, sir—You didn't really see anything up there, did y-you?"

"Just Janet."

"I—I'll bet it's in the note tomorrow morning."

"You've mentioned that once or twice, Mr. Mordag," observed the psychologist. "Just what do you mean by note in the morning?"

"I get a note from him every morning," said the sandy haired man, his uneasiness taking a new tack.

"You don't mean it?" exclaimed Poggioli with vivacity in his voice.

"Yes, I do. Why?" queried Mordag, catching the docent's hopeful inflection.

"Why, my dear man," cried Poggioli, "that puts the fellow squarely in the hands of the Federal postal authorities. You won't have to go an inch farther to lock him up in Atlanta anywhere from ten to twenty years."

"Why will the postal authorities do that?" asked Mordag, all at sea.

"For using the mail to threaten, blackmail or put in fear—"

"Oh, he doesn't use the mail."

"If he doesn't it seems the hotel management ought to catch him."

"He doesn't use the hotel boxes either—they're in my pockets."

"The notes?"

"Yes."

"Every morning?"

"Yes, I look for one every morning. If I can't find it, I—it makes me nervous. I—I just keep looking till I do."

"For God's sake!" ejaculated the psychologist. "He gets into your room every night—leaves a note in your pockets—"

"Yes, sir."

"You never see him when he comes in?"

"He doesn't come in till I'm asleep."

"Can't you pretend you're asleep?"

"Oh, Mr. Poggioli, you know Professor La Plesse would know it if I was pretending that I was asleep. That's ridiculous, Mr. Poggioli."

"Did you ever have any one else watch for him instead of yourself?"

"Y-yes, sir," explained Mordag, lowering his voice. "Last night I asked the matron on my floor to watch my door. I paid her three dollars to move her chair where she could see if anybody went in."

"And she saw nothing?"

"Nothing at all."

The docent in criminology pondered.

"Let me see, a bellboy brought up your bags; another, possibly, some ice water—"

"Some cracked ice," corrected the sandy man. "I'm Scotch."

"H-m-m—there were two chances there."

"Yes, but how would they know what to put in the note?"

"Have you got one of the things?"

For answer Mordag reached in his pocket and brought out a folded handkerchief. He handed it to Poggioli gingerly as if he were afraid of it.

His manner caused the psychologist to unfold the handkerchief with care. Inside was a strip torn from the edge of a newspaper. On this edge was written a message as cryptic as its mode of appearance. It bore the following rigmarole—

7200—2.37—3645—BLASHFIELD—
VINE—23—POPLAR—LOISETTE—VENDIG.

Beneath this was a sentence written in French.

The docent read the figures twice.

"Do you understand what this means?"

"Well, no-o—not all. My train was due to get into Columbus at 2.37 this morning—" He stood studying his own note over Poggioli's shoulder. "I'm rooming at the Vendig and I think the Vendig is on Loisette Street, isn't it?"

"Yes, and the station is on Vine," added the psychologist. "The other streets must have been on your route to the hotel."

"I suppose so—I hardly ever understand all of a note."

The docent had become interested in the missive.

"Look here, 7200 could easily be the number of the locomotive that pulled your train; 3645 Blashfield might be a street address."

"Yes, it might."

Suddenly Poggioli held the note perfectly still.

"Do you happen to read French?" he asked in a different tone.

"No, I don't know French."

"Do you know what this bottom sentence means?"

"No; what does it mean?"

"I was just asking you," said Poggioli. "I'm as ignorant as you of French—" He looked around him, then refolded the note in the handkerchief and placed it in his own pocket.

"This is more interesting than a dead cat," he said in a different tone. "I've decided to go down with you after all. Now I've got to run back up to the office for a moment and leave word that I'll be absent from the laboratory for three days."

"Three days!" ejaculated the sandy man, looking curiously at Poggioli. "Why three days?"

"Oh, I have to set a time limit and I might as well be liberal with myself." He turned toward the stairs.

"Do you want me to wait here for you?" called Mordag, with a sharp protest in his voice.

"Do you want to come with me?"

"N-no—not with the windows and everything—"

"Listen," said Poggioli cheerfully, "you stand here in the cloakroom. I'll lock the door from the outside and take the key with me. When you hear me put this key in the door again you may know that it is I, and you needn't feel jumpy about it."

"Well, all right," agreed Mordag.

The atmosphere the fellow had wrought caused Poggioli to look up and down the hallway in both directions. He would not have been greatly surprised to see a heavy man; but the corridor was empty. The docent started quickly up the steps listening intently as he went. On the upper floor it suddenly occurred to him that he had not searched the closet to make sure it was empty. He believed it was. He was morally certain it was empty, but the note Mordag had showed him was so extremely odd, and sinister—for the fellow to know the very locomotive number that brought Mordag to Columbus . . .

If this Professor La Plesse were hanging about the university waiting for Mordag to come out, it was not impossible for him to have secreted himself in the cloakroom. The sheerest possibility of caging the poor harried devil of a man with his arch tormentor stopped Poggioli, turned him around and sent him running back down the steps for another look into the room.

He paused at the door, tapped faintly and said in a low tone—

"I'm back just for a moment—"

The next instant a muffled scream broke from inside the door.

"Mr. Poggioli! Oh, Mr. Poggioli! Here he is—come at last!"

The psychologist jerked out his key, made two efforts before he unlocked the door.

When it was open he saw Mordag backed away among the cloaks, almost on the verge of collapse.

"What's the matter? Where is he?" cried Poggioli, breathing sharply.

"Oh—oh—that was you?"

"Yes, I just wanted to—to see if the cloakroom was empty; it struck me a man might be hiding—"

Mordag drew long, shaken breaths.

"No, no; he isn't in here. He—he doesn't have to get behind anything to—to hide. He just—melts away."

"I see," said Poggioli, giving a brief laugh. "I didn't know his habits."

He locked the door again and set off upstairs once more. On his way up he paused to reread the French at the bottom of the note. He had remembered it correctly. The sentence read—

"You have three more days to live."

II

IN THE taxicab on the way to the Hotel Vendig Mr. Henry Poggioli attempted to soothe the nervousness of his client. He began talking about the five hundred white rats which he had in the university laboratory. He was experimenting, he said, on their diet. It was remarkable, the influence of diet on the functioning of both rats and men.

"Now you, for example—" proceeded the docent, warming to his theme—"if you would eat more rice—unpolished rice—and fruits, you wouldn't be so jumpy."

"Not even if somebody were trying to kill me?" asked Mordag in a gray tone.

"Now, now," advised the docent, "get your mind off of that."

The taxicab in which the men rode, moved and stopped, in unison with a great flock of cars, to the stop and go signals of the traffic lights.

Poggioli observed his companion's nervous glances among the other motors, and finally he protested this also.

"Look here, Mordag; as a psychologist I advise you to shake off this continual edginess. You need a rest."

Mr. Clayman Mordag leaned back among the cushions in an attempt to relax, but every honk made him glance around.

"Listen," begged Poggioli. "At least don't watch the trucks. You know the fellow is not in a truck; nor a car, either, for that matter. It is extremely illogical, Mordag, for you to be afraid of meeting this La Plesse in a perfectly empty room and, simultaneously, in a street full of cars."

"If he wasn't in the house he is likely to be in the street."

Poggioli leaned forward with the satisfaction of a pedagogue cornering a pupil.

"That is just what I wanted you to say. There you introduce the theory of probability. At this moment there must be at least two thousand cars in this street, divided into blocks containing about a hundred and twenty cars each. Now the probability that you are in the same block with this Professor La Plesse—that is, assuming that he entered a car at the same moment we did; which, within itself, is a ridiculous assumption; but assuming he did—the probability that he would be in the same block with you, is—let me see—a hundred and twenty into two thousand—"

But the docent did not work out this ratio because he saw his client was not listening. As a matter of fact, the scientist was not greatly interested himself. He sat quiet for a minute or two, trying to think up a more comforting line of dialectic. Finally he said—

"Look here, if La Plesse really gets into your apartment every night and seriously intends to commit foul play, why doesn't he just do it and have it over with?"

"I—I think he wants it to—to look like I—killed myself," said Mordag, wetting his lips.

"This might be indicated if on his first visit he had murdered you, but after you have advertised the situation to me and to the hotel force—"

"Maybe he really hopes to make me kill myself."

There was more color to this. Poggioli mused a moment, then said:

"If that's all, we can checkmate his whole plan of terrorism by a proper diet. It may interest you to know that suicides are recruited mainly from the meat eating nations. Now if you—"

"Or he may not want to kill me at all. He may be doing this just to torture me."

Poggioli gave up his attempt to interest Mordag in impersonal speculations on the situation.

"He may not want to kill you," he suggested dryly, "for fear of getting himself hanged."

The sandy haired man looked blankly at the psychologist.

"For fear of getting himself hanged?"

"Certainly; that's not a pleasant idea."

"Why, they couldn't hang him, Mr. Poggioli."

"Why couldn't they hang him?" demanded the psychologist, losing his patience.

"Because they'd have to keep him in jail for awhile—at least they'd have to keep him in a death cell for three nights before they hanged him, and—and he wouldn't stay; he'd just walk out."

POGGIOLI drew a breath, looked at Mordag, ready to break loose; then he blew out his breath because he saw it was no use. Then, after all, on the next reaction he did fling out—

"Mordag, you are the most complete imbecile!"

The sandy man lifted a hand.

"I know it, I know it," he cried nervously. "I don't expect anybody to believe it unless they've seen him do it hundreds of times, like I have."

"Get out of the cells of the condemned?" cried Poggioli.

"Once he got out of a death cell," said Mordag. "I believe it was at Leavenworth. Lemme see—" He reached in his pocket and drew out his leather case of clippings again.

"Put 'em up! Put 'em up!" snapped the psychologist. "And don't look at those damned things any more!"

Mordag put back his case.

"I thought you wanted to know where he did it."

"It was an exhibition trick, wasn't it—to draw a crowd to his performance. The sheriff wasn't really trying to hang him, was he?"

"No, of course not. But the understanding was that the turnkey would keep him in the death cell until after the performance at the theater that night—if he could."

"And he got out and arrived at the theater on time?"

"Yes, and they had the death watches and everything right by the cell. The men said they could see him lying on his bunk right up to ten minutes of nine—that was when he was to go on the stage. Then, all of a sudden, he wasn't there. And out he steps in the theater in full evening dress, a good fifteen blocks away, and went on with his performance—Here, I'll read you what the Leavenworth papers said—"

"For God's sake keep those clippings in your pocket, or chuck 'em out the window. You know how that was done, don't you?"

"No, of course I don't."

"By *famuli*."

"Family?"

"No, *famuli*—I mean confederates, assistants, helpers."

The sandy haired man picked nervously at the upholstering and glanced about at a passing car, then he said—

"I was his assistant for two years."

"Oh!" ejaculated Poggioli in an altered tone. "And you say you don't know how he did it?"

"Why, no-o. All I did was to put his tables and balls and boxes and things on the stage at the right time. Once I had seen him buried in the cemetery in a casket, and the casket in its box. And I thought sort of creepy, 'Well, you won't show up this time;' but when I gave his cue—you know, straightened the black velvet top on his table—out of the wings in his evening clothes he stepped, looking as good as ever."

"Then he had another helper."

"Rose."

"Who was she?"

"At that time she was the professor's wife."

"But she's not his wife now?"

"No—" Mordag stared for once absently into the crowded street—"No, she's not now."

Poggioli appraised the change that had come over the ex-assistant.

"Well," he suggested, "what about this Rose?"

"I know she didn't help him. We did the same things."

"You mean to say his own wife didn't understand his tricks?"

"No, she didn't. Why lots of times me and Rose talked about his tricks and wondered how he did 'em."

"She could have pretended she didn't know."

Mordag gave his momentary twist of a smile.

"I think she would have pretended to him before she would to me."

"Oh, I see." Poggioli nodded, looking steadfastly at his client. "And you say, I believe, that finally he—divorced her?"

"Yes," nodded the thin man, staring. "Rose and me were very good friends—she never really got along with the professor. You know he was one of those heavy men who—who really never need anybody much."

"I see; but you and Rose were—friends?"

"Yes, we were friends." A muscle in Mordag's lean cheek twitched.

"And that's the reason—well, of the trouble between La Plesse and his wife. That's why you jump off of the New York train at Columbus—and find your water glass poisoned next morning?"

"He didn't treat Rose right. You needn't look at me that way, sir, I—"

Here Mordag broke off his stammering defense. His jaw dropped. He stared at something in the street and gasped in a whisper.

"Oh, my God, sir—"

The fright of the man sharpened Poggioli's nerves. The whole street of cars were standing still under a red light. The docent searched among them.

"Which one's he in; where is he?"

"That blue car—right there . . ."

POGGIOLI saw a blue limousine. In it were three persons—a man, a woman and a child. The man was a heavily bodied person of the type who has become corpulent through success. He held a coin toward the child. As the little girl reached for the piece of silver the coin simply vanished, in full view, without any screening of the fingers whatsoever. It was an amazing enough trick to have made the docent marvel if the situation itself had not been so extraordinary. The psychologist heard the woman give a puzzled laugh and ask in French—

"How do you do that, Jacques? But that's a silly question."

The next moment the whistle blew and the parade moved forward.

Poggioli whirled and said to the chauffeur through the hole in the glass partition—

"Keep up with that blue limousine until you reach the first traffic cop, then stop!"

Mordag leaned forward and pulled at Poggioli's arm.

"For God's sake, don't do that. Turn off at the first corner; take me to a—a flying field."

The chauffeur had caught his fares' excitement.

"What do you want me to do, sir?" he called through the glass, at the same time watching the jam.

"Follow that blue car! Get to a cop! Mordag, the only way to end this situation is to end it!"

"The blue car," repeated the chauffeur.

"Yes—follow it!"

Just then a break in the traffic allowed the lane containing the blue car to pass rapidly up the street. The chauffeur attempted to edge his cab into this open lane. A protest of honking set up from the rear. He was forced back into his own path on pain of being hit.

"Damn the luck!" cried Poggioli, glaring at the cars with the right of way. "The damned egocentric American public; no matter how urgent a man's needs may be—life or death—no man in a car will give you an inch!"

He saw the blue car getting completely away. He pressed his face against the glass partition.

"Get the license number, chauffeur. Can you see it? Get it before he's gone."

Just then a lucky gap in the vehicles gave both men a view of the metal sheet. It was Ohio 143–734.

"Call it out to me," cried Poggioli through the glass. "I want to check up on it."

The driver called it out. The psychologist noted it down on an envelope.

"All right, my boy," he said, turning to Mordag. "That's the first step in Professor La Plesse's undoing. Hurry on, chauffeur, to that first officer you see yonder!"

The chauffeur aimed straight at the man in blue. The traffic guard jumped aside.

"Where are your eyes? Do I look like a speedway? Want to lose your license, you dumb fathead?"

Poggioli leaned out of the window and beckoned with such urgency the officer hushed his sarcasm and came to the car.

"What the hell do you want, stopping the traffic—"

"I want you to halt all the traffic—everything in sight—and arrest that blue limousine at the end of this block."

The guard looked up the street, then at Poggioli.

"Who are you?"

"A criminologist."

"A what?"

"Listen, the man in that blue limousine is a potential murderer!"

The policeman stared.

"Who did you say he had murdered?"

"Nobody yet, but he is going to murder—"

"Listen, what's your name and address?"

Poggioli gave it, then immediately wished he had not done so.

"Well, move along," ordered the bluecoat sharply, drawing out his summonses. "You can't hold up the traffic because somebody is going to murder somebody else. My Gawd, you'd never get a car through Columbus if you stopped traffic on that account!" He made a full arm swing at the chauffeur. "Move along; you ought to know better than to stop for a thing like that. Want to lose your license?"

The chauffeur jammed his accelerator so hard his car began bucking.

Poggioli was beside himself.

"Of all damnable systems—"

Mr. Mordag was immensely relieved.

"You wouldn't have got him if you had stopped his machine."

"The devil! Let up on that croak, will you? Driver, step on it; we've got to catch that car."

"Mr. Poggioli," pleaded Mordag, "let him go; I don't want to catch him."

"Well, I do. If I can get hands on him—"

"But the woman—the woman he had with him—"

"Woman, the devil. Step on it, chauffeur—and look out for the blue car!"

BOTH Poggioli and the driver were staring forward now as the taxicab stuttered at a great rate up the boulevard. They were passing car after car.

From the back of the car Mordag was exclaiming:

"But the woman was Arline! He's with Arline."

"Who is Arline?" asked Poggioli over his shoulder, giving about a quarter of his attention to his client.

"She's my cousin."

"Devil she is!" flung back Poggioli, not greatly interested in this.

"Yes. That night—the night he came into the dressing room and—and found us—he said to me—he said—"

"Say it; say it and stop stuttering!"

"He said, 'Mordag, I'm going to divorce Rose for this and I'm going to marry your cousin,' Arline Daupheny. And that's Arline with him; he done it."

"That's all right. I don't care if he married the Queen of Sheba."

"Yes, but he didn't even know Arline then—never heard of her. I don't think he ever heard of her. I'd never mentioned her to him."

"Oh, I see—another miracle he has worked." Poggioli peered ahead through the vibrating glass. "Now that man's miracles are one thing I'm not interested in. Do you see him, chauffeur?"

"No, sir; not yet."

"Yes, but that's why he's trying t-to kill me, sir," wailed Mordag. "I understand it now."

"Understand what now?"

"Arline's my cousin, I tell you. If I'm dead, she will be next in line to the Daupheny estate."

Poggioli turned around with a bit more interest.

"Oh, I see. So there's a financial end to this. How valuable is the Daupheny estate?"

"It's a sugar plantation—worth two or three hundred thousand."

"That's good," suggested Poggioli, with a bit more tolerance in his voice. "If I'm to run this man down, I'm glad his crime is complicated with a cold acquisitiveness."

"Of course, he wants me out of the way," went on Mordag in the empty repetition of a frightened man, "so Arline will get the estate."

The chauffeur interrupted—

"Yonder's the blue car, sir—parked by that house with the silo."

"Turret," corrected Poggioli.

"They're getting out and going in," cried the chauffeur. "Look at 'em; all three are going across the lawn, sir."

"You don't pay any attention to them; you drive on to the air field!" cried Mordag.

But the chauffeur had, for several minutes, known enough to pay no heed to Mordag.

"Shall I turn in by 'em, sir?"

"Yes, but check the car number first; might be dozens of blue limousines."

"Right you are, sir," called the driver through the hole. "It's a pleasure to drive a detective that knows his line, sir." He waited a moment as he rapidly drew near the parked limousine. "Ohio 143–734, sir."

Poggioli looked at his envelope.

"Check," he called back.

The taxi roared on up to the pavement and stopped with such suddenness that Poggioli and Mordag were assisted in a swift exit to the curb. The chauffeur also jumped out.

The three men ran across a slightly neglected lawn to the house with the turret. There were no curtains in the windows. Instead, "to rent" signs looked out through their blank eyes.

Poggioli ran to the front door and laid a hand on the bolt. It was locked. He looked inside and saw the bareness of an uncarpeted hallway.

"They're fixing to rent it," hazarded the chauffeur.

"Well, for pity's sake let's get away and let 'em rent it," pleaded Mordag, standing on the walk and staring at the house.

"If they walked in meaning to rent it, why did they lock the door behind them?" asked the chauffeur.

"They saw us coming," suggested the psychologist.

"He didn't have any key," said Mordag. "He didn't need any. He opened it locked, and of course when he went in and pulled the door shut it was still locked."

"What's your boy friend talking about?" asked the chauffeur, looking at Poggioli.

"He's got a lot of very shaky information in his head," smiled the psychologist.

"It's a pleasure to chauffeur for a detective like you," said the taxicab man.

"Let's try the windows," said the docent.

"Which ones?" asked the chauffeur.

"Why, these right here," said Poggioli, going to the nearest light. "You walk around and try the windows on that side, and I'll try 'em on this."

The chauffeur started off with the enthusiasm of a young setter on his first field trial.

"If I see 'em, shall I yell?" he asked guardedly. "Or shall I break in and nab 'em, or call the police or what?"

"Come back to me without making any noise," advised Poggioli.

The two men set off testing windows. Mordag went with the psychologist.

"What are you going to do if you get him?" he asked apprehensively.

"Arrest him for attempted poisoning."

"Won't do any good to arrest him; he'll—"

"Yes, I know all that," replied Poggioli with patient satire; "but it annoys them to have to keep percolating out of jail. I don't care how good a sleight-of-hand man gets to be, percolating is hard work."

Mordag became silent and simply followed his adviser. Presently Poggioli felt sorry for him.

"Look here, Mr. Mordag," he began more seriously. "You don't seem to realize that you have changed from the rôle of a fugitive to that of a pursuer. Don't be nervous any more. By the time this Professor La Plesse has been given the third degree—"

THE DOCENT was interrupted by footsteps coming around the house. He became alert and the next moment a policeman turned the corner of the building.

Poggioli did not know whom he expected to see; possibly La Plesse himself; but the sudden appearance of the bluecoat was a little disconcerting. At the moment he was trying to pry a window open. He had an impulse to quit, but he felt the best thing to do under the circumstances was to keep on. So he continued running the blade of the knife under the bottom of the window trying to get at the catch which he could see inside.

"Can you get in here, Officer?" he asked, jabbing in the blade. "There's a murderer in this house."

The policeman simply looked at Poggioli and Mordag for a moment, then he said:

"Are you birds color blind? Can't you tell day from night?"

"I didn't want to come here at all," began Mordag in a complaining voice.

"Shut up," snapped the docent. "Officer, we've got to get in here at once; there's a man in here—"

The patrolman saw that Poggioli had only a pearl handled pen knife, with a blade rather short even for a penknife. He became less menacing. He said:

"Better shut up your jimmy and put it in your pocket. It's against city regulations to break open houses in Columbus with burglars' tools like that."

Poggioli put his knife in his pocket.

"Listen," he repeated earnestly, "there is a man in this house who has attempted to take this man's life. I want him arrested."

"Who are you?" interposed the officer.

"This man's name is Mordag—Clayman Mordag."

"Don't *you* happen to have a name?" demanded the policeman. "If you wanted to call yourself up on the 'phone, who'd you ask for?"

"Your hypothesis is improbable to say the least of it," returned Poggioli with dignity, "but my name is Henry Poggioli, M.A, Ph. D. I teach criminology at the Ohio State University."

The officer stared, actually at sea now.

"Are you trying to show this man how to break into a house?"

"The devil! I'm after a criminal," cried Poggioli, quite out of patience with this mixture of ignorance and ill placed humor. "I expected you to help me instead of—"

The patrolman glanced up at the window.

"You say there's a gunman in there?"

"No, not a gunman; he's a sleight-of-hand performer."

"Thought you said he was trying to kill your pupil here?"

"This man isn't my pupil—"

"What is he?"

"He's a man whose life is threatened. He came to me as a psychologist."

"I thought you said you taught crime at the university?" cross-questioned the bluecoat shrewdly.

"I teach criminal psychology," stated Poggioli with the curved inflections of disgust.

"I see," nodded the officer, the docent's academic manner gaining a slight moral advantage over him. "Do you happen to have anything on you to prove what you are?"

Poggioli ran through his pockets and found two or three letters addressed to him in care of the university.

The officer considered these in connection with the fact that Poggioli was trying to jimmy a window with a rather short bladed penknife.

"Well, all right, you lads can go; but listen, Professor, you are not allowed to go to private houses outside the university grounds and try to teach your class how to jimmy—"

"Listen," cried Poggioli, "the academic phase of this incident weighs too heavily on your mind. I demand of you as an officer of the law that you help me break into this house and arrest the man inside for attempted murder."

The officer looked at the window again.

"Nobody lives here—it's for rent."

"I know that, but this Professor La Plesse, his wife and daughter, have just entered this house. I saw them go in."

"Professor La Plesse," repeated the officer. "Does he teach at the university too?"

"Yes," flung out Poggioli, goaded into sarcasm at last. "Murder is his specialty, and since you policemen won't let him use outside material, he was trying to kill this innocent member of his class . . . Come on, Mordag, what's the use staying here!"

The bluecoat followed the men around the building, not at all pleased at this.

"I'm a good mind to run you two in for attempted housebreaking . . ."

"Go on and do it," snapped the docent, not looking around.

"If the house wasn't as empty as a shell, and nothing in it to steal, I'd do it."

Poggioli made no reply. He and Mordag walked on around on the front lawn, where he came to a sudden halt.

"Why the blue car's gone!" he ejaculated in dismay.

"Thank God for that," cried Mordag, drawing a long breath.

"Which way did it go?" demanded the docent of the policeman. "Why didn't you tell us the car was gone instead of keeping us there talking?"

"When I came here," said the officer, "there wasn't anything at the gate but that taxi, so I came on in to see what was up."

The chauffeur was already around and was standing outside by his machine.

"Look here, see what happened?" called the chauffeur as Poggioli approached the gate.

The docent broke into a run, not knowing exactly what he expected.

"What is it?" he cried.

"Why look—" he pointed in dismay—"that cop's tagged my car!"

"You know better than to stop in front of a fireplug," reproved the bluecoat sharply.

"Well I'll be damned!" cried Poggioli. "Chasing murderers and the only cooperation the police will give you is to tag your car for parking in front of a fireplug!"

"Who's going to pay that fine?" inquired the chauffeur gloomily.

"We'll fight the case before the police judge, if he's got any sense at all."

The three men got into their respective places in the taxi. The policeman stood on the pavement, twirling his stick as he saw them off. He evidently considered that he had got the better of the situation.

"Where do we go from here?" asked the driver.

"Flying field," called Mordag.

"The Vendig," said Poggioli.

By this time the chauffeur had ceased to pay any attention to Mordag, who was paying the taxi fare, so he turned and started back down the boulevard toward the Vendig.

The docent rode along in silence. After the manner of men of theory, his personal frustration gave place presently to a gloomy philosophical outlook on the world in general. The ineptness of the policeman was exactly the sort of thing that permeated life at large. How bungling and aimless was the world of men compared to the scientific precision of his little community of rats in the laboratory. The aims and passions of men, taken as a whole, had absolutely no objective whatever. They crossed and blocked and thwarted each other. But his rats served their purpose with precision and with a sort of logical elegance. They lived to illustrate the effect of various diets. And it was a great pity, the docent thought, that the world at large could not have the same definition of direction as his five hundred rats. What the great torrent of life needed was some strict scientific supervision; a center, a focus, an experimental cleaning house, if life was ever really to mean anything. And here, weirdly enough, there drifted through Poggioli's mind the primitive folk notion of a god!

The psychologist straightened up.

"I declare!" he thought. "Fancy such an idea in the mind of an instructor in the Ohio State University!"

THERE was quite a stir at the Vendig when the taxicab drove up. The doorman ran out and asked if this was Professor Poggioli's cab. When he learned it was, he called out:

"Professor Poggioli has arrived! Professor Poggioli is here!"

Two or three men came running out of the hotel to the cab. One had a camera and began getting his head under his black cloth. Some one called:

"Hold that a minute in the cab door, Professor. Try shaking hands with Mr. Mordag."

Poggioli automatically tried shaking hands with Mordag.

"What for?" he asked.

"Picture for the *Times*; and a thousand thanks." He bobbed from under the cloth.

"Look here," cried the docent, moving hastily from in front of the camera. "I don't want my picture in the—"

A small man in a wine colored suit hurried up to the docent.

"Professor Poggioli, my name is Tapper. I'm with the *Dispatch*. The police turned in a remarkable story. I hurried up here to verify it. Have you been employed to discover the murderer of a cat?"

"That's right," nodded Poggioli hastily, beginning to back away.

"One moment. Have you any clues? Why did the man want to murder the cat? Was it a prize cat? Was it a case of one cat fancier jealous of another?"

"Correct! Correct!" The docent retreated with a feeling that he was being let down into a sensational quagmire.

"Look here," cried Mordag indignantly. "That poison was meant for me. I just happened to pour some water in the cat's saucer—"

Tapper turned to the sandy man.

"Oh, I see; and Professor Poggioli—"

"I'm not a professor," snapped the psychologist. "I am simply a docent."

"Pardon me, but I understand you ran the murderer to earth in a vacant house at 2714 Johnson Boulevard?"

"We saw him drive up to that number," said Mordag, "but while we searched for him—"

"Why, a Columbus policeman came up," interpolated Poggioli hotly, "and kept us answering questions—"

"Till the criminal got out the front way and drove off," concluded Mordag.

Mr. Tapper gave a snort, jerked out his handkerchief and muffled a rather long, keenish nose. A second later he asked soberly—

"What is your opinion of the general efficiency of the Columbus police, Professor?"

"I'd rather not go into that—not for publication."

"The real story here," said Mordag, "is about my room being entered every night and poison left in it. Does the *Dispatch* want a picture of me, too? The *Times* has got one."

"Who enters your room every night?" cried Tapper.

"Why Professor La Plesse."

"La Plesse, La Plesse—where have I heard that name?"

"He's a sleight-of-hand man," explained Mordag. "He played Columbus about five years ago. Here, I've got a clipping out of the old *Times-Record*—"

"I knew it!" cried Tapper. "I never forget a name or a face. I remember they sewed him up in a sack and dropped him off the bridge."

"Sure, that was one of his stunts; here's the clipping."

"Say, keep my name out of this, Mr. Tapper," asked Poggioli in extreme discomfort.

"Leave it to my discretion, Professor. I understand the academic conventions—" he turned to Mordag as a more untrammeled news source. "Where did you first catch sight of the La Plesse?"

"Downtown."

"Then where did he go?"

"We followed him to the house out on Johnson Boulevard and lost him."

"M-m-m—did you get his car number?"

"Yes, we got that. It was 2—3—4—What was it, Mr. Poggioli?"

The docent drew out his envelope.

"Ohio 143–734."

"Bill, call up the department, see who owns that car and where he lives."

Bill went to a telephone booth.

Tapper turned to Mordag again.

"Now that's fine. We'll soon have a line on him. Say he comes to your room every night and tried to poison you?" He turned to the cameraman. "Jimmy, give us a shot of Mr. Mordag by himself."

The shot was given.

"Now how about a shot of the dead cat—spot where cat was poisoned, saucer, glass—they're not trick glasses, are they? I mean the sort a sleight-of-hand man uses?"

"No, they're the glasses the hotel furnished."

"Good! Come on, let's get the shots."

THIS sudden burst of publicity drove away Mordag's fear. He led the crowd toward the elevator. Poggioli followed with a feeling that it would be wise not to follow. He knew he ought to get away with as little notice as possible. Already he sensed the sort of story Mr. Tapper was going to write. But the reporter had the air of a man who momentarily expected to unearth wonders, and Poggioli wanted to see what Tapper was about to uncover.

The crowd, for it really was a crowd by this time, jammed into an elevator. Jimmy, with the camera and tripod, created quite a diversion getting inside. At the top Mr. Mordag squeezed out and pointed out the floor matron. He explained that he had paid her three dollars to watch his room, and she had seen nothing. Mr. Tapper was enthusiastic. He directed Jimmy to take a shot of the woman who had watched Mr. Mordag's apartment all night long and had seen nothing.

"We have a real mystery here," he said to the floor matron. "What's your name and address? Married? Live with you husband? How many children have you got? All right, now, Mr. Mordag, we'll look at your cat."

As Mordag led the way to his room, Poggioli deserted the crowd and went back to the elevator. The docent at least knew when he had enough. He was going back to the laboratory and write a note to Mordag withdrawing from the case. Then he would have Janet up on the carpet and when he was through with her, she would never, so long as she worked in the laboratory, bring him another card.

He was pushing the elevator button when he heard a single sharp thump in Mordag's room, and abruptly the chatter of the crowd ceased.

After an interval he heard a voice say—

"Where the hell did that come from?"

And Tapper's voice replied sharply:

"Don't touch it! Let it alone! Let the detective see it!"

The docent turned and walked rapidly back to his client's apartment. The crowd was grouped around a knife that stuck, still quivering, just inside the entrance of Mordag's apartment.

The sandy man had lost completely his access of bravery.

"For God's sake!" he chattered, staring at the weapon. "Throw a knife at me—right through the ceiling!"

The crowd stared up at the ceiling.

"It couldn't come through the ceiling," said somebody.

Mordag looked at the man with the quivering open mouth of the terror-struck.

"Couldn't throw it through the ceiling! Why, I've seen him throw 'em through iron, wood, people—just anything."

"And not leave a hole?" cried the skeptic.

"My God, no! He don't leave a hole!"

Mordag walked feebly over to his bed, sat down on it gingerly as if afraid some knife might launch upward through the floor.

Mr. Tapper was writing rapidly. His man Jimmy was already training his camera on the knife.

Somebody said—

"Then he must be in the room right over this one."

This caused a diversion. Three or four men hurried up to the next floor to see what they could find.

"What happened?" asked Poggioli, looking at the knife stuck in the carpet.

"Just as Mr. Mordag entered his apartment," said Tapper, reading the words from the paper he had written, "a mysterious knife was thrown at the unfortunate man before the eyes of the whole crowd—" He broke away from his script to say to Poggioli, "If he hadn't stepped back just when he opened the door to let me in, he'd 'a' got hurt."

"Where did the knife come from?"

"He says through the ceiling," said Tapper. "You understand, this is a sleight-of-hand man we're after." He began scribbling again and repeating aloud, "When interviewed concerning the mysterious assault, Mr. Mordag stated that his enemy, Professor La Plesse was an adept in Rajah Yoga and could throw knives through iron, wood, stone, without leaving any visible—" He broke off to ask, "Is that a regular conjurer's knife?"

"It's the sort he always used," said Mordag weakly.

"If he's in the upper story here, how could he have been in 2714 Johnson Boulevard?" queried Tapper.

"We were there and now we're here," said Mordag.

"Yes, but we saw *you* come in," said Tapper.

"Look what a crowd's in—You don't know La Plesse."

"That's true," admitted the reporter.

Poggioli stooped over the knife without touching it. Then he drew a chair, stood on it and examined the top of the door.

"I have a feeling that La Plesse didn't go to the trouble of flinging his cutlery through ferro concrete," he began.

"Mr. Poggioli, he can," assured Mordag earnestly. "I've seen him throw knives through a steel screen and stick 'em around a woman."

"I don't doubt that he can," said Poggioli. "But he didn't take the trouble to do it this time."

"One moment," interrupted Tapper. "How thick were those steel screens, Mr. Mordag?"

"About an eighth of an inch—I could roll them around on the stage."

"You never saw him throw a knife through six inches of concrete?"

"No, I never did."

"Here's a silk thread glued to the top of the door," said Poggioli. "It undoubtedly pulled the knife from the transom."

The docent handed the thread down in the manner of a pedagogue exhibiting a specimen. Every one passed it gravely from hand to hand.

"When the door opened it pulled the knife off the transom," repeated the docent.

This left the crowd flat. How the knife had got on the transom was a small mystery compared to flinging a steel blade through the ceiling. The thread finally came to Mordag on the bed, and he sat looking at it.

While every one was still talking the man named Bill came back from the telephone.

"Tap," he said, "Ohio 143–734 belongs to the Oldham Drive-It-Yourself Garage."

"And who did the floorman say was using 143–734 today?"

"He said nobody wasn't using it; he said it was standing there in the garage."

"Who did he say had been using it?"

"Nobody. He said that car was under repair and hadn't been out of the garage all week."

III

MR. HENRY POGGIOLI did not give the information about the blue limousine having been on the streets and not having been on the streets at one and the same time the consideration that was really due it. He was so disgusted with Tapper, and Bill and Jimmy, the photographer, and especially with Clayman Mordag, for his cheap publicity seeking attitude, that he had decided to have done with the whole affair.

The docent was in his laboratory feeding his rats. As he went about this chore he thought of the crowd in the Vendig. Why did ordinary human beings wallow and grovel in a mystery of any description? Why did the Vendig aggregation want to believe that La Plesse had thrown a knife at Mordag through six inches of concrete flooring?

Men always had been like that, and it suddenly occurred to the psychologist that mankind as a whole must have greatly benefited by this attitude of awe and passive acceptance of the miraculous, or the trait would not be so deeply ingrained in the human race. If that were true, then the awful, the mysterious, the unknowable must, on the whole, have bestowed upon the world of men some great and immeasurable good. And that, of course, was religion . . .

The psychologist was really amazed at his own inference, and he might have followed it heaven knows where, possibly to orthodoxy itself, had not Janet come into the laboratory and ended his train of thought.

The girl held a damp, newly delivered paper in her hand. She entered rather uncertainly and asked, without much hope for a good reception in her voice, if the docent were busy right then.

Poggioli said not only was he busy but that he had told her never to bring him another card—never.

"This isn't a card," said the girl. "It's a paper."

"Well, what about a paper?"

"The men in the office were talking. I—I've come to say, Mr. Poggioli, I'm awfully sorry I brought you that man's card."

"Let your repentance point toward the future. Don't bring me any more."

"Oh, I won't."

There was a pause and Poggioli said—

"Well?"

"Why I—I wanted to ask," stammered Janet, "do you really believe Mr. Mordag's name brought all this bad luck on him, or did you just tell the reporter that?"

"What! What!" cried the psychologist, reaching for the journal.

The girl pointed hastily at a subheading—

NUMEROLOGIST ASSERTS CLAYMAN MORDAG'S MISFORTUNES
PRECIPITATED BY UNHARMONIZED MONIKER

"What is a moniker?" asked the docent, looking at Janet.

"It's a slang word; it means a person's name."

"Of course I didn't say such an idiotic—" He searched down the paragraph with his forefinger. "Here, it doesn't say I said it. It says Professor Wordenbaum, the famous international numerologist, said that."

"I didn't notice the exception," said Janet. "You said nearly everything else on the front page."

The docent stammered, hushed, saw the red streamer printed across the top of the page with a delicate goose flesh running over his skin.

PSYCHOLOGIST POGGIOLI SAVES CLAYMAN MORDAG FROM MURDERER'S VENGEANCE

Then followed a whole column of decks which read as if the public to which the paper catered were incapable of understanding an English sentence with the ordinary connectives and articles:

Celebrated Criminologist Pursues Poison Bug Along Johnson Boulevard.

Runs Miscreant to Earth in Deserted House. Explains Theory of Crime to Police at Back Door While Criminal Escapes Out Front.

Necromancer La Plesse Makes Second Attempt on Mordag's Life. Flings Knife Through Six Inches Concrete at Wife's Paramour.

Notes from Unseen Husband Found Daily in Mordag's Pockets.

Police Now Searching for La Plesse After Letting Him Slip Through Fingers Yesterday.

Last Seen Driving a Car on Johnson Boulevard While at Same Moment Car Was in Drive-It-Yourself Garage Undergoing Repairs.

La Plesse an Adept in Art of Hindu Magic.

Psychologist Poggioli of Ohio State Pits Western Science Against Eastern Occultism.

The second page of the paper was devoted to the elucidation of these multiple decks.

Mr. Poggioli laid the paper on a rat cage and swore with sincerity of sentiment and variety of diction. He reached a conclusion finally with—

"Janet, don't you ever again, so long as you live—"

And the girl interrupted to say:

"Goodness, Mr. Poggioli, I wouldn't again for the world. Why they say in the office this has put off your professorship ten years, if it doesn't lose you your job!"

"It isn't my job I mind losing, it's my decency. Look—look at that page—" he flapped it with his hand—"it's full of me. And I told that lying rat of a Tapper—"

"Well, you don't have to take a commission like that any more."

"No, I don't. Nothing will ever move me again into such a quagmire of indecent sensationalism; money—love—ambition—Well, what in hell do you want?"

This last was not addressed to Janet, but to a blue capped telegraph messenger.

"I have a telegram for Professor Henry Poggioli. They told me in the office that he—"

"Well, I don't want it," snapped the docent, "if it's anything about this damned affair."

"I don't know what it's about," said the messenger. "I haven't read it, sir."

"Well I know; it's about this affair!"

Poggioli shook the paper at him.

The boy opened his eyes.

"Oh, are you that Mr. Poggioli?"

"Yes," said the docent. "I am even worse than *that* Mr. Poggioli; you might say, I am *the* Mr. Poggioli."

This went over the telegraph boy's head. He stood for a moment.

"Won't you sign for it, sir?"

"No, I tell you."

The boy blinked his eyes and scratched an ear.

"If you won't, sir, I'll have to keep on bringing it back every two hours until you do."

Poggioli looked at Janet.

"The Pilgrims came to this country to win freedom; now look what we've come to."

The boy took this to be a serious thrust at himself.

"The boss says I must make every effort to deliver them the first trip out to pep up the service," he explained apologetically.

"Hand it here," said Poggioli. "I never before heard of a telegraph messenger trying to pep up the service. Janet, I'm beginning to think the comic strips misrepresent these young men." He signed for the telegram and tore it in two.

THE MESSENGER caught his breath at this unusual reception of a telegram, but continued standing where he was. "Well, do you want me to pay you anything?" asked the docent.

"Oh, no, sir; it was prepaid."

"Then what do you want?"

The boy blinked again at the torn envelope on the floor.

"Er—the regulations say, I'm to stand here, sir, till you read it and see if you want to answer it, sir."

"Well, I'll be damned . . . Janet, the American people are the slaves of system. System has elevated the message far above either the receiver or the sender. As far as the telegraph companies are concerned, the human race are merely points of origin and destination of the great central fact of telegrams. The obscure source from which telegrams spring, their equally nebulous recipients, the question of whether telegrams have a meaning, or are simply a fortuitous concourse of letters; these are probably points of acrid debate among telegraphic metaphysicians."

"Yes, sir," said Janet vaguely.

"Or take the point of free will. Since the receiver has no free will, has the sender any free will? Do telegrams hurtle over the wires in blind obedience to a mechanical necessity . . ."

"I never before heard of a gentleman not wanting to read his telegram, sir," said the boy.

"Certainly you don't hear of it, because the receiver's desires in the matter are what Huxley calls epiphenomenal."

And Poggioli stooped and picked up the torn halves of his telegram. The docent read:

TAPPER READ FRENCH NOTES STOP WILL BE MURDERED TOMORROW NIGHT STOP EXPECTED YOU ALL MORNING STOP AFRAID TO LEAVE VENDIG STOP GOD'S SAKE COME
—MORDAG

The docent read it again.

"Who's it from?" asked Janet curiously.

"Him—" Poggioli nodded cityward.

"He wants you to come to him?"

Poggioli gave a long sigh.

"Yes, he's frightened nearly to death. He really thinks he's going to be killed tomorrow night."

"Poor man—and he looked so thin and bad, too, Mr. Poggioli, when he came here to see you."

"Any answer, sir?" asked the boy.

"Tell him I'm coming. Just say, 'Will arrive in thirty minutes—Poggioli.' "

The docent started for the cloakroom out front. He turned to the girl who followed him—

"And now you see, Janet, the sort of thing your damned cards get me into . . ."

At the Vendig Poggioli found a crowd collected before the hotel, and in the lobby. As the docent went up to the clerk's desk he caught bits of conversation. A voice was saying—

"What good will it do to change his name?" And another answered, "Why, that may be like faith healing; you just think it's going to do some good."

Near a marble column an oldish man was saying to a youngish man—

"He deserves what he gets—running off with the fellow's wife." And the youngish man, who probably was not married, said, "If a wife gets tired of her husband I say she's got a right to run off. She's not his property, is she?"

At the desk Poggioli had to wait a couple of minutes while the clerk finished telephoning. He was saying—

"The Vendig roof is a hundred feet long by fifty wide; an airplane never has been landed up there."

He glanced around and saw Poggioli, and ended his conversation. He came forward, offering a key to the docent.

"Mr. Mordag is expecting you. In fact, he has been telephoning down every two minutes to know if you had arrived."

"What's the key for?"

"To let you in his room; he doesn't open his door to anybody."

At the expression on the docent's face the clerk ejaculated—

"You can't blame him with a man like La Plesse floating around somewhere in the hotel!"

"You don't mean La Plesse—"

"Yes, Mr. Mordag saw him going into a room."

"What room?"

"1728. He saw him from the elevator."

"Isn't that the room under Mordag's room?" queried Poggioli in surprise.

"Yes; everybody was expecting him to be over Mordag's room."

"He wasn't registered under his proper name?"

"Oh, he wasn't registered at all. He wouldn't be, you know."

"Probably not," agreed the docent.

The clerk leaned across the counter and said in a low voice—

"It's my opinion La Plesse showed himself and raised all this publicity for a purpose."

"What purpose?"

"Why, to get the crowds milling in here so he can come in with 'em and go out with 'em, and never be noticed. He can go upstairs or come downstairs with the crowd, and how're you going to pick him out? Our house man has spoken to three or four gents who answer the description. One was from Pocatello, one from Ripon, California, one—"

"How did he get a key to 1728?"

"From what Mr. Mordag says he doesn't need any key."

"After Mordag saw the fellow, did some one go at once to 1728?"

"Certainly; quite a bunch. But the room was empty. It was mussed up; it had been occupied, but it was empty."

"You don't know who mussed it?"

"No, I don't know whether it was La Plesse or my last registered guest. You see, with twenty-two hundred rooms to be kept in order, and chamber maids soldiering or getting sick on you, you can't be sure a room is ready because it's checked ready."

Poggioli nodded understandingly.

"But may I ask you to go on up as quick as you can," suggested the clerk. "Mr. Mordag is in a bad way, Professor. He's on the edge of a breakdown. You know he thinks he's going to be murdered tomorrow night."

The docent took the key and went up to the eighteenth floor. At Mordag's door he announced himself through the panel and let himself in.

THERE were three men in the room; Mordag lying on the bed; a large man with puffy eyes and a pasty complexion sitting beside the bed, and Tapper very busy at a telephone.

The reporter lifted a hand genially at Poggioli and went on arguing into the instrument.

"But look here, Millman, one of your little Sanson-Brevuet monoplanes can light and take off inside a hundred feet . . ."

"Professor Poggioli!" cried Mordag, reaching his arms toward the docent. "I thought you had deserted me."

The man was so haggard and worn the psychologist was ashamed of ever having given up his case.

"I was delayed on account of my rats," he explained. "When I got your telegram I came right on."

"I had telephoned and telephoned—"

"Professor Poggioli," began the large pasty man, "I also am glad you have come. I needed a man of science to help me press my solution of this situation upon Mr. Mordag."

"I can't see what earthly good it will do," complained Mordag, at his nerve's end.

"Introduce us," suggested the docent.

"This is Professor Wordenbaum, Mr. Poggioli," said the sick man.

"I read of Mr. Mordag's plight in the papers," proceeded Professor Wordenbaum in an assured and greasy voice, "and I knew I could disperse his troubles, eradicate his difficulties, remove the financial, mental, moral and spiritual obstacles in his path toward success and happiness."

"What are you?" asked Poggioli, looking at the man.

"I'm a numerologist."

"What's a numerologist?"

The man presented a card. In the center in Old English script was a catch line—

WHAT'S IN A NAME?

And below it in one corner in small Roman capitals:

HAVAH WORDENBAUM
NUMEROLOGIST,
DEVISER OF FORTUNATE NAMES,
TRADE MARKS, PATRONYMS, MATRONYMS,
PSEUDONYMS, SLOGANS, MOTTOES, APHORISMS,
APOTHEGMS AND CORRELATED PHRASES.

"What do you want to do?" asked Poggioli in mystification. "Fix this man up a slogan?"

"Devise him a more harmonious patronym, so that every time he speaks it or it is spoken to him he will vibrate to the rhythm of success. I will tune his subconscious to opulence, power, harmony and realization."

"Realization sounds as if it ought to be good," said the docent.

Professor Wordenbaum looked a little carefully at the newcomer.

"What's wrong with opulence, power and harmony?" he asked.

At this point Tapper turned from the telephone.

"I told Wordenbaum that Mordag couldn't change his name bang-off like that without an act of the Ohio Legislature; and he can't, either."

"What name do you suggest?" asked the docent of the heavy man.

Professor Wordenbaum considered.

"Well, now, his original name, Clayman Mordag, is very unlucky. Look at what the words mean; Clayman, a man of clay. Mordag, the day of death. Could anything be more unpropitious?"

"Can you better it?" inquired the docent.

"Now let me see; I would suggest 'Gaylord Morning.' That has buoyancy, optimism—"

"All right, he takes it," decided the docent at once. "Good day, Professor, and call around sometime next week and see how the new name is working."

Professor Wordenbaum was a little disconcerted at this swift decision.

"Well, all right," he agreed. "My fee is ten dollars a name."

"Mr. Mordag will be only too glad to pay you next week—if the name keeps him alive that long."

"Don't call him Mordag, call him Morning," coached the numerologist.

"Certainly; Morning—"

"And don't say if he is alive; make a positive assertion that he will be alive."

"Certainly; he'll pay you next week," asserted Poggioli positively, floating the pasty man toward the door.

"Go into this seriously, Mr. Morning," called back the professor as he went away. "Say to yourself, 'I am Gaylord Morning.' Write it on a piece of paper a hundred times. Inhale slowly and think, 'Gaylord Morning!' "

"I will," said the sick man. "It can't hurt me."

"Can't hurt you! It will cure you; dispel terror, danger, apprehension—"

"I'll do it," repeated Mordag.

"But look here," interposed Tapper. "It requires an act of the Legislature to change a man's name."

"Does it?" snapped the numerologist. "If I should call you a meddling, sharp nosed busybody, would the Legislature have to indorse that to make it true?"

"Do you call me that?" demanded the reporter sharply.

"No, I am simply trying to show you the power of suggestion requires no legal action. Language was used before laws were thought of. Well, good day, gentlemen. I'll be back for my fee next week, Mr. Gaylord Morning."

"I hope to God I'm here to pay it," said Mordag fervently.

When the man was gone, Poggioli turned to his client.

"What's this I hear about La Plesse being in this hotel?"

"He's just here," said the sandy man gloomily. "Of course he would come here."

"You saw him on the floor beneath this one?"

"Yes, sir."

"But you rather expected to find him the next story up, didn't you?"

"That's where he threw the knife from, sir."

AS MORDAG said this he got himself out of bed and walked across to the desk containing the hotel stationery.

"I got his note this morning as usual," he continued shakily. "Mr. Tapper here can read French. He read it to me." The ex-helper sat down at the desk and reached into a pigeonhole for the note.

"Let it alone, Mordag," said the psychologist. "I don't want to see it—That knife that dropped from the transom yesterday, did you ever see it before?"

The sandy man sat down and began writing weakly.

"Yes; it used to be one of his throwing knives."

"Used to be! Whose is it now?"

"Why, it's mine, sir."

"How came it yours?"

"He had fifteen of 'em, sir. He gave me one and Rose one when we broke up our act."

Poggioli looked at his client in amazement.

"Then at the time when the gravamen of—of your offense was fresh on his mind, he wasn't so terribly angry either at you or at Rose!"

"No, sir, not so terribly. At the hotel where we are all packing our things to leave, I happened to need a knife. He handed me this one and said I could keep it. Then he handed Rose one, too. He said he thought it would make an appropriate gift for parting."

"And you haven't offended him in the meantime?"

"I haven't even seen him in the meantime, except, you know, just glimpses as he followed me around."

"Why, that's the most extraordinary thing—after a wait of two or three years, then grow angry enough to take revenge."

"I suppose so," murmured Mordag.

"Listen; in the meantime had you been brooding over the injury you had done him, Mordag?"

The sandy man winced.

"Mr. Poggioli, would you mind not calling me that name?"

"What name?"

"Mordag, sir."

"What do you want to be called?" inquired the docent in surprise.

"If you don't mind, Morning—Gaylord Morning."

Poggioli was amused and slightly contemptuous.

"Oh, all right—if I can remember to call you that."

"It can't do me any harm, sir, and it might do good."

He got up and walked slowly over to the telephone and called down and asked the clerk to change his name on the register. After a pause he straightened up and said—

"Professor Wordenbaum had it changed on the register as he went out."

Then he went over and laid down on the bed again, repeating—

"I am Gaylord Morning; I am Gaylord Morning—" in the queer voice of a man who speaks while he is drawing in his breath.

At this Tapper turned and hurried to another telephone which stood in the room and which Poggioli had not observed before. Tapper picked up the transmitter and said:

"Take this, Bill. . . . At the suggestion of Numerologist Havah Wordenbaum, Clayman Mordag has changed his name to Gaylord Morning. Professor Wordenbaum has in a way guaranteed Mr. Morning's new moniker to save his life as he supplied the name on a contingent fee of ten dollars, payable in event Mr. Morning lives to pay it. Psychologist Poggioli of Ohio State approved the change of names—Put that in a box on the front page."

"What's that?" cried the docent. "You say I approve such an idiotic—"

"Certainly you did," cried Tapper, turning from the telephone defensively. "I told Mr.—er—Morning it was all damned stuff and nonsense; but you advised him right off to do it."

"That was simply to get the fellow out of the room."

"You approved," persisted the reporter doggedly. "There's a human interest story in that, but if I say you did it just to get him out of the room, no story there. Anybody would have done that."

"But damn it, you will absolutely ruin my reputation—" The docent caught up the receiver from the second telephone. This proved to be a private wire to the *Dispatch* office. "Hello, who is this? . . . I want to speak to Bill—Tapper's assistant. . . . Yes, listen, this is Henry Poggioli, the psychologist in the Mordag— I mean Morning—case. I absolutely forbid you to quote me as approving the change of Mr. Morning's name. . . . Yes, I did sanction it, but that was simply to rid the apartment of—You will take it out or I'll sue you for libel. I'll—" Poggioli snapped down the receiver in its fork. "Damn you, Tapper, I'm half a mind to pitch you out that window!"

"Well, by Jiminy," cried Tapper spunkily, "other men have tried pitching me out of windows—"

AND the two men apparently were about to fight when Mordag called:

"Men, for God's sake, don't. You two are the only friends I've got now. If you get to fighting—"

"Well this damned little snake printed a paper full of libel about me yesterday and he's starting another edition today!"

"I never printed a line you didn't dictate yourself, either in word or substance!" snapped the reporter.

"Listen," cried Poggioli, "either Tapper goes or I go, Mordag."

"Please, please, Mr. Poggioli, say Morning."

"All right, Morning—you can decide which you want, me or Tapper."

The sandy man looked at his incompatible aides.

"Uh, M-Mr. Tapper," he stammered, "h-has thought of a p-plan that may s-save me if he can get—"

"I can get it," snapped Tapper belligerently. "I've just received assurance from the air field they have a helicopter coming over from Akron."

"A what?" ejaculated Poggioli.

"Helicopter," repeated Tapper impatiently. "It can light on the Vendig's roof. We plan to take Mr. Morning up tomorrow afternoon on an endurance flight. We mustn't let out a word so this La Plesse will have no idea of what is about to happen. Then we'll take Morning up and see if the magician can break into an airplane somewhere over Ohio and murder one of the passengers. I'm going to stay with Morning straight on from now till the flight ends."

The reporter's voice had become friendly again with enthusiasm over his plans.

"Did you think of this?" asked Poggioli, taken off his feet.

"No, it was Morning's idea. It hit me hard, however, and the city editor O.K'd it. We'll have a wireless in the plane. I'll keep in touch with the office and write the story as we go." The little man paused. "Won't you go along, Professor?"

"No, no, I couldn't."

"Listen, we'll say you suggested the whole idea. Think of the scareheads—Western Science Versus Eastern Occultism. Psychologist Takes Threatened Victim in the Air. Leaves Magician Stranded on Earth."

"I wouldn't go unless I was prepared to hand in my resignation at the university."

"I wish you would. Be a great advantage to have you if anything should happen up there. You know, if another airplane came and chased us; or La Plesse should—you know, just form in the air and shoot Mordag—we'd like a scientific explanation of it."

"For God's sake, don't call me Mordag!" squealed the sandy man.

"Beg pardon, Mr. Morning."

"I believe if both you men will remember to call me Morning, and I ever get up in that plane, I think I can live through tomorrow night."

"We'll both remember it, Mr. Morning. And you won't go with us, Professor?"

"No, I wouldn't think of it. I'd like to, but I can't. You say you are going to remain here with Mr. Morning in his apartment tonight, Mr. Tapper?"

"Yes; the city editor wants a line on whoever it is writes these notes."

"Will you have a policeman or some one to sit up with you?"

"No, we are afraid if you put two or three men in the room nobody would appear."

"He'll come and write the note," said Mordag with certainty. "And Mr. Tapper won't see him—you know, he'll just come in and write it in my pocket without being seen."

"You mean La Plesse will get into your pocket?" queried the docent.

"Oh, no; I mean he will cause the writing to appear in my pocket. Many a time I've seen him put a blank sheet of paper in a glass and pass his hand over it, and when he pulled it out it was full of writing."

"Don't you know how he did that?"

"No, I don't know how he did it."

"He had already written the message on the paper in invisible ink."

"Invisible ink wouldn't cause the notes to appear in my pocket every morning."

"Oh, no, I'm simply explaining the trick you saw him do; about how your notes get in your pockets—that's something else."

"It certainly is something else," assented Mordag in the greatest depression; and he began repeating to himself in the odd tone of an indrawn breath—

"I am Gaylord Morning; I am Gaylord Morning—"

Since he was tacitly let out of his uncomfortable situation by the entrance of Tapper's flying machine, Poggioli made his *adieus*, expressed his sincerest well wishes and washed his hands of the whole matter. He went away from the Vendig in better spirits than when he had entered.

IV

IT WAS highly characteristic of Mr. Poggioli, that after he had severed his connection with the Mordag mystery, it bedeviled him all night long. Not only did the enigma itself seduce him, but he wondered whether or not he had acted wisely in withdrawing from the problem. If Tapper attempted a world's record airplane endurance flight and at the same time preserved a victim from attempted murder, it would bring every one connected with it into nationwide publicity. And such publicity was so much money in hand. If he had gone up in the airplane he could have written a book, appeared in a motion picture, spoken over the radio, sold his name for a cigar brand . . . The docent could not help reflecting that he had thrown away a fortune.

As he passed through the office on his way to the laboratory, the girl, Janet, jumped up excitedly and followed the docent in among the rat cages. Evidently she had something on her tongue's end, but she bit it back. Finally she asked tentatively—

"Have you found out anything more about the Morning case?"

"You mean the Mordag case."

"The newspapers are calling it the Morning case now. He's changed his name for luck. I think that's silly."

"It's tommyrot."

"But those notes he gets aren't silly. I think they are the eeriest things I ever heard of; just imagine, getting a note every—"

"They aren't mysterious at all compared to that knife," growled the psychologist.

"Why aren't they mysterious?" demanded Janet, vaguely offended.

"Because La Plesse either puts them in Mordag's pockets—or he does not."

"Why certainly," agreed Janet, a little confused.

"Well, there you are; any proposition that can be reduced to one of two alternatives is not mysterious; it's simple."

"But how does he get them in there?" demanded Janet, ruffled.

"That's a detail—a trick of some sort."

The office girl gave a short laugh.

"I'll say it's a detail." She looked at Poggioli with a touch of satire. "Maybe you don't consider there is anything mysterious about this case."

"Oh, yes, there is—the knife."

"You mean the one thrown through the concrete ceiling—I don't believe that."

"Neither do I. I happen to know the knife was laid on top of the transom over Mordag's door. It was pulled off by a silk thread. I found the thread."

"Then that isn't mysterious either," said Janet. "That's just another detail."

"Certainly how the knife got on the door is a detail, but the knife itself casts the most mysterious complexion over this whole affair that has ever fallen under my observation."

Janet looked at him blankly.

"I don't see how a knife—just a knife—"

"Why the knife was given to Mordag by La Plesse."

"Yes; I read that in the papers yesterday evening."

"It was given to Mordag immediately after Mordag and La Plesse had had trouble over La Plesse's wife."

"So I understand; what's strange about that?"

"Why, it involves a paradox, a contradiction," ejaculated the psychologist. "For La Plesse to assume the ironic attitude of giving his wife and her lover a knife apiece when he has just been wronged, and send the couple about their own devices, is, I think, one of the most cynical things I ever heard of a man doing."

"I—I suppose it is," hesitated Janet, "but it isn't mysterious."

"That part isn't, but look at this. Five years later he is imbued with such a hatred for Mordag that he is trying to kill him with all this red fire and melodrama."

"But La Plesse's wife will inherit a fortune if Gaylord Morning is put out of the way."

"That's true, but La Plesse was a popular magician and he must have had money. And then your genuine cynic would never turn into a murderer. Cynicism is a shield, not a sword. A cynic is a man who has no more fight left in him.

Since life rides him hard, he says his galled withers are trifles; since he can't win love that love is ridiculous; since he can't keep a wife, that he never cared anything about her. Such a man would never go out and commit murder for a fortune. He would tell himself that fortunes were tiresome things and that he was glad he had none."

The office girl looked impressed.

"He would do that, wouldn't he?"

"Certainly. That is why the knife throws such a blank mystery over the whole affair."

"You don't believe the man who would give away a knife would now try to murder Mr. Morning?"

"I know he would not—but he did. Now that is what constitutes a mystery."

"Then what do you believe about it?" cried Janet excitedly.

"Personally, I don't believe La Plesse has anything to do with this."

The office girl was logically outraged.

"The idea of such a thing; the notes, the knife, the poison! You've got to account for them somehow. Besides that, you yourself saw La Plesse and his wife and child on Johnson Boulevard."

"They are details that will have to be worked out separately," said the docent.

"But La Plesse has followed Morning around from city to city."

Poggioli smiled.

"Suppose I should suggest to you that Mordag has been following La Plesse around from city to city . . ."

"What!"

The psychologist nodded slowly with the faint smile of one who deals in oracles.

"Exactly. Mordag, or Morning as you call him, was La Plesse's assistant. Mordag still carries around with him a pocket full of old newspaper clippings extolling the showman. The poor devil genuinely believes that La Plesse can perform any sort of miracle whatever. Now here are some of the things Mordag believes La Plesse can do; read your thoughts, get out of a grave, fling one object through another without leaving a trace, produce writing on blank paper without any physical means of doing so. And I feel sure that Mordag was hypnotized by La Plesse for exhibition purposes every evening for two years. When the helper was discharged, he was, you might say, left without his divinity."

"Why, Mr. Poggioli," ejaculated Janet with horror in her face, "that is the crawliest thing I ever heard of."

"Or take another theory; if La Plesse hypnotized Mordag for such a long time, it is within the bounds of reason that wherever La Plesse decides to go, Mordag automatically makes up his mind to go to the same place. That is why they are eternally meeting one another, on trains, in the street, in hotels. Mordag always chooses to stop where La Plesse is stopping."

"And doesn't know that he is doing it," ejaculated the office girl.

"No, he thinks he is trying to get away from the man—his conscious side thinks that, while his subconscious side is following him."

"That nearly makes me sick," cried Janet.

"That's merely a theory," said the docent. "It explains part of what we know. But if La Plesse really is trying to murder Mordag after having given him that throwing knife, I must say this is the most blindly mysterious affair I ever encountered."

"So you don't believe the magician is after Mr. Morning at all?"

"I do not."

As the docent said this they heard the faraway tinkle of the office telephone. The girl started, then said:

"They have been ringing for you, I don't know how long, Mr. Poggioli. The janitor said they were ringing when he swept out."

The docent frowned.

"It's something about that case."

"I imagine Mr. Morning has gone quite mad because you aren't with him."

Poggioli smiled.

"No, he and Tapper have hit on a plan that entirely dispenses with me."

"What are they going to do?" asked Janet.

"You'll see it in the afternoon papers."

Here the janitor entered the laboratory from the office.

"Mr. Poggioli, they've been calling for you about every three minutes since before I came. Shall I muffle the bell or will you answer it, sir?"

A curiosity moved Poggioli to know what Mordag wanted with him now.

"I'll answer it, Henderson," he said, and went out front to the telephone.

When he put the receiver to his ear a man's voice asked in nervous haste:

"Has Professor Poggioli come in yet? Has he a telephone? What's his street address? How can I get into communication—"

"This is Poggioli," interrupted the docent with a discomforting premonition.

"Thank God I've found you, Professor. This is Manderby, city editor of the *Dispatch*. You know more about this case, I believe, than any other man in town. You have *carte blanche* to hire anybody, draw on us for any amount, but run the murderer to the earth."

Poggioli's heart suddenly dropped into his chest.

"You don't mean Mordag has been killed?" he gasped.

"No; it's Tapper!"

"Tapper! What happened to—"

"La Plesse shot him through the window. We knew Tapper was a good friend of yours—the way he protected your name in his stories. You'll go, won't you?"

"Oh, yes; yes, I'll go. Starting right now."

He hung up. On his way out he said to Janet—

"La Plesse killed Tapper last night in Mordag's room."

"Oh, my Lord," ejaculated the girl. "The man who wrote—"

She followed the docent out to the door and watched him signal a taxi to the curb.

POGGIOLI motored to the Vendig, confounded by this swift and certain proof that Herman La Plesse had concealed himself in the hotel with murderous intent. He tried to construe some rationale that would transform a cynical man into a murderer, but failed.

As the psychologist approached the desk at the Vendig, the clerk turned to a tall athletic man standing nearby and said—

"This is Professor Poggioli, Mr. Olsen."

The two men shook hands.

"I'm with the *Dispatch*, in Tapper's place," explained Olsen in lowered tones. "I wanted to meet you in the lobby so I'd know it was you."

The docent nodded and started to the elevator with the new reporter.

The two men got out on the eighteenth floor.

"Have you any theories about this, Professor?" asked Olsen. "I've got to go through the case with you. I'd like to know what we're trying to do?"

"It has been a tentative theory of mine that Mordag was following La Plesse, and not La Plesse Mordag," began the docent.

"What?" ejaculated the reporter, staring at the psychologist.

Poggioli ceased his explanation and concluded with a perfunctory—

"Of course I'll have to discard that idea now."

"I should think so," nodded the reporter, "after what has happened to poor Tapper."

The two men went on to room 1827. Olsen produced a key and let himself and his companion inside.

In an easy chair by the bedside Tapper still sat. He might still have been watching except for his stonelike stillness. Under the covers of the bed, Poggioli saw the outline of a man's form which occasionally shook or jerked.

As the two men entered Olsen said in a lowered tone—

"I have brought Mr. Poggioli, Mr. Morning."

The man in bed put his face out from under the quilts and looked at the reporter. The thin man was ashen.

"W-when are you going to bring the h-helicopter, Mr. Olsen?" he chattered.

"Right away—at once," soothed the big man in the tone one uses to a child.

"You are really going to take me?" queried Mordag suspiciously.

"Of course I am."

The thin man looked at the figure sitting by his bed.

"Oh Lord—to kill him just to frighten me. What a fiend! I wish the airplane would come on."

Poggioli glanced at Olsen interrogatively. The big man shook his head slightly.

"The story is here now," he said, guarding his meaning as if Mordag were a very young child.

The thought came to Poggioli that fear would kill Mordag that night if nothing else did.

"Well," said Olsen in a muted voice, "nothing has been touched. Everything here is exactly like it happened."

The psychologist took in the ensemble—the body, the little hole in the window where the bullet had entered the room, the lesion where it had entered the skull, the place on the other side of the head where it had come out.

"Let's locate the bullet in the wall," suggested the docent, "and get its line of trajectory."

The reporter got his bearings from the window and the body and began searching for the bullet. But the closet stood in its path. The closet door was open and in the confusion of this closet the missile was impossible to locate.

"Get a window cord," directed Poggioli, "and we can approximate its line of flight by the wound and the hole in the window."

Mordag sat up in bed watching them with a colorless face. The two men used chairs, a walking stick, the throwing knife, and so maneuvered the line into position; one end pointing at the wound, the other at the hole in the glass. The line was leveled on a window across the court.

"Describe the location of that room to the desk clerk," suggested Poggioli, "and see if it was occupied last night." Olsen went to the house telephone and began talking. The psychologist turned to the man on the bed.

"Did you hear anything in the night, Mordag, a shot—"

"Mr. Poggioli, please—"

"I'm sorry—Morning—Did you hear a shot last night?"

"No, I went to sleep."

"He would hardly have heard it anyway, coming from a room across the court," interposed Olsen. He began talking to the office again. "A room on this floor on the opposite side of the court. . . . Has two windows in it . . . What number? Oh, 1875. And you say it was empty last night? . . . Empty but locked. Well, we supposed it was locked; that's running true to form. . . . Yes, if you'll send the key up, we'll cross over."

HE PUT the instrument on its hook. Poggioli was examining the pane of glass itself. The ball had struck from the outside, taking off delicate slivers on the inside. It really had been shot from across the court. He gave up the examination.

"Well, let's go around to 1875 and see what we can find there."

Mordag began getting out of bed hurriedly.

"I'm not going to stay in here by myself. I'll go with you."

The ex-assistant was so shaken that Poggioli begged him to stay where he was, but his fear overcame his weakness.

"No, I can walk; I'm all right." He repeated, "I can walk."

"We're going to hunt for La Plesse," warned the psychologist, hoping to discourage him.

The cadaverous man gave the wannest twist of his skeptical smile.

"I'm not afraid of you finding him."

The two men helped Mordag get on his socks and shoes and tied his tie, then the three walked out of the room and started along the corridor that led around the court.

When the matron at the floor desk caught sight of the thin man, she threw up her hands.

"Poor Mr. Mordag—they've poisoned him at last!"

"No," said the docent, "it's the strain. He's under a terrible strain."

"Poor man," consoled the matron, arising from the desk and following the trio. "Here are the keys. The clerk telephoned me to go with you. Just pick out any room you want and I'll let you in."

"Thanks," said the docent.

"Have you found out anything new—what does Mr. Tapper think about it?"

"Mr. Tapper—" the thin man's mouth made mussitations of Tapper's name when Olsen said—

"Oh, Tapper remains hopeful of getting Mr. Morning out of his trouble; so do I for that matter."

The three men and the woman walked on around the turn in the corridor. As the room numbers neared 1875 Mordag became more and more nervous.

"There's not any use looking in that room," he complained. "You know he won't be there after he killed Mr. Tapper."

"What! What!" cried the floor matron.

Olsen turned sharply.

"Don't pay any attention to him," he advised significantly. "He has murder on the brain."

At this moment a door behind the group opened and a man came out into the corridor and walked past the four in the direction they were going. The searchers lined up along the wall to allow the man to pass. The stranger walked rapidly and was ten or twelve doors ahead when suddenly Mordag caught the psychologist's arm.

"O God!" he gasped, on the verge of collapse. "That's Professor La Plesse!"

A kind of shock traveled through Poggioli. He started forward.

"La Plesse! La Plesse! Stop there!"

The next moment Olsen and the docent began running. The man down the corridor broke into a sudden dash without a glance over his shoulder, and swung suddenly aside into a door. They saw him work a moment at a bolt and vanish suddenly into a room.

Poggioli dashed up to the door with Olsen at his heels. He tried the bolt and found it locked.

"Matron! Matron!" he shouted. "Come on!" He ran back to her and met her down the corridor while she fumbled at her keys.

"What room?" she puffed.

"What room, Olsen?" called the docent.

"The one we were hunting—1875."

The woman selected a key and Poggioli went running back with it.

"He won't be in there," chattered Mordag, stopping two or three doors down the hallway and staring after the men fearfully.

"Why," cried Olsen, "I saw him go in." The reporter twisted at the key in the lock. He looked at Poggioli. "He's holding the knob from the inside."

"What'll we do?"

"I believe I can break in the panel of the door . . ." Olsen looked at the convex hardwood finish.

"You won't find him if you break in," cried Mordag. "I've seen it tried before."

"But I tell you he's holding the door," snapped the newspaper man.

"He does that—holds it up to the very last second, then turns it loose and he's gone."

"Keep up the pressure," cried the psychologist. "As long as he twists against you you know he's there. Matron, go get help!"

THE woman went waddling down the corridor in a great hurry.

At that moment the lock on the door suddenly gave. The bolt snapped back and almost at once Olsen and the docent found themselves inside.

The room was one of those uncompromising cubicles with one door and two windows such as a single room in a large hotel usually is. It was obviously empty.

"Look in the closet," suggested Poggioli, glancing about the blank interior.

Olsen jumped for the knob of the closet and tried to turn it. This also stuck. Then after at least a half minute of straining, it gave way. The door swung open so suddenly that Olsen half fell. Poggioli stepped inside with hand out ready to grapple with anything inside, but beyond the musty warmth of an unaired closet he felt nothing.

The psychologist groped around, found the switch of the closet light, turned it on. The interior was empty except for two or three whisky bottles and an old shirt some guest had discarded.

The two men reentered the room. The window on the court was raised about six inches.

"That's where he went out," cried Olsen, running to it. "He tried to pull it down after him but didn't have time!" The reporter jerked up the sash and thrust his head out. He looked up and down. "He might be one of these human flies—"

"You don't see him?" asked Poggioli, running to the same window and looking out.

"No, but he's had time to climb down three stories and crawl in a window below."

Poggioli was somehow not at all surprised at the magician's escape. He looked up and down in the futile fashion of the reporter. Then he observed that the dust and soot on the window ledge and on the fillet of masonry below it were not marked. He reached down his finger and touched the film. It made a clear cut dot. Poggioli glanced at Olsen. The reporter was not watching and did not get the significance of the untracked dust.

The psychologist leaned out of the window, looking this way and that. Across the court, in one of the opposite windows, he presently picked out the form of Tapper still sitting by the bed. Just then the docent's fingers felt a little roughness on the outer edge of the ledge. He leaned out and looked at it. It was a bullet hole. He reached in his pocket, drew out his penknife. He began digging in the wood. Presently he touched steel and a few minutes later had the missile in his hand. He turned it about, looked at it.

"Olsen," he said slowly, "this is why we couldn't find the bullet in Mordag's closet."

"What do you mean?" asked Olsen, mystified.

"I mean La Plesse was standing in the closet across the court when he fired at Tapper. This is his bullet."

"But look, man," cried the reporter. "La Plesse's bullet entered that window across yonder, you can tell by the fracture of the glass."

"M-m-m, yes; that's true."

They heard a sound at the door and both men whirled.

It was Mordag. He was leaning against the side of the door giving an impression that he had crawled up the corridor to that point.

"You didn't catch him—he wasn't in here?"

"No."

"I—heard what you said. If—if he had already got into my room, why did he kill Mr. Tapper?"

"He advanced that idea merely on the strength of one bullet," explained Olsen comfortingly. "He found a bullet here in the window ledge; it may have been shot across the court a long time ago."

"And if he fired a bullet in my room, why didn't it wake me?" complained Mordag.

"Well, you might have been hypnotized," said the psychologist.

"Hypnotized?" cried Olsen.

"Hypnotized—" wavered Mordag.

"Yes, damn it, hypnotized," ejaculated the psychologist in an annoyed tone. "Merely because hypnosis is somewhat unusual, you want to rule it out of the evidence. He has hypnotized you, hasn't he, Mordag?"

"That was a long time ago, sir."

"Really," said Olsen, "this is getting too melodramatic even for the *Dispatch*."

There was nothing more to be found on that side, and the three men walked back to Mordag's room. Poggioli went at once to the window with a hole in it. The bullet seemed to have entered from the outside. He lifted the sash and looked at the outside of the pane. Then he saw the putty had been pried out of the mullions and the pane taken out and reversed. This reversed the apparent course of the bullet.

HE THEN examined the body of Tapper in the chair by the bed. A stain on the carpet which must have trickled down one of the chair legs fitted to a leg with no stain on it. The stained leg was at the opposite corner of the chair. He showed these things to Olsen.

"You see, the window pane and the chair have been reversed."

The reporter stood nodding slowly to these findings.

"That's one of the cleverest tricks I ever heard of."

"It seems to be a crime of some complication," admitted the docent. "For example, why should a man who can disappear so easily take all these pains to shift the direction of his bullet?"

"I don't think he disappeared so easily," said Olsen. "Climbing up or down a skyscraper isn't easy."

"He didn't climb a skyscraper."

"Why didn't he?"

"Because there were no marks on the dust on the ledge."

The reporter went blank.

"You—you don't suppose the fellow had some sort of pocket parachute so he could jump out?"

"No, I think you can rule that out."

"Then he escaped somehow inside the closet—it was really he holding that door?" inquired Olsen incredulously.

"Apparently—and, also, apparently that is how he entered this apartment last night and shot Tapper; through the closet. If he had ever come out of the closet, you know, Tapper, sitting there watching, would have moved."

Olsen pondered—

"Then I see just one thing left for us to do, Mr. Poggioli."

"What's that?"

"See if he comes out of this closet tonight."

"You mean, watch as Tapper did?"

"With greater precautions, of course. We understand it's dangerous now. We'll be on our guard."

At this point he was interrupted by a sudden knocking at the door. It startled all three of the men. The next moment the bolt clicked and the door swung open. Three policemen, the coroner, the hotel clerk, the floor matron, and behind them a rabble blocked off the room. One policeman kept the crowd out of the doorway.

"The paper is out," said Olsen in an aside to the docent. "We kept this quiet until the 1:15 edition."

Sure enough, from the court, they could hear a newsboy shrilling:

"Mysterious murder of reporter! Newspaper sleuth shot by Professor Herman La Plesse from empty room across court! All about the new murder in the Gaylord Morning mystery!"

V

THE LATE evening editions of all the Columbus papers carried a revised version of the Tapper murder mystery. The origin of the bullet was located not across the court of the Vendig, but in Gaylord Morning's own clothes closet. The coroner's verdict was that Tapper met death at the hands of an unknown person.

Newsboys were crying these new facts up and down the streets. Their calls echoed now plainly, now faintly, in the tall, chimney-like court of the hotel.

A drizzling rain set past the windows of Mordag's apartment, a gray descending veil with its suggestion of some melancholy eternity.

Three men sat in the apartment, watching the man in bed. Each was buried in his own thoughts concerning the sinister surroundings. The sick man was asleep.

"What I don't see," said Olsen at last, "is how Mr. Morning gets to sleep—expecting a terrible visitation the moment he drops off—yet he always does and seems to rest profoundly."

"Rests?" questioned the third man sitting by the bed—he was a physician.

"Sleep is supposed to rest one," said Olsen.

"Look at him now; does he look like a man who has been getting rest?"

Both Olsen and Poggioli glanced at the emaciated figure on the bed. The man had grown more drawn even within the forty-eight hours Poggioli had known him.

"Is there really nothing physically the matter with him, Doctor?" inquired Olsen incredulously.

"Complete exhaustion, that's all. No organic weakness; heart, lungs, nerves normal within the physical limitation of his exhausted condition."

"So all that troubles him is shock and fear?"

"That's enough," said the physician dryly. "It has killed thousands of men and will kill thousands more. It would not surprise me greatly if he doesn't get through the night."

"Would the fact that he thinks he is going to die tonight have a bad influence?" asked Olsen.

"Why certainly."

"Even when he is sound asleep, as he is now?"

"I would hazard that his fear would operate more devastatingly, more uncontrolled asleep than awake." The physician stared out into the darkening drizzle. "It has sometimes occurred to me that what you might call reality is not the houses and air and men and women which surround us. They are more in the nature of walls cutting off reality, making us, for the moment, oblivious to reality."

"Then what is reality?" queried the reporter.

"It is our unconditioned selves, our subconscious. When we sleep we are lost in reality; possibly, when we die."

Olsen shook his big shoulders.

"I think I'll stick around with the unreal boys and girls as long as I can." He paused a moment and then added gloomily, "If he dies of simple fright after all this melodramatic prologue, that will be one hell of an anticlimax from a journalistic point of view."

The physician arose and smiled.

"There's a lot of journalistic waste goes on in the world . . . Well, I don't believe there is anything further that I can do here, and I certainly don't care to sit here all night considering the surroundings. You gentlemen mean to?"

"That is our intention," said Poggioli.

"You have a better courage than I have. I certainly hope nothing untoward happens tonight."

"Thanks, Doctor."

The medical man bowed slightly and let himself out the door.

Olsen looked after him in the gloom.

"Untoward—he hopes nothing untoward happens tonight. I like that untoward; it certainly is a hell of a decent wish he made us."

"Scholastic," said Poggioli.

The docent arose briskly.

"Well, let's make ready to receive our guest in event he does come, and try to see that nothing untoward does happen here tonight."

"What are you going to do?"

"First, I'd like to find out exactly what is in this room."

"What's the idea?"

"You may remember that was Mordag's own knife that fell off the transom. It had been given to him by La Plesse."

"That's true."

"Well, doesn't it seem odd that a man who came into an apartment intending foul play should depend upon his enemy to furnish him a knife?"

"He visits the apartment every night; he knew about the knife."

"But he writes his notes on strips of Mordag's newspapers. Apparently if Mordag would just hide his things he would have this fellow checkmated."

Olsen nodded in the gloom and made a note in his book.

"I wonder if he has used anything else?"

"That's why I want to search the apartment—to find out."

THE TWO men set to work, paying no attention to the figure on the bed. There was no use in asking the thin man's permission. When Mordag had discovered no flying machine was to be provided him he had collapsed.

In the room was a box with a green cover. The docent searched Mordag's pockets, found his keys and opened the box. It contained a number of bizarre red and black suits which the thin man evidently had worn during his employment as the magician's *famulus*. A lower tray contained a *pot-pourri* of used magical equipment. Probably La Plesse gave his discarded equipment to his assistant.

In one compartment were bottles of chemicals, and among these was a vial of prussic acid.

The docent picked it up.

"This would have disposed of the cat without a quiver," he said.

Olsen looked at the tiny bottle in surprise.

"You don't really suppose La Plesse comes here empty handed?" he asked.

"He had a pistol last night," said the docent.

"Well, there's nothing more in this box. Let's see if we can find it somewhere else."

The room obviously contained nothing else, so they went into the closet. Here was a wardrobe trunk. The docent swung it apart and began going through the drawers. Pretty soon he paused with a whistle.

"All right, here it is."

"The gun—the automatic?"

"Yes, a .38; that's the caliber."

The reporter shook his head.

"That's ridiculous. You know a criminal wouldn't enter a room hoping to find a pistol to commit a murder with!"

"La Plesse didn't come into this apartment last night to commit a murder," argued the docent. "He came to terrorize Mordag. When he saw Tapper in here he resorted to violence."

"But how did he get this pistol if it was locked up?"

"Mordag says bolts and locks are not in his way. He probably got the automatic out of this trunk as easily as picking it up off a table."

"This may not be the gun after all," said Olsen. "There must be thousands of .38 automatics."

"No, it may not be." The docent drew out his handkerchief, made a twist and thrust it into the muzzle. The cloth came out clean. He said, "Smokeless powder leaves almost no fouling at all."

"You mean it may have been fired."

"It's clean, but I'm not sure."

"We could fire it, get its bullet and compare its rifle lines with the one you found."

"That would be microscopic work for a technical man," said Poggioli. "We couldn't get a report for another forty-eight hours."

"And this performance concludes tonight," said the reporter.

"Yes, and tonight I'm going to hold this particular automatic in my hand. If La Plesse shoots me he will have to bring something with him for once."

"I imagine," said Olsen slowly, "that he will bring it." After their search the two men fell silent. As night deepened in the windows on the court, the watchers could hardly distinguish each other.

At last Poggioli said—

"What had we better do about lights?"

"My idea is to stay as much in the dark as we can. Tapper had a bright light."

"There are two spots I want brightly lighted," said the docent in an undertone.

"Where's that?" inquired Olsen. "The closet and the door?"

"The closet's one," assented the docent softly, "but I don't believe he comes in the door—the matron never has seen him enter."

"How does he get in then?"

"Haven't the faintest idea."

"Well, we'll light up the closet."

The dark bulk of Olsen moved silently across the gloom and a moment later the closet was full of light. The reporter repassed against it in silhouette.

The light in the closet gave the creepy impression that it was about to be used and that it was really the entrance to the room.

"Look here," whispered Olsen. "He got out of the window on the other side. Better put our second light there."

"He got out of the closet on the other side," stated the psychologist. "You felt him twisting the bolt against you, didn't you?"

"Ye-es—Then he isn't human," ejaculated the reporter.

"Now you've seen dozens of illusionists do cabinet tricks on the very same principle," whispered the docent satirically, "but when you see a single instance off the stage, you say it isn't human."

"They were trick cabinets," said the reporter in an injured tone.

"You assumed they were trick cabinets."

"Why, they have to be."

"Did you ever hear of the fourth dimension?"

The reporter remained silent a moment.

"I hope you are not going to bring that in."

"Why not? We have every mathematical proof that it exists. It is mathematically no more difficult to step inside of a completely enclosed cube than it is to step inside a completely enclosed square drawn on the floor."

"Oh, my God!" whispered the reporter.

"That is if a man has the intelligence to do it, and, possibly, some practice."

The reporter gave a grunt of stifled mirth.

"Must be hell—getting the practice."

AT THAT moment a faint noise in the closet snapped off the low conversation. The psychologist arose noiselessly with that tightening of his muscles that precedes violent action. He moved around the closet door to see inside. The faint noise continued. Presently Poggioli stood looking steadfastly at something.

"What is it?" whispered Olsen at last.

"A mouse."

After another wait, the reporter whispered a trifle nervously—

"Well—what of it?"

"Why if a man should step through the wall it would be no more terrifying to the mouse than if he stepped through the door. What it feels isn't in our realm of consciousness at all."

"Of course not," agreed Olsen in a nervous tone. "I wish you wouldn't—" He broke off and finally added, "Expecting to be killed by a superman is bad enough. I don't want to sit here and wonder what a mouse would think about it."

"Excuse me, when I'm excited and nervous I—I think of things."

Both men broke off in a silence tense with listening and watching.

"I wish I knew the sort of tricks La Plesse could do," whispered Olsen. "I never realized before what a touchy job it would be trying to catch a—"

"By the way!" rapped out Poggioli in an undertone, "that second light—I want it over Mordag's bed."

"Mr. Morning's bed!"

"Yes, the person who visits this apartment has really never harmed Mordag in any way."

"No, that's true," agreed the reporter.

"Whoever it is comes in here writes notes, leaves poison, shoots poor Tapper; but the man he ostensibly wants to murder has slept through it all—slept."

"Hypnotized as you suggested," said Olsen.

"I don't know about that. At any rate he has never received a scratch or a blow."

"What do you make of it?"

"At present I don't make anything of it. But that is my reason for wanting Mordag's bed in full light—his reading lamp will do."

The psychologist moved across to the bed to turn on the light when the faint noise stirred in the closet again. It caused both men to start, when at the next moment a blurred tapping began at the window.

Poggioli instinctively got the automatic out of his pocket.

"That's the buzzer of our private line," explained Olsen sharply. He strode across to it in the shadows.

"Hello . . . hello . . . hello . . ." he began saying in a barely audible voice. "This is Olsen, Mr. Morning's apartment. . . . What? . . . You don't mean—"

He broke off; Poggioli could see his bulk standing motionless with the receiver to his ear. Finally he turned to the docent and said in a bleak voice:

"Manderby, the city editor says—" he began speaking in the receiver again— "you say you have received a facsimile of the burial certificate by telegraph?"

"What is it? Who's buried?" cried Poggioli, staring at the shape of the reporter.

"Manderby's been tracing down La Plesse," whispered Olsen in a shocked voice. "The fellow died three years ago. He's buried in the cemetery at Olagoula, Louisiana."

The psychologist made a single step across and switched on the reading lamp at the head of Mordag's bed. The bed was empty.

What happened next Poggioli never clearly knew. Olsen shouted:

"He's in the closet! Got a gun! Dodge!"

The docent made a headlong leap to get out of range of the door. He heard two deafening reports. He saw Mordag firing the pistol from the brightly lighted small room. Olsen lunged at him from the shadows. His powerful form went straight into the thin man. The two crashed back into the closet out of sight.

Poggioli suddenly became aware that the pistol he had had in his hand was gone. He lunged into the closet where the two men were struggling. He saw Olsen trying to twist the automatic from Mordag, who was trying to fire it. Poggioli rushed in as the reporter wheezed out—

"For God's sake get that gun!"

The psychologist bent aside from the muzzle of the automatic, caught the body of the weapon and began trying to break it loose from the thin man's fingers.

Olsen suddenly loosed the gun hand and struck at the fellow's jaw, evidently hoping to knock him out. The next moment all three men were down on the closet floor with Poggioli being swung back and forth by the terrific arm that held the automatic. It might have been a beam of some machinery. The thin man was prodigious. Poggioli curled up and got the wrist in the crotch of his legs and began twisting the gun in the man's steely fingers. Olsen was under Poggioli trying to get a strangle hold on this devil of a man. The two had him at full length with his head out the closet door.

"Get a rope! Get a strip of sheet! Get something!" panted the reporter.

"Got to get this gun!"

"Hell, haven't you got that gun yet!"

"Not yet."

Olsen detached a hand from the business of choking the thin man and reached up to help.

The next moment Mordag began a swift crawling out of the closet and across the room by some inhuman movement of the muscles of his back. He went toward the bed. He dragged his captors sprawling after him with the resistlessness of a caterpillar.

"For Pete's sake!" yelled Olsen. "Let's hold him!"

At that instant the rail of the bed struck Poggioli's skull. His hold on Mordag broke. Half stunned, he tried to grab his legs but they whipped under the bed and out of sight.

The docent jumped to his feet. He grabbed Olsen, who he thought was hurt.

"Get up quick; he'll shoot from under the bed."

"No he won't," puffed the reporter. "I've got his gun. I'm trying to see him."

"Why, he's right under the bed!" cried Poggioli, bending down.

"No, he isn't under here!"

"He's in the shadow."

"No, I see the light on the other side!"

Poggioli was now staring under the bed himself. He did see the light on the other side.

"Well, where in the devil—"

"His hand didn't wrench loose from mine," panted Olsen. "It sort of melted out—it left the gun in my fingers."

"Thank God you got that."

A rustle from the closet behind them caused Poggioli to knock his head on the rail and he jumped up and whirled. Then he stood on his feet, holding his bruised scalp and staring into the closet. Olsen was beside him with the automatic ready.

"It—it's that damned mouse again." The reporter shivered.

The big man turned back to the riddle of the bed and gave a gasp. Poggioli wheeled quickly.

Under the bedclothes, motionless, with his eyes fixed, lay Mordag. Olsen advanced with automatic ready, but as he leaned over the bed and touched the man's face with the back of his fingers he lowered his weapon.

In the closet the mouse pursued its tiny irrational gnawing at the foot of the clothes rack. And queerly enough while Poggioli looked at the dead man he thought of the mouse.

In reality the little rodent eluded him as completely as did his uncanny adversary on the bed. Their whole human tragedy was removed so utterly from the realm of the mouse. The struggle of the men with Mordag; the melting of Mordag's hand in Olsen's grip; his vanishing from beneath the bed; his reappearance under the cover smoothed out in the cold formality of death; all this had swirled about the tiny animal unknown, undreamed of while it pursued its meaningless nibbling on a piece of varnished wood. The universe of the mouse, whatever it was, stunned Poggioli with its unthinkable simplicity.

Olsen turned to the docent and began in a bewildered voice—

"What I don't understand—"

Then he hushed.

AFTERWORD

THE ACTUAL report which Mr. Henry Poggioli made of this material in the *American Journal of Psychology* and which led to his requested resignation from the Ohio State University, need not be copied here. The article he wrote was as tedious as his adventure itself had been strange and diverting.

However it did embody an attempted explanation of the foregoing episode. And also it shows Poggioli's absurd blunder in university politics in setting down on paper what he really thought about the incident.

Afterward, at the trial in Dayton, Ohio, one of the greatest criminal lawyers in America tried to prove that Mr. Poggioli's written words did not mean what they appeared to mean; but he was not altogether successful in his attempts.

It is needless to state here that a docent in an American university could not afford to employ the best legal talent in America. And as a matter of fact that eminent counselor was furnished *gratis* by the American Society for the Advancement of Free Speech in America. For while not a single member of this society believed in the antiquated tenet Mr. Poggioli put forth, still, as the attorney so forcefully phrased it—

"The Society would spend its last dime in defending Mr. Poggioli's inalienable American right to express an egregiously incorrect opinion."

Still it was the advocate's equivocal tactics to soften Mr. Poggioli's expressions where he could. One sentence which the attorney found impossible to reduce to doubtful English was the following:

"The theory of dual personality will never completely cover this case, even if one gives to that theory the usual *miraculous scientific stretch* which modern psychology is forced to give to all such cases in order to avoid a presumption, if not indeed a positive proof of the *survival of human personality after death*. (Italics, the transcriber's.)

"Take the classical psychological theory of split personality. According to that theory, the murderous half of Mordag's mind was aware of the normal half and was continually plotting to murder it. But the normal half was entirely unaware of this abnormal murderous half.

"Why should not have such intercerebral knowledge have been mutual? Materialistic psychology has no reply to make save that this does not fit the theory of materialism.

"How did the abnormal half of Mordag's split personality know the engine number of the train that bore him to Columbus, the name of every street which he passed in a closed taxicab after midnight? Conventional psychology answers: He noted these data subconsciously. That to the writer's mind is too flagrant an appeal to the miraculous to be admitted. He feels it is better to allow our modern materialism to fall flat than to have it propped up by such dubious miracles as that.

"Take the reappearance of Professor La Plesse in the blue automobile. That was probably an hallucination superinduced by Mordag's nervous apprehensions. But La Plesse's bodily reappearance in the corridor of the Vendig Hotel, his grip on the keybolt when Olsen attempted to turn it, proves that here La Plesse was a concrete physical fact. What sort of fact was he? A mediumistic exteriorization produced by Mordag to his own undoing without any relation to the surviving personality of the deceased La Plesse? Or was it, what would be far more rational and less supernatural, *the soul of La Plesse reassuming human form* to revenge itself upon Mordag?" (See transcriber's note below)

"The final and completely insoluble riddle when viewed from the conventional angle is Mordag's assumption of magical technique in his death struggle. First, how did Mordag, if he were not a trained prestidigitator, take from the hand of the writer the automatic pistol? This was done at a distance and without the writer's being aware of its removal. It was a magician's trick, but Mordag was no magician. How did he drag two heavy men across the floor by the muscles of his back? How did his hand melt from Olsen's grip? How did his whole body melt into nothing under the bed and reappear a moment later, stretched out in death in the bed? All these are simple enough illusions for a practised thaumaturgist. But the writer repeats, Mordag was no practised thaumaturge!"

"So here is the lion in the path of conventional psychology.

NOTE: In a conversation with the transcriber the eminent attorney for the defense said, "I knew my case was lost when I read that damning sentence."

"Mordag's untrained brain, muscles, nervous system, must suddenly have assumed the technique of a trained adept in legerdemain. He had no practice, no instruction, no talent, and no reason for doing such a marvel.

"The conventional reply to this certainly will be, that in his work as a magician's *famulus*, his nerves, brain and muscle acquired all this training subconsciously by merely *watching* La Plesse.

"This explanation places such a vast burden on the reader's *faith* that the whole structure must fall.

"Faith certainly has its uses, but the writer does not feel that faith should be the sole touchstone of the materialistic theory. Reason should have its day in court, even if it should destroy some of the pious miracles, not to call them the pious frauds of science. Science can be only all the better for allowing reason to check up on the operation of beautiful scientific faith." (See transcriber's note below)

Mr. Poggioli's article then went on to show how simply all these enigmas and riddles could be solved by accepting the hypothesis that Professor La Plesse's soul did survive his death. He further wrote:

"Not only can we explain how it was done, but why it was done. The facts cease to be an amorphous and incomprehensible riddle, but become a logical, straightforward course of action.

"La Plesse was a cynic, a passive wielder of sarcasm. He inhibited his grievance against Mordag with the sardonic gift of a knife.

"But at his death this repressed hatred broke all bonds and drove him to consummate his vengeance by taking demoniac possession of his ex-assistant's body. La Plesse's paradoxical situation of trying to slay the body of Mordag after he himself had relinquished it must have formed a horrible tantalization for his unquiet soul. To have committed suicide while he himself was in possession of Mordag's body was no revenge. That is why he pursued him with knives and poisons and what not, and finally frightened him to death with notes.

"This tragedy not only justifies the religious command to forgive your enemy quickly, but it strongly suggests the existence of an actual spiritual hell after death, for those who die unforgiving and unforgiven."

This ends the docent's fantastic paper.

THE EMINENT counsel for the defense used the following strange words in his peroration before the court:

NOTE: This paragraph the counsel for the university alleged to be ironical and full of disrespect for science, which indeed was the gravamen of the action against Poggioli. But the counsel for the defense was able to prove to the court that all scientific advancement has been a product of pure faith acting under inspiration, and the above was simply Mr. Poggioli's way of stating that well known fact.

"And may it please your Honor, last, but not least, this action is a true bill against our whole world of Western science.

"The aim of Occidental science, your Honor, has always been the mastery and subjugation of nature. Its aim is to make man supreme. It has sought to subdue every natural power to his dominion; the lightning that emblazons the tempest; the waterfall hurling seas over rainbowed heights must bend and toil for man.

"Now I submit to the discretion of the court does not such an attitude beget in the subconscious mind of man the impulse to subjugate, subdue or to deny every power that thwarts, estops or overshadows it?

"Scientists may not be aware of this profound anti-deistic tendency in their own psychology. But it is impossible for it not to exist.

"The persecution of this ignorant, ill-advised and perhaps insane young man, must show these scientists the enormous lengths to which the subconscious intolerance goes.

"I appear before you, your Honor, not representing this young man primarily, but as an advocate of free speech. My society clings to the ancient American belief that the expression of thought, even in a university, should be encouraged and not forbidden.

"Because who really knows where the truth lies hidden? Take the quaint old theology which this young man has so anachronistically resurrected—suppose it were true? Suppose by way of a momentary hypothesis, that every man and woman in this court room today possessed a soul (laughter). Then it would not be inapplicable for the regents and faculty of Ohio's great temple of learning to remember that once there was an angel named Lucifer, who vaulted in the face of Almighty God to his own eternal destruction; Lucifer, too, was a Bearer of Light."

ADDENDA: All evidence as to the facts of the case was ruled by the court as incompetent, as it did not bear on the point whether or not Henry Poggioli had committed scientific heresy. The decision of the lower court was affirmed. Mr. Poggioli lost his position in the Ohio State University and is now teaching in Tennessee.

The Resurrection of Chin Lee

GALLOWAY, superintendent of the Everglades Mill & Manufacturing Company, and Professor Henry Poggioli, his weekend guest, were discussing at the breakfast table in the superintendent's bungalow the rather didactic subject of recognition. The mill official did not expect, it did not even occur to him, that an immediate personal relevance could arise from so detached a theme. He was simply saying that he himself never could tell negro babies or Cubans or Chinamen apart.

Poggioli, the psychologist, was about to make some reply when a tall, raw boned white man came up the conk lined walk and halted just outside the screened breakfast room.

"Jim," he called to the mill official, "them last potatoes I got from Tampa ain't fitten to feed hawgs on, much less mill han's. What am I goin' to do about it?"

"Write to Farburger & Company and tell them about it."

"Yeh, and they'll think I'm tryin' to flim-flam 'em and next time they'll want cash with their order."

"Just when did the Everglades Mill Company lose its reputation for honesty?"

"These ain't mill potatoes. They're mine. I bought 'em for the ships."

"Oh, I see. Well, that's different."

"So I figgered I'd send one hamper back by Chin Lee when he goes up to buy supplies today, just to show 'em what rotten stuff they tried to put off on me. The freight won't be nothin'. Chin Lee can take one hamper along with him as personal baggage."

"M-m . . . Well, all right, do that. Good plan to show folks you're on the level when you happen to be—helps out at other times when you don't happen to be."

The superintendent opened his teeth but kept his lips closed with the expression of a man inwardly laughing at his own jest.

The man outside the screen wall was not amused.

"Then I'll tell Chin Lee to take a hamper with him."

He turned back down the garden path under the red flaming boughs of some poincianas.

The superintendent bestirred himself to make amends for a possible discourtesy.

"Wait a minute, Erb. I want to introduce you to Professor Poggioli. Professor Poggioli is one of the greatest criminal psychologists in America. He was attending a convention in Miami and I got him to come visit us over here in

Everglades. Now I want you to spread yourself in the kitchen while he's here. Mr. Poggioli, this is Erb Skaggs, our cook."

The sun tanned man peered at the guest through the wire.

"You say he's a criminal psychologist?"

"That's right."

"What's he done?"

Both gentlemen laughed. Galloway said—

"What he does is to find out what other folks do."

"Oh—you mean he's a detective?"

"In a way. He bears the same relation to an ordinary detective that the president of the Everglades Company bears to one of our lumberjacks."

"Gosh, he's a high priced man," said the cook soberly. "Who's he after down here?"

"Nobody at all. Just down for the weekend to eat and fish."

The rough faced man pulled down his lips in a grimace meant to be humorous.

"Hope he uses jedgment in what he fishes after."

And with that he turned and walked back toward the mill kitchen.

"Good old Skaggs," remarked the superintendent half affectionately. "Always in hot water about a little ship chandlery business that he runs on the side, and he brings me his troubles."

Conversation paused for a moment and then the psychologist said:

"By the way, what were we talking about a moment ago? I had a question to ask."

"You mean just before Skaggs came in?"

"Yes."

"Well, now, lemme see—what *were* we talking about?"

For a moment or two the breakfasters sat trying to think back, but they came to nothing.

"I recall what I wanted to ask you," said Poggioli. "I wanted to know if you were especially fond of chop suey?"

"Am I fond of chop suey?" Galloway smiled at the oddity of this question.

"Yes," Poggioli said, "but I can't remember why I wanted to ask it."

"That's funny. Why, no, I don't believe I ever tasted chop suey. I wonder why you wanted to ask that?"

POGGIOLI shook his head with the air of a man giving up a problem, then ejaculated:

"Certainly I remember! What you said about not being able to tell negro babies, Cubans and Chinese apart. I understand how you came to use Cubans and negro babies, but I wondered where you had met enough Chinese to choose them for examples?"

"Why, Chin Lee, our kitchen boy."

"Just Chin Lee? Don't you know other Chinese besides Chin Lee?"

"No, none at all," said the superintendent, rather amused at the psychologist's problem.

Poggioli puckered his brows.

"Why, that makes it more extraordinary than ever!"

"I don't see why."

"Because you seriously say you can't tell one Chinese from another, and here you never have known but just one Chinaman. You were serious, weren't you—you were not trying to be funny?"

Galloway broke out laughing.

"No, I wasn't trying to be funny. I meant what I said."

"Well, that's absolutely amazing. Have you any idea how you arrived at the generalization that all Chinese look alike when you have known only one?"

The superintendent became humorously thoughtful.

"Now, lemme see: Chin Lee—Chin Lee—What could there be about Chin Lee?" He pondered for some moments and finally nodded. "Yes, it must be that."

"Be what?"

"This may strike you as funny. I suppose it will. I never had thought of it myself before. The truth is I never have really known Chin Lee. I see him only now and then, and I don't remember how he looks from one time to the next. Of course I recognize his Chinese generalizations. I know he has a yellow face, slant eyes and wears his shirt outside his trousers; but the actual man himself—honestly, I can't recall his features at this moment."

Poggioli was astonished.

"How long have you known him?"

"He's worked here two or three years."

"That really is odd. I suppose it is a race obsession. You are so obsessed with Chin Lee's Chineseness, if I may coin a term, that your recognition stops there and doesn't reach the individual. It is probably based on our Anglo-Saxon superiority complex."

The superintendent laughed.

"I didn't know I felt that way until you asked me about it."

"Oh, well, a man is so accustomed to his own biases and slants that he never knows he has them."

Professor Poggioli sat considering the further queer fact that Galloway had decided all Chinese looked alike because the one Chinaman he did know never did quite resemble himself. A droller *non sequitur* he had never encountered.

He was smiling faintly when he saw a negro man hurrying up the garden walk. The black man's expression caught the scientist's attention. His dark face was drawn and of a grayish cast. The whites of his eyes circled his black irises. He came to a halt some distance down the path and called in an unsteady tone—

"M-Mist' Jim, kin I see you a m-minute?"

"Now, Sam, why do you want to come bothering me when I've got company?"

The negro made a desperate gesture.

"Mist' Jim, I jes' got to see you a minute."

The mill man gave a hopeless shrug and explained to Poggioli—

"Sam's the night watchman; somebody's probably been stealing lumber while he was asleep and now he's all cut up about it."

He opened the screen door, went as far down as the third poinciana, put a hand against its bole and asked in a bored tone—

"Well, what is it?"

The negro's answer was in a voice too low for the psychologist to catch, but he nodded toward the mill and the docks with a terrified expression. Presently Galloway ejaculated:

"What! Chin Lee?"

Sam explained something more.

"How did it happen? Is he still there?"

Here the black man went into a long rigmarole, pointing at Poggioli on the porch. Galloway shook his head.

"No, no, I wouldn't bother Professor Poggioli with a little thing like this. Besides, he didn't come down here to work; he came down to rest up and fish."

THIS reference to himself induced the psychologist to call out—

"What is it he wants with me, Mr. Galloway?"

"Oh, he says he's heard about you," deprecated the superintendent, with an apologetic laugh.

"Is he uneasy because I am a criminologist?" inquired Poggioli, amused.

"Oh, no, Sam's all right. It's not about himself. He's begging me to have you take a look at Chin Lee."

"What's happened to Chin Lee?" inquired the psychologist with more interest.

"Why, he's lying over there on the lumber dock, Sam says, with a bullet hole in his head."

Poggioli arose quickly and came out into the garden.

"When did you find him, Sam?"

"J-jes' a li'l while ago."

"You were night watchman, I understand. You yourself didn't have any trouble with Chin Lee—catch him stealing lumber or anything like that?"

"Lawdy, no, suh; no!" cried the black man in a panic. "Theah you is, Mis' Jim, jes' whut I was tellin' you! He think 'cause I'se night watchman, I mus' 'a' shot Chin Lee. Why, I di'n' even know he was shot tull I walk up on him."

"You must have heard the shooting."

"N-no, suh—take mo'n a pistol to wake me up when I'se night watchin'."

The criminologist paused a moment, and then said—

"Let's walk over, Mr. Galloway, and see what we can find out."

The superintendent cleared his throat.

"Well—I suppose we ought to go and take a look around, Professor."

Poggioli was a little surprised at his host's attitude.

"You would naturally go, wouldn't you?"

"Oh, certainly, I'd have to go!"

"Well, you—don't mind my going with you?"

"Why, no-o—" Galloway cleared his throat again. "But if you don't object, Professor, may I say here that I hope your interest in this matter will be—uh—purely academic?"

Poggioli looked at his companion in amazement.

"Academic!"

"Y-yes—if you don't mind."

"What am I to understand by academic?"

Galloway blinked.

"Well if you should find out who the murderer is, I—I hope you won't feel it necessary to—to make a great to-do about it."

"You mean not tell it—keep it quiet?"

"Well, baldly, I'd rather you would—keep it quiet."

Poggioli stood looking at his host for several moments.

"That is the most unusual request I have ever had made of me."

The superintendent moistened his lips.

"I suppose it is. But I have a good reason. These killings happen every now and then around the mill here. If the newspapers get wind of this one, they'll feature it because you're on the case. Then they'll get busy and dig up all the other killings and feature them, too. That will go all over the United States, and it will be damn rotten publicity for Everglades. It will prejudice investors against the place. So I do hope you'll keep quiet anything you find out. It's business with me."

The scientist listened in surprise to this odd reasoning.

"I had never thought of murder as adverse advertising."

"Well, if you had promoted as many boom towns as I have," said Galloway earnestly, "you'd know enough to hush up any little killing like this. Now if it were a big killing—like a banker or a preacher or a millionaire sportsman—I'd say go to it. A big murder trial would draw a lot of people to Everglades, and we'd sell 'em homes or business sites or something of the kind; but a dinky little killing like this—" Galloway shook his head. "It would do more harm than good."

Poggioli smiled dryly.

"Well, that's a Florida viewpoint. Come on, let's walk over for our private curiosities."

Here a discussion came up as to whether the three men should walk or ride to the lumber dock. The superintendent wanted to ride, because Everglades was laid out on the gigantic scale of a Florida boom town, and the houses in it which were actually built were so far apart that a neighborly call between any two residences was impossible without the aid of a motor car or a passing bus. The superintendent was about to send Sam for his automobile, but Poggioli said the walk would do them good, so the three set forth afoot.

AFTER a long hike they reached the dock full of racks of lumber with the planks standing on end in order to season in the hot sun without warping. As they entered the vast lumber yard, Sam walked more and more slowly. Finally he stopped altogether and said the dead man was right around the next rack. It was clear that Sam did not mean to walk around the rack himself.

"When did you find him?" asked Poggioli.

"'Bout a hour ago, suh."

"Did you move or touch the body?"

"No, I can tell you he didn't," interposed Galloway, walking on around the rack.

"Sam, do you know of anybody around here who had a grudge against Chin Lee?"

Just then he heard Galloway, from the other side, call out in annoyance—

"Sam, where in the hell is the thing?"

"Why, right theah befo' yo' eyes, Mist' Jim, layin' wid his face down an' a hole in his haid."

"Well, I don't see him."

"'Fo' Gawd, I ain't gwi' have to come aroun' an' point out a daid Chinaman undah yo' nose, is I?"

"If I'm going to do anything about him, Sam, I've got to see him. I don't see what the hell you wanted to walk off and leave him like this for, anyway."

"Wh—whut you speck me to do wid him?"

"Well, there was the edge of the dock, wasn't it? Just what do you imagine the duties of a night watchman are?"

Poggioli came around the rack.

"Is it gone?"

Galloway drew a long breath of relief, got out and lighted a cigaret.

"It certainly is gone, and thank heaven that ends our problem. Got a match?"

Poggioli supplied a cigar lighter.

"I don't see how that ends the problem; it strikes me that it makes it more complicated."

"Oh, no—you don't know what problem I was talking about."

"Well, just what were you talking about?"

"Why, how to avoid an inquest and keep the mill from being held up half a day. You know every man jack in our plant would have to be questioned. Why, it would cost the company ten or twelve hundred dollars—just for a dead chink." Galloway stood looking up and down the dock. "I imagine the man who killed him came back and rolled him in the water."

Poggioli looked more carefully at the planking.

"I suppose he was lying here on this stained place?"

"Yes, suh, yes suh." The negro nodded.

"Then he hasn't been rolled off the dock," said the psychologist.

"Why do you say that?" inquired Galloway antagonistically.

"Because there are no stains on the boards or trail in the dirt where he was dragged."

The mill official glanced about in his turn.

"There are no stains or trail in any other direction, either."

Poggioli stood pulling at his chin, looking up and down the dock's edge. After several moments he replied absently to Galloway:

"Yes, yes, so I had observed . . . How big a man was Chin Lee—about what did he weigh?"

Both white man and negro began pondering this odd question.

"I figgahs 'bout a hun'erd an' fifty or sixty," hazarded Sam. "But I don' see whut diff'unce dat makes now, seein' as he's daid."

The professor continued musing over the situation.

"Did Chin Lee go with any women here in Everglades?" he inquired.

Here Galloway caught the drift.

"Oh, no, Chin Lee hasn't been seen with a woman since he came here . . . Would you say he had, Sam?"

"No, suh," corroborated Sam.

"Not being seen with a woman is not identical with never being with one," pointed out the psychologist. "Could you give me a list of the women here in Everglades, either white or colored, who are large and strong enough to lift a hundred and sixty pound man clear of the dock and carry him away without so much as a heel dragging?"

"Whut you gwi' do wid any sich list as dat?" asked Sam, thrusting out his head and dropping his mouth half an inch.

"I thought we might take such a list and just walk around among the more powerful women here in Everglades, and tell them that Chin Lee had been shot. We could watch how they take it."

"Just why do you think it was a woman who killed him in the first place?" inquired the mill official.

"Because whoever killed Chin Lee did it for a sentimental reason."

"How do you get that?"

"Because she didn't throw the body over the dock to the sharks. I can easily understand how in the excitement of homicide, any person, man or woman, could run away and forget to dispose of his or her victim; but here is the revelatory circumstance: This murderer escapes, but returns, not simply to destroy the evidence of her crime, but to pick it up and take it away with her.

"She could not endure the thought of her lover's body being thrown to the sharks or given over to any stranger who found it, or to the callousness of a coroner's jury. She even bound up the wound her own pistol shot had made. On this point I am undecided.

"Did she tie a piece of cloth around his head out of a useless tenderness, or was it merely to keep from leaving a trail of drops to betray her direction? Of course, that has nothing to do with finding the person, but it is an interesting point in criminal psychology."

Both men were amazed at such detailed deductions from the mere fact that the body had been removed without leaving a trail. Still both remained equally sure that Chin Lee had never gone with a woman in Everglades.

Poggioli spread his hands.

"If what you say be true, this becomes one of the most puzzling murders in my experience. If he were not spirited away from this dock for a sentimental reason, I am forced to doubt that Chin Lee was ever killed at all."

"Why couldn't he have been killed by crap shooters, or cock fighters?" demanded Galloway impatiently. "He gambled heavily on both sports."

"Because such a murderer would have tossed him over the dock automatically. It would be the most natural reaction in the world. You even reprimanded Sam for not doing it himself, and getting rid of the whole unpleasantness at a stroke."

"M-m, yes, that is a fact, I did," admitted the superintendent. "But, of course, I didn't exactly mean it."

"So my thoughts keep coming back to a woman," concluded the psychologist. "Now while you and Sam think up that list, suppose we go to the dining hall and look through Chin Lee's things. We might find a letter or a woman's picture— something to throw light on who shot him."

The scientist's theory had a logical solidity which the superintendent was unable to shake, so he contented himself with saying rather emptily that he didn't believe it was a woman, and the three set out back for the kitchen.

The January sun was higher now and beat down with a sticky heat. Galloway complained again that he had not brought his car. Once, as the men trudged through the sunshine, Poggioli said—

"If there were any bloodhounds near here, this would be settled in an hour or so."

"No, no," repeated Galloway. "The sheriff and his dogs would be too much publicity—sorry."

The Resurrection of Chin Lee 93

THE grub shack of the Everglades Mill & Manufacturing Company was a great wooden structure whose walls were made up mainly of screened windows and doors. The only solid things about the place were a big electrical refrigerator run by current from the mill's dynamo, and the kitchen stove, which was an old ship's range that the New York manager of the company had bought at a marine auction in Brooklyn.

In the kitchen the two white men found Erb Skaggs directing two negro helpers in picking chickens. They had twenty or thirty fryers piled in a tub for the noon meal. A tin pan held the livers and gizzards.

"I was just wonderin'," said Erb, meeting his visitors, "if Mr. Poggioli likes livers. Thought I'd fry him a chicken and stuff it full of livers."

Galloway nodded.

"There you are, Professor. When Erb decides to do you proud he does you proud . . . By the way, Erb, where does Chin Lee bunk around here?"

The cook changed his expression completely.

"Where does Chin Lee bunk?"

"Yes, I'm checking up on the men to see how they are billeted. I've got to send in a report."

The cook frowned and stood looking at the superintendent.

"Is that why Mr. Poggioli come down here?"

Galloway laughed shortly.

"No, it doesn't require the help of a psychologist to describe what a lot of mill hands' bunks look like."

"Well, my bunk's in that little screened off space yonder in the corner of the kitchen. And you can tell the comp'ny when too many other things git in it with me, I take to a hammock that I got strung up outside."

"Yes, I know where yours is. Now where is Chin Lee's?"

"Mr. Galloway," cried the cook, "I be doggone if it ain't a shame for you to have to poke around lookin' at the dirty stinkin' bunks of these mill hands. Say so, an' I'll do it for you."

"No, just show me—"

"I'll go with you—I'll take you to it."

"We can get there all right if you'll just point it out."

The cook jiggled about, moved a skillet on the range, but finally complied.

"Well, Chin Lee bunks right yonder in that little shack yonder—" He followed them irresistibly for a few steps. "You didn't want to see anything about Chin Lee hisse'f, did you—whether he had any complaints to make or not?"

"I don't imagine he has any complaints to make," said Galloway.

Skaggs dropped behind.

"Well, n-o, I reckon not . . . That little shack, right there."

The shack in question was a trifle more than a large goods box. It had in it three shelves. The bottom shelf was spread with a dirty mill blanket, the middle one contained two bags.

"Now you want to look into those for a picture or a letter or something?" questioned Galloway.

"If you please."

"Sam, swing 'em down."

The black man lifted one gingerly to the dirty floor.

It was an ordinary pigskin bag, rather worn from travel. When the valise was open, a variety of odds and ends lay spread before them: Chinese shirts and trousers, a set of eight ivory chopsticks, a Chinese print in a silk folder, a carved opium pipe and some tiny porcelain teacups, without handles, nested together.

The psychologist squatted on his haunches in the chairless shack, turning through the collection. Presently he opened a small ivory box filled with tiny gold trinkets. He held it up to the superintendent.

"Know what these are, Mr. Galloway?"

The mill official picked one up.

"Look like gold gyves for a game rooster to me, but they are too blunt."

The psychologist squatted, looking at them with a puzzled expression.

"They're too much for me."

"Don't you know what they are?"

"Oh, yes, they're fingernail guards. They protect the fingernails so they'll grow long."

"What's the idea in that?"

"Why, it's a Chinese mark of high caste—it proves the owner doesn't do any manual labor."

"Then what are you puzzled about?"

"Why a kitchen helper here in Everglades should own a set of gold nail protectors. What would a coolie want with nail guards?"

Galloway considered this proposition.

"Chin Lee might have brought them over as curios."

The psychologist shook his head slowly.

"If an American had brought them to this country, yes; a Chinaman, no. They are no more of a curio to a Chinese than a cigar clipper would be to you."

Galloway agreed to this.

"Then I would say at some time or other Chin Lee had been a man of leisure."

"Then what's he doing here in your kitchen, surrendering his caste?"

"Oh," cried Galloway, "that's nothing. What a man is in Florida is no sign at all of what he was where he came from. One of the biggest racetrack men in Miami was once an eminent Episcopal minister in Connecticut. And then, on the other hand, I know a Chicago gangster who is trying to reform our school system. He makes speeches about it and says the children of

Florida ought to have the same chance to make good men and women as the children of Chicago."

"Well, at any rate," pondered Poggioli, "these nail guards give Chin Lee a background where one is likely to run across any sort of motive. Why was he in hiding? Was this a murder of revenge? If so, why should the man save the body? Was it the riddance of an heir to some large Chinese estate? In that instance the murderer might want to produce the body somewhere to prove his victim is dead."

"Oh, you're giving up the woman theory?"

"No, not at all; but if he has been a very wealthy man, it introduces other possibilities. Look here; I would really like to find the body. Suppose we have over the sheriff and his hounds?" The psychologist glanced at his host interrogatively.

Galloway was tempted.

"TELL you what I'll do," he offered. "If you'll guarantee to me that Chin Lee was a millionaire and that somebody murdered him while he was at work in the company's kitchen, by George, I'll not only agree to the bloodhounds, but I'll telephone for the brightest newspaper reporters in Miami to fly over here and help you on the case. I'll do that if he's rich."

"Not if he has *been* rich?"

"No; he's got to be rich right now. There's no news value in the murder of a man who has been rich—at least not in Florida after the boom."

"But look at it this way," said Poggioli. "Suppose I showed you a spot on the ground bearing traces of petroleum; wouldn't you be willing to sink a well there, even if I couldn't absolutely guarantee that you would strike a gusher?"

The superintendent of the mill company shook his head.

"Not now. Five years ago, Mr. Poggioli, I'd have backed you to the limit if I had caught a whiff of oil, but since the boom I wouldn't put a nickel into a speculation of any kind unless it was guaranteed by the United States Treasury and insured by Lloyds."

The scientist shrugged.

"Well, all right. It's just that sort of psychology that is keeping this depression functioning, Galloway; but you fellows refuse to see it. I do wish I could find the body and examine it. It would be more revealing than these bags."

"I see that," agreed the superintendent, "and I'm really sorry I am not in a position to do anything about it."

This apology of the superintendent for not being able to assist in capturing the murderer of any cook's helper with a rating of less than AA1 in Bradstreet, was interrupted by a shadow falling over the group.

The negro Sam glanced about, gave a sort of grunt as if some one had struck him violently in the stomach, and abruptly scrambled up into the top bunk.

Galloway moved back from the valise and gave an odd kind of laugh.

"Well, I'll be damned—Chin Lee!" he exclaimed. "We thought you were dead. This damn fool, Sam, here—" He nodded angrily at the pop eyed black man in the upper bunk.

"Me no dead," said Chin Lee. "Me fall, get hurt, wake up by me by, come back klitchen."

Galloway was outraged.

"Sam, you black ignoramus, you're a thunder of a night watchman! Run off and leave a wounded man lying on the dock!"

"He was daid!" cried Sam. "Yo' sho' was daid, Chin Lee, wid a great big hole in yo' haid!"

"Me pull out big fish," explained the cook's helper simply. "Foot slip, fall, hit head, by me by wake up again."

The head of the cook's boy was tied up with a great bandage.

"Well, Chin Lee," said Galloway, "sorry we mussed up your things."

"Allee lite," rattled the Chinese. "Me dead, somebody mus' open bag."

"That's true. Well, we're glad you're no deader than you are."

Chin Lee lifted a hand to his bandage.

"Big bump—feel allee lite now."

The negro climbed down from his bunk and the visitors were about to go.

"Why did you come here, Chin Lee?" inquired Poggioli. "Skaggs send you down?"

"You say you look at my bunk. Me come say bunk good bunk."

"You heard us talking as we came through the kitchen?"

"Yes."

"What were you doing at that time?"

"Fix potato. Mis' Skaggs say fix potato go Tampa."

"I see. When do you go?"

"On 'leven."

The psychologist glanced at his watch.

"That isn't far off. We'd better go back and let you finish."

The four men moved out of the shack for the kitchen. In the big screened shed, the two negro helpers were now pouring bread dough in an electric kneading machine.

"How do you fix the potatoes to go back to Tampa?" Poggioli inquired of the Chinese.

"Fill up hamper, put him in ice box till go," explained Chin Lee.

He led the way to the potato bin and resumed the simple business of filling a split basket with potatoes. The criminologist watched the work for a few moments, and a little later the white men set off for the superintendent's bungalow.

ON the way back Galloway fell to bemeaning Sam for cowardice—too cowardly to walk up to a man on the dock and see whether he was dead or not.

"He sho was daid then, Mist' Jim; he ain't now, but he was then."

"Oh, you're not only a coward, you're an imbecile!"

"Don't be too hard on Sam," soothed the criminologist. "It seems to me there are some very odd things about Chin Lee's resuscitation."

"What's that?" inquired the superintendent sharply.

"Well, for instance—where did he get his head bound up?"

"In the kitchen, I suppose. Why?"

"Then why didn't he leave a trail of drops from the dock to the kitchen?"

"His head probably had stopped bleeding by that time."

"But if it were an arterial cut, wouldn't it have broken out again when he got up?"

"Well—it didn't do it."

"Apparently not," agreed the psychologist.

The two men entered the superintendent's garden and passed under the blue-green leaves and yellow melons of a papaya shrub.

"It's odd," went on the scientist, "after such a wound, he goes right back to work sorting out samples of spoiled potatoes and, apparently, he is going to Tampa on the eleven o'clock just as he had planned."

"I don't suppose he was hurt as badly as Sam thought."

"That's possible, too," admitted the psychologist. He walked on a space and then said, "There are two things about the way Chin Lee sorted out those potatoes that seemed very odd to me!"

"And just what were they?" inquired the superintendent, beginning to feel faintly ironic about his guest's finical logic.

"One thing was, his hands were perfectly steady."

"You mean if he had just been knocked out, he should have been shaky?"

"I think so; don't you?"

"Well, I don't know. He may have extraordinary recuperative powers."

"All right, I agree to that temporarily. Now how do you explain this final contradiction? Chin Lee picked up his sample potatoes and put them in the hamper in a very ordinary manner—in fact, just as you or I or Sam would have done it."

Galloway looked at his guest and then broke out laughing.

"Really, Professor, is that a matter for suspicion—filling a hamper with potatoes in an ordinary manner?"

"Certainly!" said the scientist tartly. "If a man has spent years and much care in growing long and delicate fingernails, don't you know he would have formed motor habits to protect those nails? He would have picked up the potatoes with fingers and thumbs held straight, and not bent at the knuckles in the usual manner."

The superintendent was a little bewildered at this.

"Look here, where is all this getting us, Mr. Poggioli?"

"Well, all these slight contradictions mean very little taken by themselves; but put together they amount to a great deal. However, I think they might be construed logically enough, if Sam's first diagnosis had been correct."

"Sam's first—what was Sam's first diagnosis?"

"That Chin Lee was dead."

Black Sam began to nod.

"Boss, now yo're shoutin'—you sho is shoutin'."

Galloway smiled incredulously.

"Look here, what sort of a fellow are you anyway? When Sam came and told you Chin Lee was dead, you looked around the dock and decided if Chin Lee wasn't killed by a big strong woman, then he wasn't dead at all. Well, that was a good guess. You were right—Chin Lee turns up alive. But now, by George, you look at Chin Lee alive, sitting there picking up potatoes, and decide he must be dead. You are the hardest man to get to agree with anybody I ever saw. You won't even agree with yourself."

The psychologist disregarded this complaint, but after a moment asked gravely—

"Why is it so necessary to send a hamper of spoiled potatoes back to Tampa today?"

"It isn't necessary at all so far as the potatoes are concerned, but Chin Lee has to go anyway, so Erb might as well send the potatoes along."

"What does he have to go after?"

"For supplies for the *Mayaguez*. She is expected in tonight, and Skaggs must deliver her a lot of green groceries and such-like stuff. As I told you, he's a ship's chandler in a small way."

The psychologist nodded with a sharpening of attention.

"When was the last Cuban boat in?" he inquired quickly.

"Why, I think the *Ponce* pulled out of here last night. Why?"

"Nothing, nothing; I was just curious . . . By the by, Mr. Galloway, I'm afraid I'm going to have to start home on the eleven o'clock train, if you don't mind my cutting my visit short a trifle."

The superintendent began the usual protest, then followed Poggioli up to his room and stood talking while his guest packed his personal belongings.

A FEW minutes later the two men got into the superintendent's car and set off.

When they came in sight of the station, Poggioli saw a solitary figure on the platform standing beside a large basket. Galloway saw him too.

"Yonder's Chin Lee with his potatoes—very faithful fellow."

A minute or two later they drove up to the station and entered the waiting room. At the office window, instead of purchasing transportation, Poggioli signaled the agent to him and asked *sotto voce*—

The Resurrection of Chin Lee   99

"That Chinaman on the platform—did he pay for his ticket in American gold?"

The agent looked at the criminologist and said that he had.

The investigator thanked him and turned to the outer platform. As the two men walked out, Galloway asked curiously—

"Why did you put such a question as that, Mr. Poggioli?"

"I wanted to see if your kitchen boy was just over from Cuba."

"Is he?"

"Yes."

"How does his paying for a ticket in gold show that?"

"Because a great deal of American gold is used in Cuba, while here in Everglades you pay off your men in bills."

"But Chin Lee hasn't been to Cuba. He must have had some gold of his own."

"Yes, but he wouldn't have spent it if he had had anything else. People don't spend gold when they can avoid it. No, he's just over from Cuba. He arrived on the *Ponce* last night and now he's on his way to New York."

Galloway stared at his companion, bewildered.

"Look here, what do you mean? Isn't that my Chin Lee standing there?"

"That is your present Chin Lee. You'll have another tonight when the *Ponce* comes in; but the Chin Lee you are thinking about is dead."

"Poggioli," said the superintendent in a shocked tone, "you're crazy!"

The criminologist said nothing more; the two men walked out on the platform and joined the kitchen boy. Poggioli placed a hand on the rim of the hamper.

"Boy," he asked in a casual tone, "why did you shoot Chin Lee?"

The yellow man looked at his questioner with an expressionless face.

"Me Chin Lee."

Poggioli nodded.

"I know you are now; you are one of a long line of Chin Lees, but why did you shoot the Chin Lee we had here yesterday? Why didn't you let him go on to New York, or Chicago, in his turn?"

The man with the bandaged head said blankly:

"No savvy. Me Chin Lee."

The scientist began throwing the decayed potatoes carelessly across the track. They were still cold from the ice.

"If you don't savvy now, you will in a minute or two." He began scooping out handfuls of the tubers. The Chinaman watched the performance for a few moments, then said casually—

"Me savvy."

"I thought you would. Now, why did you kill Chin Lee?"

"Him likee this," said the kitchen boy impassively. "Some Chinaman velly bad man—big general—fight Chinese government—velly bad—get run out of country. Try to come back, deserve die . . ." The Chinaman hesitated.

"That's all good and well," agreed the psychologist, "but why didn't you shove him off the dock when you had the chance? Why are you lugging him around in that hamper of spoiled potatoes?"

The Chinese lifted a brow as if he had no hope of making his questioner understand.

"After allee, Chin Lee Chinaman. Send him back to own country to sleep. No let him come to his fathers from land of barbarian."

The psychologist nodded.

"Simple enough. Odd, I didn't think of that myself."

Galloway interposed:

"What in the thunder is all this about! Chin Lee dead, and in that hamper?"

"Skaggs is smuggling Chinese into this country from Cuba, and one of them happened to be after the man just before him. That's all there is to it. And by the way, it also explains why you were never able to recognize one of your collective kitchen boys when you saw a sample of him before your eyes."

BULLETS

AT THE door of Munro's General Merchandise store in La Belle, Florida, Sawyer, the deputy sheriff, stopped an old negro woman and the white man who followed her.

"You can't come in," he explained patiently. "They're holding an inquest in here."

The old crone quavered out that she knew it, that she was bringing in Slewfoot's lawyer.

The deputy looked at the well dressed white man disapprovingly.

"I hope you're not stoopin' to defend a nigger cowhand that shot his own boss?"

"No, I'm neither defending nor prosecuting," assured the stranger.

"You have to do one or t'other if you're a lawyer."

"I'm not a lawyer, I'm a psychologist. I told this old woman if her son were guilty, my services would simply assure his conviction, that I would be a much greater danger for him than a jury itself."

The officer frowned and looked at the stranger as if he had not heard him aright.

"A psychologist," he repeated vaguely. "I don't exactly see how a psychologist would come in on a murder investigation."

"I'm afraid," snapped the stranger in Yankee impatience, "that I can't explain to you the connection between murder and psychology in two words."

"Well, that's all right," drawled the Florida man leisurely. "Take four words if you need 'em—take as many as you want. You ain't goin' to git in noway, so you've got all the time there is to tell me what you would do if you could git in."

The man gave the faint grin of a rustic who feels that he has put a city man in his place.

The psychologist half turned away, but the old woman began pleading:

"Oh, Mas' Poggioli, please don' fly off de han'l' an' leave Slewfoot by hese'f. Please tell Mistuh Sawyah whut you gwi' do inside fuh my po' boy Slewfoot."

The well groomed gentleman controlled his temper, studied the guard for a moment as if reducing his thoughts to words sufficiently simple for the fellow to understand.

"Let me see. Murder—murder is a physical action impelled by some motive or motives, is it not?"

The deputy sheriff of Hendry County blinked his eyes.

"I mean," said the psychologist impatiently, "if one man kills another he has a reason for doing it, hasn't he?"

"Oh, yes, yes," ejaculated the guard, suddenly seeing that this was what the first sentence meant.

"Very well; when you put a thought into action, you leave traces of your motive in every object you have touched; to choose a musical analogy, shall I say that every detail of your instrumentation reflects the dominant chord of your purpose—do you know what I'm talking about?"

The deputy scratched his head.

"Not yet."

"Tchk! Tchk! Listen: When you do anything, your motive impresses itself on everything you touch. You go through an action such as this murder, say. Very well; every trace you leave points to your mood, your motive and your identity as plainly as a trail of torn paper. There is no way to avoid it."

The deputy became somewhat interested in what, up to this point, he had considered a meaningless jargon.

"Couldn't a man watch out an' hide his trail?" he inquired shrewdly.

Mr. Poggioli dropped his hands hopelessly.

"Don't you see what an absurdity your proposition involves? When you say 'watch out,' you mean 'take thought.' That introduces a second motive. This second motive produces results in its turn which are just as easily read as the first. In other words, no matter how many times a man goes over his own trail, putting out his own tracks, he must finally leave his last footprints quite open to view. Now, surely, you understand that."

Mr. Sawyer was astonished to catch a ray of light in the limbus of the psychologist's reasoning.

"Well, now, I'll be darned," he ejaculated. "That does sound reasonable. A man couldn't put out his own tracks, could he, because he'd make some more when he went back to put 'em out." He pulled at his chin. "Yes, sir, that's plumb reasonable."

He paused, thinking, then started off with a new breath:

"Howsomever, this murder ain't anything so complicated as all that. Slewfoot shot old man Jake Sanderson twict because the old man wouldn't advance him any money on his wages. That is, either Slewfoot or Finn Labby, a white man, shot him. They was both workin' for the old man an' both of 'em was in the store here when he was killed. Two shots were far'd an' the jury has jest about decided the nigger far'd both of 'em."

The psychologist stood pondering this statement of the case.

"You knew both of these cow herders?"

"Shore—worked with 'em before I got app'inted deputy sher'ff."

"Was the negro the sort of fellow who wanted to give orders, or was it his habit to wait and do what he was told?"

"He waited, of course, an' done what he was told—he was a nigger."

"Mm-m! Then if that was his mental habit, don't you think it reasonable to assume that he followed the lead of the white man in this as in everything else? Isn't it probable?"

The deputy frowned and twisted his mouth in a fashion that showed he was thinking.

"Now, by George, that's a p'int," he decided slowly, "an' a very plain one, too. I believe the jury ort to hear that."

"It's slight," disclaimed the originator.

"Big or little, I say it's so. Slewfoot was a triflin' nigger an', if for onct in his life, that's a p'int in his favor, I say the jury ort to know it. Jest you keep this crowd back, mister, for half a minute, an' I'll step in an' tell 'em."

He lifted his voice and called to the villagers in front of the door:

"Hey, you folks, this man's my deputy while I'm inside. Don't nobody come past him!"

WITH that he went inside to the jury at the back end of the store. The psychologist could see him talking and gesticulating, and presently he came back with a smile of satisfaction on his brown face.

"Well, they had to swaller it." He nodded. "They were fixin' to return their verdict that old Jake was shot by Slewfoot, but now they've changed it to either Slewfoot or Finn Labby."

"I believe you said Mr. Sanderson was shot twice," observed the psychologist.

"No, jest onct."

"You will excuse me, but your original statement was twice," insisted Poggioli.

"No; I said they shot at him twict—an' they did—but the first shot missed him. They jest hit old man Jake one time."

"Mm-m," murmured the psychologist. "And where did the other bullet strike?"

"In the wall."

"Were both bullets fired out of the same gun?"

"I don't know—how could you tell?"

"Cut them out and compare them; if they're the same caliber, with the same rifle marks on them, then one man shot both bullets and you can excuse the other man."

"Shore, shore, that's a fact, an' it runs right alongside ol' man Munro's argument, too."

"Who's Munro?"

"The man who owns this store."

"What's his argument?"

"Why-y—er—derned if I know. He's got a clippin' out of a paper tellin' how this thing ort to be done. He's tryin' to git the boys to dig out the balls, an' Doctor Livermore is cuttin' the ball out of the body, but the jury figgers since the bullet in the wall didn't hit nobody, it don't make no diff'runce. I see now it does an' I believe I'll step back an' tell the boys what you say about it."

This was carried out and Poggioli was again placed in the deputy's stead at the door. The old negro woman edged up to him and said in a shaky voice—

"See dah, Mas' Poggioli, you 'bout to git my Slewfoot out o' dis trouble wid one word."

"If the bullet in the corpse is different from the bullet in the wall, your son will be in worse trouble than ever," cautioned the psychologist.

"Why?" asked the old woman, mystified.

"Because that will show both men shot at Mr. Sanderson."

At this the old crone puckered up her brows and began a low praying that the two bullets would be alike when they were cut out.

Poggioli listened to this for a few moments and finally said—

"Aunt Rose, there is no use praying for the bullets to be something when they are cut out, because whatever they are, they are that now; and while the Lord might conceivably change a future condition, I should think it would be beyond even His power to change what has already happened."

The old woman nodded.

"Yes, suh, yes, suh, Mas' Poggioli!" She then went on mumbling, "Oh, Lawd, let dem bullets be jes' alike an' save po' Slewfoot!"

Her prayer was interrupted by a white woman attempting to enter the door. When the psychologist explained that no one was allowed inside, she said she wanted to do some trading.

At this a heavy old man with a square cut face came forward and called to the psychologist to let her in, that his trade had to go on, inquest or no inquest. The woman bought a package of soda and handed the old man a dollar bill. The storekeeper started to his cash drawer, but paused halfway, turned and came to the door.

"Any of you fellows got change for a dollar?" he inquired.

There was a general thrusting of hands into pockets. One of the onlookers produced a handful of small change and counted out the dollar.

The psychologist watched this incident without much attention when the old man looked at him and asked—

"Air you the stranger who told Sawyer to have them bullets cut out?"

The scientist said that he was.

"Well, by gum, I'm glad there's one man o' sense in this crowd. I been ding-dinging at them boys all mornin' to cut out them bullets. Suppose you come on back here with me an' tell 'em yourself, why it ort to be done."

Poggioli nodded.

"Certainly, that suits me; I've been wanting to go in, but—"

He was following the storekeeper to the rear of the building when the deputy called out.

"Hey, there, mister, you cain't come back here. I deputized you as guard."

"Aw, thunder an' nation!" exclaimed the storekeeper. "This man's got good ideas. Let him come back, Sawyer, an' it'll save you prancin' up an' down the store ever' two minutes."

"That's with the jury, it ain't with me," disclaimed the deputy.

"Oh, all right, let him come on," called the foreman of the jury.

When Poggioli reached the rear of the store, the spokesman of the jurors asked just what he meant about the bullets being alike, and what did it mean if they were alike.

This was interrupted by old man Munro, the storekeeper, saying:

"Why, he means jest exactly what I was tellin' you boys. I got a clippin' that explains it. They call it—lemme see—they call it ballistics, don't they, mister?"

"I believe so."

"Well, the clippin' is right over here in my desk. I cut it out of a Sunday paper six months ago. I'll show it to you."

He shuffled to a tall desk near the back door and returned to the psychologist with a yellowed clipping.

POGGIOLI glanced at it out of courtesy to the old man, but he was really attentive to the scene before him. The dead man lay on the floor quite close to the counter. Over him stooped the village doctor probing for the bullet.

Some of the jurymen were talking among themselves—

"Curious thing for a cowhand to shoot his boss over a little money—"

The foreman asked the storekeeper—

"You say they was quarrelin' amongst theirse'ves when you left them in here for a minute, Mr. Munro?"

"Yeh, Finn an' Slewfoot was both devilin' old man Jake for some money, an' he kep' puttin' 'em off, sayin' he didn't have any."

"An' fin'ly they shot him?" questioned a juror.

"That I don't know. I reckon they did. Jest then ol' man Ike Newton drove up with a truckload of oranges. I went out to count the crates an' while I was outside countin', I heard two booms in the store. They was so muffled I wasn't shore they was shots, an' me not expectin' anything like that either; so I finished my tally. When I went back in the store there was ol' man Jake down on the floor, openin' an' shuttin' his mouth, an' his two cowhands was gone. I run for Doc Livermore here, but when we got back, ol' Jake was dead."

The physician glanced around, nodded at this and resumed his work.

"So it's a question of which of the two hired men shot him?" queried the psychologist of the foreman.

"That's right, sir."

"Were you jurymen acquainted with these two cowhands?"

"Oh, yes, we're all cattlemen. Finn an' Slewfoot have worked for every man on this jury at one time or another."

"Then of these two men which was the more irritable and high tempered?"

Another juror answered—

"Why, Finn Labby. He was always flyin' off the handle."

The psychologist nodded.

"Taking this case on its face value, then, gentlemen, isn't it probable that the higher tempered man of this pair shot Mr. Sanderson? Isn't it reasonable that the waspish Finn Labby shot him and the easy going negro did not?"

The foreman of the jury hesitated for several moments.

"That sounds pretty good, mister," he said at last, "but if you must know—we think Slewfoot done it."

"Slewfoot!" ejaculated Poggioli, astonished and puzzled.

"Yes, sir, we jest about know that Slewfoot done it."

"Why?"

"Because he was jest the kind of nigger you described—easy goin' an' biddable."

The psychologist stood silent for several moments. Finally he said:

"Gentlemen, either my sense of logic is bad or my viewpoint doesn't agree with yours. I produce a reason which seems to me to clear my client; you gentlemen use the very same reason to condemn him. If we have no common ground of understanding, I think I had better withdraw." And he made a slight bow and turned to the door.

The old negro woman fell into a visible trembling and began praying aloud for God to cause the white man to stay and talk for Slewfoot. The foreman turned to the old negress.

"Don't be so noisy, auntie." He then glanced at another juror and said, "S'pose we tell him?"

The juror addressed blinked his eyes.

"Well, all right—but there ain't a bit o' tellin' what that man'll figger out from it."

The foreman turned to the deputy sheriff.

"Mr. Sawyer, tell him."

At this the deputy beckoned Poggioli to follow him. He led the way to the back door and when the two were out of earshot, Sawyer nodded sidewise at the jury and said in a low tone—

"Them fellers think Slewfoot was put up to shoot ol' man Jake."

"Put up to it!"

"Why, shore; you know, pickin' a quarrel about money was jest one way to start trouble."

Mr. Poggioli was suddenly enlightened.

"Oh, yes, that's why Slewfoot would have to be—biddable?"

"Why, of course," agreed the deputy. "An' it's dollars to doughnuts that one o' them jurymen theirse'ves paid Slewfoot to kill ol' man Jake. Shoo! We jest know one of us done it—but we don't know which one; an', really, we don't want to know which one."

The psychologist stood staring at the foreman, moved by a sense of ghoulish humor.

"Do you mean to say that just any member of that jury had sufficient cause of animosity toward Mr. Sanderson to murder him?"

"That's exactly what I mean to say, an' it's what I am sayin'."

"What did Sanderson do to infuriate everybody?"

"Why, ever' man on that jury is a cattleman, an' ol' man Jake was what we call a 'open range man.' If any of us fellers fenced up our pastures, he'd cut our wires an' let his own cattle range on our lands. He's treated dang near ever' man in La Belle like that from Doc Livermore an' ol' man Munro clear up to the Yankees that come in with the boom an' thought they could run things down here like they done up North, but ol' man Jake showed 'em they couldn't do it. No fences, that was his motto, an' he stuck by it till somebody paid a nigger to kill him."

POGGIOLI grunted as the oddness of the investigation dawned on him. He stood looking out the back door. It gave on an expanse of creeping palmettos. The bayonet shaped leaves bristled as high as a man's chest. Then he observed some tracks in the sand under the door. The prints were of hobnailed shoes and larger shoes with broken soles. The toes of these tracks were pressed deep in the ground while the heels scarcely touched the sand.

Poggioli called the deputy's attention to them.

"Have any of the jurymen come out the back door since the inquest began?" he inquired.

"Why, no-o, I don't reckon they have," said Sawyer. "One of 'em had to go across the street to the garage."

"M-m! Has the crowd out in front there been milling around this end of the store?"

"No; these scrub palmettos ain't a comfortable place to mill in. What are you askin' about that for?"

"I was just wondering if those tracks there were made by Slewfoot and Labby?"

"Oh, shore, they're bound to be. That busted shoe is a nigger track, an' you know no nigger ain't been around here since ol' man Jake was killed. Yes, I noticed 'em there when I closed the door on the jury, an' I thought about layin' boards over 'em to preserve 'em for the criminal trial, then I thought ag'in, 'Now they's no use in that. If you jest almost see one man shoot another 'n with your own eyes, you don't have to go aroun' identifyin' his tracks.' "

Poggioli nodded slowly and grunted again.

"Yes—I see."

The footprints visualized for the psychologist the two cowhands tiptoeing silently away from the store into the palmettos. But there was something about the picture in contradiction to the deputy's theory of the crime. The scientist was thinking about this as he turned and went back to the jury.

When he stood before the group again he saw one of the men with a chisel, about to cut the bullet out of the wall.

Suddenly the position of the corpse impressed itself on Poggioli. It lay quite near the counter, directly across from the bullet hole. A possible defense struck him and he called out to the chiseler:

"Wait just a moment. Give me half a second before you dig out that bullet."

He drew a match from his pocket, walked across and thrust it into the hole.

"Gentlemen," he said to the group, "this match stick is pointing in the direction from which the bullet came; straight across the dead man. But Mr. Sanderson is lying almost against the counter. The murderer, therefore, stood just behind the counter to fire that shot; do you agree to this?"

The jury assented, after a moment, by grunting and nodding.

"Very well; now you men know negroes. You have hired them, worked with them, been with them all your lives. Now I ask you as a group, did any man here ever see a negro behind any counter in any store in La Belle?"

"I—I never did," drawled the foreman, looking around among the others.

"Neither did I," put in two or three more.

"None of you ever did. Negroes don't walk behind white men's counters. They have been accused of stealing too many times when they were innocent for them to take a chance of being seen behind a white man's counter. Besides, there was no reason for Slewfoot to go behind the counter to shoot Mr. Sanderson. There was every reason for him not to go. Behind the counter he would have attracted the old man's attention. And when it came to the actual shooting, he could have shot just as easily from in front of the counter. No, Slewfoot would never have walked behind the counter.

"With Finn Labby the conditions are exactly reversed. He was white. He had the white man's privilege to walk around for a bite of cheese. There's the cheese hoop. Once behind him, Finn could have shot his employer in the back of the head—where he *was* shot. This murder could have been a murder for anger, because Finn was high tempered. This view of the crime, gentlemen, removes suspicion from any other man in Hendry County, and I recommend it to your discretion. Return your verdict that Jake Sanderson was shot and killed by Finn Labby. It will be a widely acceptable solution to this crime. I thank you for your attention."

THIS speech created quite a stir among the jury. They glanced at one another with relief in their faces. The old negro woman began clapping her hands and praising the Lord and had to be hushed by the deputy. Then the officer came around to the psychologist.

"There's a lot to what you brought out, Mr. Poggioli," he said admiringly. "Of course a nigger wouldn't walk behind old man Munro's counter, an' of course Finn Labby would.

"Besides that, you send all these boys home with a clear conscience for each other. That was quite a stroke of yours."

"Thanks," said Poggioli.

The jurymen were standing up now, turning around and around after the manner of men who wish to retire for consultation, but who have no retiring place selected.

"Suppose me an' Mr. Poggioli an' Mr. Munro go out front an' leave you men in this end of the store to ballot on this thing," suggested the deputy.

The foreman agreed.

"An' you go along with 'em, Aunt Rose," he directed, "while we free your boy from this murder charge."

"Gemmen, I thanks you all. Oh, Lawd, I thanks you!"

"Yes, yes, that's all right—just go along with Mr. Sawyer."

Sawyer, the deputy, was beside the psychologist and was still in a congratulatory mood.

"By George, I would never have believed you could get a Florida jury to free a nigger of a murder charge jest by stickin' a match in a bullet hole."

The scientist pulled at his chin.

"I wish it were as clear to me as I made it to the jury."

"What do you mean?" asked the deputy, looking at him curiously.

"Those tracks at the back door, where the two cowhands came out—"

"Well, what about their tracks?"

"Why, they tiptoed away—both those boys went off on their tiptoes."

The deputy pondered a moment.

"Ain't that nachel, for 'em to go sneakin' away from their murder?"

"A man wouldn't try to tiptoe and keep quiet immediately after he had fired a pistol twice," said the psychologist.

"Well, now, that's a fact, too," admitted Sawyer, puzzled.

These observations were interrupted by a stir outside the door. Voices shouted out:

"Hey, Lang, got one of 'em, did ye?"

"Where'd you ketch him, Lang?"

"Slewfoot, what ye let the sheriff git ye for?"

A negro's voice blubbered out. The crowd outside the door parted and a wool shirted man entered, leading a handcuffed negro.

When Sawyer, the deputy, recognized the negro he shouted back to the jury to hold their decision as more evidence had been brought in. Old Aunt Rose looked at her son and wailed out—

"Lawd, Slewfoot, go an' git caught jess when Mas' Poggioli 'bout to sot you free!"

Slewfoot blinked at his old mother and said nothing. The jurymen who were standing now went back to their seats. The sheriff brought his prisoner before them and the foreman motioned the black man to sit on a nail keg.

"Sheriff," asked the foreman, "did Slewfoot have a gun on him when you caught him?"

"Oh, yes—" the officer nodded, "here it is." And he drew from his pocket an ancient single action Colt revolver.

The spokesman took the weapon, turned it in his hand.

"Smith," he said, "better finish up your work chiselin' out that bullet. You've got yours, have you, Dr. Livermore?"

The surgeon indicated a pellet of lead lying on a piece of wrapping paper on the counter.

"Now, Slewfoot," said the foreman, "we want you to tell us exactly how old man Sanderson was shot an' who did it. No use in your tryin' to lie about it. If you did it, say so; if you didn't do it, tell us who did."

THE black man became very frightened. He wet his lips with his tongue and stammered:

"W-wuw-well, Mistuh Tim, Ah di'n' do hit. Ah sho di'n' do hit!"

"Then who did?"

"Ah—Ah don' know."

"Wasn't you in the store here when he was shot?"

"Yessuh, Ah guess Ah was."

"An' you say you don't know who shot him?"

"N-n-no, suh, Ah don' know who shot him. Ah—Ah di'n' see nobody shoot him."

"Hand me that bullet, Smith, soon as you get it out," directed the spokesman, "an' let me have that one on the counter now."

The chiseler presently brought his bit of lead and handed it in. The foreman compared the two bullets with the revolver.

"Well, gentlemen, there you are," he said to the other jurors. "Two old style .38 balls shot out of this .38 Colt." He swung the cylinder of the revolver to one side and added, "Here are a couple of exploded shells in his gun. The damn fool didn't even have brains enough to reload."

"Well, that ends the investigation," said one of the jurors.

"I think so," agreed the foreman.

At the sudden and simple turn of the evidence the old negro woman began weeping and praying the Lord to save Slewfoot.

The psychologist called out above the stir—

"Wait, gentlemen—wait just a moment before returning a final verdict."

One of the jurors was impatient.

"Thunder! What more do you want? Here's the bullets that done the work exactly fittin' the nigger's gun."

"Still, I'm here representing the prisoner, in a way. At least let me have opportunity to look over the evidence."

"Are you still thinkin' about the shot from behind the counter?" asked the foreman.

"I am; I am also thinking about Slewfoot's tracks just outside the back door. He didn't leap out as a man running away from a murder. His heels did not hit at all. He tiptoed away from the door. He was evidently under some sort of restraint."

"Restraint!" ejaculated a voice, and gave an incredulous laugh.

"Exactly; restraint—some sort of restraint."

The psychologist took up the two cones of lead and began examining them.

"I think this is a plumb waste of time," complained a juryman.

To this Mr. Poggioli made no reply, but continued examining the two missiles that had been recovered. Finally he came to a pause, frowning in concentration over the pieces of lead. His expression caught the attention of the whole group.

"Now what in the hell d'ye reckon he sees in them two bullets?" asked a juror querulously.

The psychologist glanced up and answered for himself—

"One of the most intriguing mysteries it has ever been my good fortune to encounter," he replied gravely.

The foreman arose from his chair.

"What is it, Mr. Poggioli?" he asked curiously.

"These bullets. The one that struck the wall and the one that hit Mr. Sanderson—which one do you gentlemen think was fired first?"

"Why, the one that hit the wall, of course—he missed him."

"On the contrary, it was fired last. The bullet from the body has reddish rust in its old fashioned lead grooves, but the one out of the wall is fouled with the black residue of smoke powder."

The coroner's jury looked at him in silence. Finally one of them said—

"Well, what do you make of that?"

"I make this of it: The man who killed Mr. Sanderson first shot him down, and then for some reason or other stood over his dead body and fired a bullet into the wall."

"Why, he may have shot at him twict and jest missed the second shot," suggested the foreman.

"Impossible; Sanderson was shot in the back of the head. Death was instantaneous. He dropped like a beef. This old pistol is a single action gun. The murderer had to recock his weapon, then he pointed it again and deliberately fired a bullet into the wall with his victim lying at his feet."

"What in the thunder did he do that for?" demanded the foreman.

Poggioli drew a long breath.

"Gentlemen, there could have been but one reason. The murderer wanted the bullet to be cut out and identified. He was afraid the ball in Sanderson's body would not be found, so he fired another into the wall. He had thought out his whole plan of action before he fired a shot."

"What would Slewfoot want to have his own gun identified for?" demanded a juror.

"Slewfoot didn't do the shooting. Such a plot was far over his head. The murderer gave Slewfoot this revolver after he had killed old man Jake. He had plotted to give it to Slewfoot; that was why he was so anxious to have the gun in Slewfoot's possession identified. He thought it would save his own neck."

At this the foreman of the jury got hastily to his feet.

"Here! Here!" he cried. "This way of savin' a nigger, first by stickin' a match in a bullet hole, an' then by punchin' a pin in the grooves of two bullets—they ain't no sense to that!"

"No!"

"No, they ain't!" cried two or three voices.

Poggioli was about to protest this logical outrage when the spokesman of the jury nodded at him:

"Wait a minute, boys," he called. "Let me an' Mr. Poggioli have a word about this."

The session again had fallen into disorder. The foreman led the way to the back door. Poggioli followed him, wondering what would come next. When they were outside the door on the sand, the excited man asked in an undertone—

"Looky here, mister, do you know which one of us shot old man Jake?"

"Why, certainly," said the scientist.

"Well, which one of us—No, no—don't tell me! I don't want to be goin' aroun' knowin'—Yes, damn it, do tell me! I'd jest like to know the man that could think quick enough to bang another bullet into the wall."

"He didn't think that quickly," returned the psychologist. "He had been studying out that plan for over six months—ever since he clipped that article on ballistics out of some Sunday paper."

The foreman stood staring blankly at his companion.

"I'll be derned," he whispered. "Old man Munro!"

"Certainly. He had been holding a grudge against Sanderson ever since old Jake ran him out of the cattle business twenty years ago. He read this article on ballistics and made up a plan to murder Sanderson and place the blame on a negro.

"His chance came. He shot his enemy and then told the negro he would shoot him if he ever told it. Then he paid the negro his pistol and all the cash in his cash drawer to leave the country. That is why he couldn't change a dollar bill for that woman awhile ago. It also explains why these tracks here show two men tiptoeing away from the store and not running. They stole away with old man Munro whispering instructions."

The foreman stood shaking his head.

"I jest be danged," he said slowly. "You said a fellow couldn't cover up his tracks without makin' a lot more—" He thrust his head inside the door and called out, "Oh, Sheriff, has that nigger Slewfoot got any money on him?"

The officer called back:

"Yes, he's got a pocketful of small change. I thought it was cartridges when I first searched him, but it turned out to be nickles an' dimes."

"Well, then," called the foreman, "we'll have to turn Slewfoot loose, because you know he wouldn't have shot old man Jake for some money when he already had a pocketful." He looked at Poggioli and winked. "You see, I'm a pretty good reasoner myse'f, when I git started."

"What are you going to do about old man Munro?" inquired the psychologist.

"Why-y—er—nothin', I reckon. A jury of cattlemen like us ain't goin' to give old man Munro any trouble for killin' a skunk like old man Jake Sanderson. We'll return a verdict that he died at the hands of unknown parties for well known reasons. You see, out here on the Floridy prairies the law has its limits, an' old man Jake was one of them."

He gave the wink of a rustic who feels he has said something clever before a city man.

The Cablegram

IN THE course of his evasions over the telephone, Mr. Henry Poggioli, investigator in criminal psychology, said apologetically—

"Mr. Slidenberry, my work here in Miami is purely theoretic, and if I devote any time to practical crimes . . ."

"But this is theoretic," pressed the voice in the receiver earnestly. "The *Stanhope* is due in today and we want you to go aboard with us and—"

"If the trouble is aboard a ship it must be smuggling," surmised the scientist. "I am really no expert as a baggage searcher."

"Oh, it isn't that at all. It's an A. J. P. A. cablegram."

"Let's see—that's the American Jewelers' Protective Association?"

"Right you are, Doctor, and the trouble is we can't quite decode it."

There was something whimsical in the Miami customs force receiving a cablegram which they could not decode. Mr. Poggioli smiled over the telephone as he suggested—

"If you have it by you would you like to read it to me over the wire?"

"M-m—we'd a lot rather you'd come down to the docks, but if you think you can decode the thing right off . . ."

Came a pause, and after about a half minute interval the voice began again: "Here it is:

"BARBERRY. EXTREME CARE. STANHOPE. 36-B—FEATHERS—CONSULAR REPORTS 1915 PP. 1125–6. REWARD CLAIMED.
—J. DUGMORE LAMPTON, CARE AMERICAN CONSULATE, BELIZE, B. C. A."

"What is it you don't understand?" inquired the psychologist.

"Feathers—do you know what feathers means?"

"I don't know what any of it means."

"The rest is simple. Barberry means a diamond smuggler. *Stanhope* is the name of a ship that will dock here in half an hour. The 36-B is his cabin number. The rest is just plain English. If we capture him J. Dugmore Lampton wants the reward offered by the American Jewelers' Protective Association."

"What about the consular reports?"

"Don't know yet. I set a clerk to looking up the reports for 1915. We keep them in the attic of the customs house in goods boxes. This is the first time anybody ever had any reason to refer to them."

"You don't suppose consular reports could be another code word?"

"No; we suspected that at first. We searched through all the codes, but 'consular reports' seems to have no meaning beyond just—you know, the actual reports themselves."

"That's an extraordinary detail of your telegram," Poggioli admitted after a pause. "It creates a kind of puzzle as to the sender of the message."

"How's that?"

"That he should not only quote the consular reports, but he is so familiar with them he actually refers to a particular page."

"The man is probably in the consular service himself," returned the customs officer.

"That doesn't alter anything. Every consul knows that the consular reports are never read, are never filed away properly and are seldom even preserved. Really, Mr. Slidenberry, your cablegram is not only puzzling, it is enigmatic."

"Really, Doctor," interposed the inspector, "we wish you'd come down here yourself and see—"

"I think I will; yes, I'll come. But while I'm on the way down, please cable Belize and get a report on J. Dugmore Lampton. I would like to know something more about a man who refers in a cablegram to a particular page in the American consular reports."

Fifteen minutes later a group of three uniformed men met Mr. Poggioli's taxi at pier 26. Captain Slidenberry gripped the arrival's hand.

"She's just swinging in now, Dr. Poggioli," he said gratefully. "Come on inside. The passengers will be down immediately."

"Now, as I said," cautioned the psychologist, "I am utterly inexperienced in searching baggage."

Slidenberry held up a hand.

"The boys will take care of that."

"Then what do you want me to do?"

"Well, I want you to look over the passenger who occupies cabin 36-B and tell me if he is the type of man who would hide his diamonds in his baggage, or drop them in the pocket of some fellow passenger to be retrieved later—or would he wrap his gems in meat and feed them to his pet dog?"

Poggioli smiled and shook his head.

"There may be some physiological index to classify the different types of smugglers; they say it's true of murderers. I haven't gone into the matter yet."

"How would you like to make your headquarters here and measure all the smugglers we arrest?"

"I'll think that over. By the way, you cabled for the information about J. Dugmore Lampton?"

"Certainly, but I don't see how that information can aid us here."

"Well, don't you think it queer to quote a consular report?"

"Mm—ye-es—queer enough, but what is the connection between a diamond smuggler at this end of the line and a man quoting the reports at the other?"

"I have no idea. That's what we want to see. When anything seems queer, Mr. Slidenberry, that is merely a psychologic signal that it has connections with something we do not understand. In any crime queerness may very well be a clue."

THE psychologist's theory was interrupted by cabin boys streaming down the gangplank of the *Stanhope* bringing luggage and arranging it in alphabetic piles. Captain Slidenberry went aboard to the window of the ship's purser and asked who occupied room 36-B. The purser ran his finger down the passenger list.

"Dr. Xenophon Quintero Sanchez—what's the matter with Dr. Sanchez?"

"That's what we are trying to find out, Purser."

The purser touched his cap.

"His bags will be in the S pen, sir."

Slidenberry was searching among the S's for the initials X.Q.S. when a cabin boy came up and touched his cap.

"Excuse me, sir, but the passenger in 36-B asks if you will please come to his cabin?"

The inspector became suspicious at once.

"What's the point in that? Why doesn't he bring down his keys?"

"His bags are not down yet," explained the boy. "He sent me to ask if you would please examine them in his cabin."

Slidenberry lifted an eyebrow at Poggioli, and the two men started aboard the *Stanhope*. When they reached stateroom 36-B Slidenberry tapped on the door, and a man's voice called—

"Enter, señor, and pardon my occupation."

The shutter swung open and Poggioli saw a heavy man of dark complexion and dissipated features sitting on his bunk apparently cutting up his wardrobe with a pair of scissors. Two or three garments already were in pieces, and he was taking out the lining of a coat. The two visitors stood looking at the queer sight.

"Are you a tailor, Mr. Sanchez?" inquired Slidenberry.

The heavy man on the bunk made a deprecatory gesture.

"A kind of analytic tailor, señores. I am preparing to make my declaration in customs."

"Just how?" inquired the inspector dryly. "Are you trying to reduce the value of your wardrobe?"

Sanchez shrugged.

"I am trying to find out what my portmanteau contains, señores."

"Don't you know already?" asked Slidenberry in a brittle voice.

"I do not," stated Sanchez sharply. "I know what I put in my baggage, but what others have slipped into it I have no way of knowing except by some such method as this." He jabbed his shears into a garment.

As Mr. Poggioli viewed this irrational scene there seemed a touch of something familiar in the old Latin's somber face. He stood trying to recall where he had met the man while Slidenberry went on with his astonished questioning.

"Do you mean some one has slipped something in your bags?"

"That's what I mean, señor."

"Why didn't you find out before the *Stanhope* entered customs?"

"Because I did not want to sit in my cabin all day long to make sure nothing else was added. I wanted to go to my meals, take the air, sleep."

Slidenberry looked at the old man intently, then glanced at Poggioli, said, "Pardon us a moment," and drew the psychologist outside the cabin.

"Crazy," he said in an undertone, "or do you think it's a hoax?"

"Our cablegram shows there is a reality to it somewhere, so I would mark out insanity."

"But if it's a hoax why didn't he select a more reasonable falsehood?"

"You know, the fact that it's unreasonable is an argument for its truth," pointed out Poggioli—"that is, if he really isn't insane."

"That somebody actually planted dutiable goods of value in his bags?"

Poggioli shrugged.

"But whoever did would lose money on it," went on Slidenberry. "His reward would be only a part of the value of the goods smuggled. He would certainly lose half of his investment even if his scheme worked."

"This can't be simply a trick to get a reward," agreed Poggioli at once. "There is something—something else—" The scientist drew out a cigaret and tapped it on his thumbnail. "You know—I've seen that old man before!"

"Something criminal?" asked Slidenberry hopefully.

"Must have been, if I remember him."

"Good, good." The inspector nodded. He turned back into the cabin. "Dr. Sanchez," he began, "I want to ask you pointblank: Have you any diamonds to declare?"

"I don't know," said the old man, still scissoring away. "That's what I'm trying to find out for you."

"Do you think somebody hid diamonds in your trunk and clothes?"

"I have no idea what they hid—diamonds possibly."

Slidenberry gave a brief smile.

"Suppose you let me help you hunt. I've a knack at that sort of thing."

Dr. Sanchez straightened and held up a prohibitory hand.

"Not as you are, señor, please," he said with a dry smile.

"Not as I am—what do you mean?"

"I mean, señor, not with your coat and vest and trousers on, if you please."

The customs officer stared in amazement.

"Are you suggesting that I undress myself to inspect your—"

Poggioli interposed—

"He means he is afraid *you* will put something in his bags and then arrest him for having it."

Slidenberry looked at Poggioli, tapped his forehead and shook his head slightly.

"Listen, Señor Sanchez," reasoned Poggioli, "no matter what Mr. Slidenberry should plant in your trunk he could not arrest you for it. You have declared that you don't know what your baggage contains. All he could do would be to confiscate anything illegal he discovered or let you pay the duty on it and keep it yourself. Either way he would lose and you would go free."

Sanchez nodded.

"That is the legal theory—but if he slipped something in my pocket and I walk off the ship carrying goods on which I have paid no duty, I go to jail. That has happened to me many times, señor."

The psychologist was astonished and incredulous.

"You don't mean to tell me the customs officers themselves—"

Sanchez interrupted—

"Certainly, señor; there is no tyranny so inescapable and so difficult to prove as that of the police department."

"But why should the customs officers themselves wish to—" Poggioli broke off, studying the old man's almost remembered face.

Dr. Sanchez shrugged, then spoke in a bitter voice—

"If I were a North American, señor, I would not only tell you my story; I would also tell the newspapers and the radio broadcasters, but we Latin-Americans—" he spread his palms sardonically—"feel somewhat differently about our private affairs."

"In my opinion," interposed Slidenberry dryly, "you handle not only your private affairs with the greatest reticence, but the truth also. The idea of a customs officer planting something in the baggage of a traveler! It was never done in the history of American customs."

The old man bristled at such an insult, but the dawning quarrel was interrupted by the voice of a cabin boy paging Captain Slidenberry. The officer stepped outside to call the boy, and Poggioli followed curiously.

AS THE messenger came up, the inspector turned to Poggioli and asked sharply:

"What do you think of him now? Is he crazy, or is he just a hopeless liar?"

Poggioli shook his head.

"If he really has been framed—"

"Framed, the devil! Did you ever hear of customs men framing a casual traveler?"

"I never did, but it is the most probable explanation of this riddle."

"You don't mean it has really happened?"

"I do because the old man doesn't insist on it. If he were a simple liar he would have gone on with a long cock and bull story to prove what he said was the truth, but he simply says it's so."

Slidenberry shook his head.

"You may believe it for psychological reasons if you want to, but I'm a customs man. No such thing ever happened on the face of the earth!"

The messenger boy came running up the deck and delivered a parcel. Slidenberry signed for it and opened it.

"Oh," he ejaculated, "the clerk has found the consular reports at last. Let me see; what was the page?" He drew out his cablegram and consulted it. "1125 and 6."

The inspector turned through the pages until he found his citation, then stood looking at it blankly.

Poggioli glanced over his shoulder, then drew in his breath.

"Oh—that man!" he ejaculated.

The inspector turned sharply.

"That man? What man?"

"Read there at the bottom of the page."

Slidenberry read with an uncomprehending expression:

July 5th. Today visaed the passport of the Magnificent Pompalone. Shipped him to Guiana on the French Line.

"Of course! Of course! Of course!" shouted Poggioli in amazed remembrance. "Dr. Sanchez is the Magnificent Pompalone—or once was. Heavens, yes, I remember him now!"

Slidenberry looked around.

"Who is he—or was he?"

"Why he's an ex-dictator of Venezuela."

"Is what he says true?"

"I suppose it is. In fact, I'm sure it is."

"But, Mr. Poggioli, how is it possible—"

"Why, you see, a group of nations—America, England, France, Holland and some others—went into an agreement not to allow the ex-dictator to return to his country because he would start another revolution. That would upset business and cost everybody money and time. When I knew him the Dutch authorities were trying to keep him on Curaçao, but he got away during a storm."

Slidenberry was amazed.

"Then there must be some truth in what he's telling. I suppose the authorities got tired of following him about and just lodged him in jail on some charge or other as the easiest way to keep him."

"Certainly. And what could be simpler than a customs offense?"

The inspector was moved at the old man's trials.

"Well, I'm going back and tell him he has nothing to fear from me."

The two men reentered the stateroom and found Dr. Sanchez sitting on his bunk, which was scattered with small, snowy, harp-like designs. The old man said acridly—

"I trust, señores, my finding these hasn't upset any plan you may have had to land me in prison."

Slidenberry exclaimed automatically—

"Poggioli, there are the feathers!"

Dr. Sanchez laughed with brief irony.

"Officer, I declare these egret feathers. I don't know how many there are."

The inspector looked blankly at the ornaments.

"You can't enter these in the United States; they are prohibited."

"I know that, señor. It has always struck me as touchingly beautiful for the American people to be so considerate of the wild birds of Venezuela while they kept a Venezuelan imprisoned year after year for fear he might go home and upset their commerce."

Slidenberry paid no attention to this.

"What are you going to do with your feathers? They can't go ashore."

For answer the old man drew out his cigar lighter, snapped a flame and began applying it to the egrets one by one. The stench filled the cabin. Slidenberry watched the destruction rather blankly.

"Have you got any diamonds in your bags?" he asked after a space.

"That I don't know," said the ex-dictator.

"Well, since you have feathers, I suspect you have diamonds too."

"Why? Do the two things go together?"

"So I've been informed."

"If I fail to find them and you do find them, will I be put in prison as a smuggler?" inquired the old man.

"Of course not," snapped the inspector. "If you actually help me search your bags for diamonds we'll be partners in the matter, won't we?"

With this agreement the two returned to the work in good earnest, rummaging through the trunks and the rest of the clothes. Slidenberry was more expert than the ex-dictator; he examined the trunks for false bottoms and double tops; he ran his fingers along the seams of the coats and trousers; he looked under the lining of Dr. Sanchez's hat. In the midst of this work he pushed aside a stray envelope on the floor with the toe of his shoe. A faint tinkle made him stoop and pick it up. He opened the flap and looked inside.

"Here they are," he said dryly.

Poggioli was astonished.

"You don't mean they were thrown around loose like that!"

"That's part of the technique," returned the inspector, "hiding it right under our eyes."

Dr. Sanchez watched this discovery impassively.

"What would you have done, señor," he inquired, "if by chance I had picked up the envelope before you did?"

The customs officer had to think twice before he knew what the old man meant, then he exclaimed—

"You think I put them there!"

"Think?" snapped the old man in sudden wrath. "I know it! Do you imagine I would deliberately help you customs men land me in jail by attempting to smuggle so much as a pin into your country?"

Slidenberry studied the exiled Venezuelan—

"You and I started searching for these diamonds together, didn't we?"

Sanchez nodded slowly and questioningly.

"You admitted you had them—or might have them—but neither of us knew where they were?"

"*Si, señor*—and what is your conclusion?" asked Sanchez in suspense.

"My conclusion is you have declared these diamonds and all that is required is for you to pay the normal duty on them and enter this country as a free man, señor."

Poggioli interrupted.

"Look here," he pointed out. "These diamonds were *not* mislaid in a chance envelope in the middle of the floor. That's impossible."

Slidenberry gave a short laugh.

"I know that, but under the circumstances I am going to rule arbitrarily that these diamonds were mislaid and found."

The scientist turned to the passenger.

"Dr. Sanchez, how do you explain this envelope?"

"Señor," said the old man, "why does so simple a thing need any explanation? Captain Slidenberry comes into my room and throws a package of diamonds on my floor. He means to arrest me, but for some reason he has a change of heart—"

"Look here," interrupted Slidenberry, "you know that's a falsehood!"

"Slidenberry! Slidenberry!" protested the psychologist. "Maybe he actually believes what he says!"

"How can he? Either he or I—"

"No, not necessarily; some third person could have stepped in here and dropped the envelope; then each one of you would think the other did it."

"What third person?"

"I don't know—the man who sent the cable; another inspector besides yourself. You see, when the United States has pledged itself to keep Dr. Sanchez out of Venezuela, what easier method would there be than to keep him in jail?"

Slidenberry nodded, unconvinced, and cooled off.

"Well, at any rate, I have agreed to let Sanchez go free when he pays the duty on these jewels. I stand by my agreement."

AS THE inspector said this Poggioli poured some of the stones out in his palm and looked at them, at first casually, then with dawning astonishment and suspicion.

"Mr. Slidenberry," said the scientist in an odd tone, "Dr. Sanchez didn't bring these stones on this ship."

"Why do you say that?" demanded the officer.

The criminologist handed over the jewels.

"Because they're glass."

The inspector received the sparkling bits incredulously, or at least with an excellent imitation of incredulity.

"Then I should say," he diagnosed slowly, "that Dr. Sanchez was fooled in his purchase."

Poggioli shook his head.

"No, an ex-dictator, an ex-millionaire, would hardly mistake paste for diamonds."

"Then what is there to think?" demanded Slidenberry, quite at sea.

"Well, if some third person didn't bring the sack in here—"

"You mean I did?" cried Slidenberry, amazed.

"What else is there to think? Sanchez didn't do it."

"Look here," cried Slidenberry, thrown for a moment on the defensive, "it's absurd the idea of my doing such a thing! I couldn't incriminate Dr. Sanchez with such brummagem as this! There's no law against bringing glass into America!"

The old Latin-American himself shook his head slowly.

"I believe this is the most complicated plot that has ever been woven around me," he said. "If it had been in a French port I would not have been surprised. Even the Dutch might have originated it; but for simple minded North Americans to hatch up anything so complicated—it amazes me."

Suddenly Slidenberry tossed the envelope on the bunk.

"I've got it!" he announced triumphantly, turning to confront the psychologist with a grim smile. "I've got it now!"

"What is it?" inquired Poggioli.

"Why, that was a blind to throw us off the trail, of course. Now let's get to work and find the real stones!"

As the inspector searched, Poggioli introduced himself to the dictator and recalled to him the matter of the murder in Curaçao. The old adventurer was immensely moved.

The Cablegram   123

"*Gracias a Dios* that I should see that clever young American again before I die," he cried. "The mystery you solved in that godforsaken island, señor, was much darker than that which surrounds me now."

The old man arose, embraced and kissed Poggioli in the affectionate Venezuelan manner.

"But still this is rather an oddly twisted case, Dr. Sanchez," suggested Poggioli.

"Puh, nothing of the sort; simply a customs inspector trying to send me to jail with glassware!"

Poggioli looked puzzled.

"But why is he searching so thoroughly now?"

"To save his face, señor."

"But, señor, look at him. That isn't the psychology of a desultory search. It isn't necessary to squeeze out your shaving cream to save his face. Then he found feathers in your room. He didn't bring them in with him."

"No-o. That is a queer thing, señor. Feathers—was the inspector expecting feathers?"

"Yes, he was. I'll tell you the truth, señor; he had a cable from Belize instructing him to search you for feathers and diamonds."

"Oh la! So those feathers were sewn into my military uniform in British America!"

"Or possibly on the voyage here. The cable could have been filed ahead of time to be sent later."

"You have a great head, señor; you think of every combination that can possibly exist. You catch the truth not in the Latin style of a burst of divination, but in the North American style of wearing her down by endless analysis, of making her surrender out of sheer boredom, Señor Poggioli."

This somewhat dubious compliment was interrupted by Slidenberry. He arose from his search, stood balked in the middle of the cabin.

"You may go," he said slowly, "I pass your trunks. I find nothing dutiable in them."

The old man looked at him cryptically.

"I can go ashore free?"

"That's what I said."

Sanchez shrugged.

"Do you imagine I would fall into so obvious a trap as that, señor?"

Slidenberry stared at the Latin.

"What the hell are you talking about now?"

Dr. Sanchez sighed wearily.

"You know very well. You find glassware; you say, 'These are not his diamonds; I will find genuine diamonds.' Well, I am as wary as you. I look at the glassware; I say to myself, 'These are not his diamonds; I will be as clever as he is and avoid his genuine diamonds.'" The old man patted himself on the chest.

Slidenberry looked at him.

"I almost thank God I don't know what you are talking about."

"I'll make myself clear. How easy it would have been for you to have hidden a real diamond in my trunk or toothpaste or clothes; then, when I step ashore, I will be searched and, la! caged up again."

"Good Lord, you don't think I'd plant a real diamond—"

"Think! I know it. Why would you make such a stir with paste if you did not intend to plant a real one?" The old man laughed.

Slidenberry looked at him.

"Really, our faith in each other is touching. All right, what do you intend to do if I can't even clear your baggage and let you go ashore?"

"This," said the old Venezuelan pungently. "By the strangest coincidence there is a man in my cabin whom I can trust. I am going to ask Señor Poggioli to take my money ashore, buy me a complete new outfit of clothes, bring them back here, let me dress and disembark from this ship in a virgin costume."

WITH this the old man went to his trunk, drew out a canvas bag of specie, silver and gold, swung it toward Poggioli and set it clinking on a chair.

The psychologist looked at the old man in amazement.

"Why any such rigmarole as this, señor?" he asked curiously.

"Señor," said Sanchez, "how can you ask me? You know how long I have sweated in prison on trumped up charges. You would be wary too if you saw ahead of you one tiny glimpse of freedom."

Poggioli stood pondering this new development when Slidenberry nodded him aside. When they were outside the cabin door the inspector whispered intently—

"Well, what do you make of that, Dr. Poggioli?"

"I think—I think that throws a new light on the subject," answered the psychologist carefully.

"How?"

"This is a positive move. Don't you see—up to this point his maneuvering has been negative and defensive; now it is for me to do something for him."

"But, listen," pressed the inspector, "don't you see it works out just right for us? If he takes absolutely nothing ashore, he takes nothing ashore—does he? Now I believe he's cracked—as you would say, got a complex, not to say a mania—on the subject of prisons. I suppose he has been driven to it by his experiences which you describe. So, if you don't mind, I wish you would go get him an outfit and let him walk off the ship in his birthday clothes as far as anything he brought into this country is concerned."

Poggioli could see why Slidenberry jumped at such an opportunity. He agreed to the plan, full of vague suspicion created by this new quirk of the ex-dictator.

Dr. Sanchez handed him the bag of Venezuelan coins, gave him a money changer's address in the Latin quarter of Miami and also a list of the shirt, suit and shoe sizes that he wore. The psychologist went ashore in an odd mood.

The money changer was in Miramar Street near the harbor. He ran a mere booth, arranged in the room of a private house, evidently one of those men who attend to the wants of his fellow Venezuelans before they learn the ways of American banks.

The fellow weighed the gold and silver coins in a pair of scales instead of counting them and gave Poggioli the exchange in American money.

An hour later the scientist took the clothes on board the *Stanhope*. Slidenberry had occupied his time by researching everything in the cabin, but without results. The whole affair would apparently remain an unsolved mystery, that is if it really were a mystery and not the maunderings of an unbalanced brain.

Dr. Sanchez had Slidenberry stand completely outside the cabin while he changed his apparel from hat to shoes. Then he pointed to his baggage.

"That I am going to leave in bond, señores, until I get ready to sail from this country. Then I'll search it myself and see what you planted in it at the last hour."

The inspector shook his head.

"Crazy as bedlam," he said, as he and Poggioli watched Sanchez go ashore.

AFTER the ex-dictator had gone the different phases of the incident simmered in Poggioli's mind. No two pieces of the puzzle seemed to fit together. Slidenberry, too, was curious, but he was relieved.

"That was a devil of a layout," he said. "Egret feathers, glass diamonds. I suppose they really must have been planted by that J. Dugmore Lampton, after all—he was an English customs officer, and he was no doubt following precedent in the consular reports when he arranged for Sanchez to be seized at this end of the line."

"Why did Sanchez wish that complete change of clothes?" pressed Poggioli, unsatisfied. "You know he could have worn ashore his shirt, undershirt, socks—"

"Oh, that was just his obsession, his craziness."

"All right. Admit that. Then why did J. Dugmore Lampton quote the consular reports? As I said long ago, if he is a consul he knows those reports go in the discard the moment they are published. For Lampton's memory to go back to 1915, and quote reports of that year, that isn't human, Mr. Slidenberry."

"Well, I'm not worrying about that end of the line," the inspector laughed. "Sanchez is ashore and he took nothing with him."

At this moment a Western Union boy came bicycling down the wharf and rounded into the inspector with a message.

Slidenberry looked at the enclosure, then puckered his brow and read aloud:

"NO SUCH PERSON AS J. DUGMORE LAMPTON REGISTERED WITH AMERICAN CONSULATE AT BELIZE. ERROR POSSIBLE. MAY BE J. HAMILTON SMITH."

The two men stood holding this second cablegram between them, looking at it.

"Well," said Slidenberry slowly, "so there was no J. Dugmore Lampton, or if there is one he is not expecting any reward after all—"

Poggioli burst out:

"My heavens! Of course, of course, that's the solution of it!"

"What? What's the solution of what?"

"The whole thing! There isn't any Lampton. Dr. Sanchez himself sent that cablegram. Why didn't I think of that at once? Of course he is the only man in the world who could quote year and page of consular reports as far back as 1915 because you see his name is mentioned in them. In fact, he was deported then. He would have no trouble at all remembering the date."

"But there's no sense to that!" cried Slidenberry. "What in the world would he want to make all this trouble for himself for?"

"He is like a sleight-of-hand performer; he wanted to center our attention on diamonds and feathers while he slipped something else past us. He wanted to make absolutely sure of it. I suppose he needs money for some new revolutionary undertaking."

Slidenberry dropped his hands hopelessly.

"But, look, man, he didn't go ashore with anything—nothing at all. Even his clothes are new!"

Poggioli laughed wryly.

"No-o, he didn't, but I did."

Slidenberry looked surprised.

"You—you went ashore—what with?"

"Why, his money, of course; I took that ashore, didn't I?"

"But money can't conceal diamonds and egret feathers!"

"Of course not, but you could take a five-bolivar piece, couldn't you, and—come on, come on, let's get to that money changer's address and look into this thing."

The two men hailed a taxi and whirled a few blocks to Miramar Street. When they reached the house, a very simple old householder met them.

"Where is that money changer, the one I traded with an hour or so ago?" hurriedly asked the psychologist.

The householder, who was an Ecuadorian, spread his hands.

"Señores, he gave up his room. He is gone. Did he cheat you? No, I hope not."

"No, he didn't cheat me! He smuggled dope—cocaine, I imagine—out of a ship down at the docks."

"Are you Señor Poggioli?" asked the householder.

"Yes, I am. Why?"

"A very fine gentleman left with me a note and a little token. He said you would call and get it."

"Well, give it to me!"

The Ecuadorian hustled away for a moment and returned with a note and a five-bolivar piece. The note said:

> *Muchas gracias, señor*, for your highly esteemed services. I am leaving you a little souvenir which will assure you that your deductions, although somewhat tardy, are correct.
>
> Always your friend and admirer,
—XENOPHON QUINTERO SANCHEZ

The souvenir was a very light five-bolivar piece. Poggioli twisted it experimentally. It unscrewed and disclosed the fact that it was a small silver container. It was empty and had been cleaned thoroughly. Legally it proved nothing.

The Pink Colonnade

WHEN Mr. Henry Poggioli, specialist in criminal psychology, stepped out of the elevator into the lobby of the Hotel Las Palmas, a man by the name of Lambert made the all-too-familiar plea for help. He began by paying what he evidently considered to be a compliment—that he had read about Mr. Poggioli's great skill as a detective in the morning papers; then he added that he had come to ask Mr. Poggioli if he would go with him to see a young lady.

The psychologist glanced patiently at the hotel clerk who had introduced Lambert.

"What's happened to her? Has she lost something, been threatened, accused, attacked, arrested?"

Mr. Lambert moistened his lips with his tongue.

"Well, no-o, she had a dream."

"A dream!"

"Yes, a very horrifying dream about her father. She dreamed—"

"Just a moment," interrupted the scientist. "Are you afraid this young lady has an Œdipus complex and you come to me as a psychologist, or are you uneasy lest something actually has happened to her father and you come to me as a criminologist?"

"Oh, as a criminologist, of course. Nobody worries about complexes as far south as Florida."

The psychologist nodded dubiously.

"All right, go ahead; tell me about the dream," he conceded.

"Well, she was awakened by it at three this morning. She is still terribly upset; she thinks something awful has happened to her father."

"Then he isn't at home?"

"No, if he were at home she'd feel all right, I suppose."

The scientist stood nodding at this; finally he said—

"If you don't mind, Mr. Lambert, I believe I will prescribe for this young lady as a psychologist, not as a criminologist."

"Dr. Poggioli, we would be more than grateful."

"Then suppose you have your family physician give her a dose of bromide."

The clerk who had introduced Lambert laughed at this anticlimax. Mr. Lambert was greatly perturbed. He walked with Poggioli toward the elevator and said in a lowered voice:

"Her father's not at home now, but he was last night. He went to bed yesterday evening. At three this morning he was gone!"

Poggioli instinctively lowered his own tone.

"Then what did his daughter dream?"

"That her father was calling for help. She jumped up, ran into his room—and he was gone."

"You have no clue as to what became of—"

"Yes, Laura heard his speedboat leaving the pier."

"Well, is there anything unusual in a speedboat trip?"

"If he was going off in his boat, why did he call for help?"

"I thought you said she dreamed that part of it?"

"That's what we don't know; maybe it was a dream, then maybe it wasn't—with kidnapping going on everywhere—"

"Look here," interposed Poggioli, "if you are really uneasy, why don't you take the matter to the police?"

Mr. Lambert hesitated, then stammered—

"We—we couldn't possibly take it to the police, Mr. Poggioli."

The scientist laid a finger on the elevator bell.

"I'm sorry, Mr. Lambert, but if you find it inadvisable for the police to look into this matter, I'm afraid I can't go into it either."

The caller was greatly disturbed.

"Wait—don't ring that bell! It isn't what you think at all." He leaned toward Poggioli and whispered tensely, "The missing man is Brompton Maddelow."

"Well, is Brompton Maddelow a gangster, or outlaw, or—"

"Good Lord, no, man! He's the biggest real estate dealer in Miami. He has more power in that game than—"

The psychologist stared.

"Then why shouldn't a real estate dealer have police protection?"

"Because if a single rumor should leak out that he has vanished, the mortgages on his properties would be foreclosed at once. They are hanging now simply on Mr. Maddelow's reputation as a business man."

The psychologist began nodding at this odd twist.

"Mm—I see—I see. But really, from what you say, I don't believe anything has happened to the man. At a guess, I'd say he is out for a cruise and will be back in a day or two."

"Why should he have left home at three o'clock in the morning?"

"I really don't know his personal habits."

"Well, it wasn't his habit to cruise at three or four or any other hour in the morning. He never took his speedboat out, because it was too expensive. He—he couldn't afford the gas and oil."

"Tut! That's nothing; it's a commonplace in psychology for men to break over from long continued economies."

"All right, suppose it is. But why should he suddenly stop working on his colonnade to go cruising in his speedboat?"

"Working on his colonnade at three in the morning?"

"Yes, he worked on his columns at night when he got restless and couldn't sleep. You see, he was a plasterer in Pocatello, Idaho, before he came to Miami during the boom and made such a splash as a realtor."

During this conversation Poggioli had walked with Mr. Lambert to the door of the big beach hotel. At the curb he stepped into an old high powered car and started northward. At the third turn of the beach Lambert directed the scientist's attention to one of the villas that lined Biscayne Bay.

"It's the pink one with the royal poincianas in front of it."

"Is that the pier where the speedboat was moored?"

"Yes, sir, that's Mr. Maddelow's private pier, six hundred feet long, water seventy feet deep at the outer end. He built it when he was worth ten million in cold cash."

"Can we reach the villa from the beach?"

"By a ramp built into the side of the pier."

Poggioli looked at the structure looming above him.

"You don't mean he built this just to hitch a speedboat to it?"

"Oh, no. Mr. Maddelow had ordered a yacht from Germany to fit his pier, when the boom broke and everything fell through. It was a hard blow for him, Mr. Poggioli. I don't blame him for working on his colonnade at night to keep from thinking about it."

THE ancient car rattled up the ramp, passed under the poincianas and stopped in front of the pergola which the owner of the place had been building. The final column of the decoration still stood in its wooden mold where the ex-plasterer had poured it just before setting out on his alarming boat cruise.

The sound of the automobile brought several persons out of the villa. A tall, sun-tinted girl, who evidently had been weeping, hurried to the car.

"Is this Mr. Poggioli? Mr. Poggioli, what happened to papa?"

"I have no theory as yet, Miss Maddelow."

"Do you think somebody made a mistake and—and kidnapped him?"

"Made a mistake—how?"

"Why his having all this—" the daughter indicated the villa with a turn of her head, "a person who didn't know him might think he was wealthy and try to hold him for ransom."

Two other men on the pergola besides the Maddelow son, daughter and mother, broke into ironic laughter at the idea of Brompton Maddelow being held for ransom. The girl turned on them angrily.

"That could easily be! Anybody who didn't know what bad luck papa has had with his property would certainly think he was rich."

The psychologist got out of the car, and Lambert introduced him to the Maddelows and to a Mr. Sandley and a Mr. Lynch who bore an air of also being permanent residents of Villa Maddelow. The scientist naturally turned to the daughter and began questioning her about the call for help that had disturbed her during the night, but she could add little to what he already had learned from Lambert. He then turned to the group at large and suggested in a comforting tone that Mr. Maddelow was simply on a pleasure trip and that they need not disturb themselves about the matter.

The man named Lynch answered dryly—

"It takes gas and oil to run a speedboat, Mr. Poggioli."

"You mean Maddelow couldn't afford it?"

"Of course not," seconded Sandley in a disgusted tone.

The psychologist walked to the end of the pergola and saw a small layout for mixing concrete. With this outfit the missing man had erected the final column of the pergola which now stood wrapped in its wooden mold. As he looked at this he asked in a more careful tone—

"Am I to understand that Mr. Maddelow built all these columns by himself?"

"James helped him," said Laura Maddelow.

"When he stayed up at night working at it," amplified Lambert. "He often said he made more money at night than he did during the daytime."

"How was that?" inquired the scientist.

"Why he figured the additional value this pergola would give the building would net him eighty-seven dollars and thirty-four cents a night—if times were normal."

Poggioli looked at the layout with a puzzled air.

"And he put up all these columns?"

"He and the man of all work. Why?" asked Lambert.

The criminologist shook his head.

"What you tell me makes this vat a rather extraordinary riddle," he said slowly.

The whole group looked curiously at the concrete mixer and asked why.

"Because of the concrete that is left in the vat unused," explained the investigator simply. "If Maddelow had poured all these columns he must have known to the half sack how much each one would take; now for him to leave this much in the vat unused—you see, it contradicts the careful, exact character of the man you describe, Mr. Lambert."

Lambert scratched his head.

"That is odd—"

Lynch spoke up dourly—

"It shows the Emperor knew he was working on his last column and didn't care if he did use all his cement."

Poggioli shook his head.

"I don't quite think so. A man who would figure the value of his night's work to the odd cent wouldn't dump out the last of his cement. He would try to come out with a sack or two left over."

"Look here," interrupted Sandley, "how is that going to help us find out where the Emperor is now?"

Laura Maddelow interrupted her co-tenant's criticism by ejaculating—

"Why look, there's something a lot stranger than a little cement left over in the box!"

"What is it?" asked her brother as every one followed the direction of the girl's finger.

"That new column is yellow! You can see smudges of it on the molds. Papa forgot to put in the pink dye. Why, that column won't do."

Lynch put forth a sarcastic idea—

"Maybe the Emperor was pifflicated when he put up this post; that's why he put in too little dye and too much cement."

Poggioli shook his head.

"If he had been under the influence of alcohol he wouldn't have gone to work at hard manual labor."

"I am sure he wasn't drinking," agreed the daughter, "but if he left out the pink color he must have been tremendously excited about something. Why, color was the main thing with papa about the colonnade."

Poggioli shook his head in thoughtful negation.

"No, Mr. Maddelow wasn't excited. Excitement is something that demands thought, but Maddelow used this pergola as something to deaden his memories of his financial losses. If he were excited about something else, he never would have worked on the pergola in the first place. Therefore he didn't leave out his dye through excitement."

"Look here," said Sandley acridly, "you seem to be able to prove our theories untrue—why don't you try one of your own and see how that comes out?"

Mr. Lambert broke into this incipient acrimony—

"Oh, Mr. Poggioli, I happened to think of something. Will you step in the library for a moment?"

Sandley looked at Lambert.

"What's in the library?"

"Something Mr. Poggioli ought to see," evaded Lambert with a trace of embarrassment.

With this Lambert stepped through a French window that gave on the pergola, and the scientist followed. A moment later Poggioli found himself in a long sunlit room with cases of books on two sides. Lambert walked quickly to a picture that was hung low against the wall. He beckoned silently to Laura Maddelow, who stood looking at them through the window.

"Let us in here, Laura," he requested in a low tone.

The girl approached, rather at sea.

"Why, Lawrence, you know papa's not in there!"

Lambert shook his head at her for silence, then drew aside the picture and displayed a small door masked by wallpaper. He pushed back the panel and displayed the steel door of a safe.

"You know the combination, Laura; open it for us, please."

"But there's nothing left in here that's valuable," protested Miss Maddelow, and began turning the combination, presently swinging open the small, heavy door.

THE vault contained an orderly collection of account books and private papers. Lambert opened a small drawer and took out a linen envelope. With a glance at the French window, he handed this to the scientist and whispered—

"There you are, Mr. Poggioli; that's why they killed him."

"Who killed him?" frowned the criminologist, puzzled.

"Why, Lynch and Sandley," whispered the fellow.

"Lawrence Lambert, what are you saying!" exclaimed Miss Maddelow in horror.

"Look at it! Read it!" pressed Lambert in hushed excitement.

The scientist drew out a crackling enclosure.

"Read a life insurance policy?" he asked blankly.

"Certainly—read the amount."

Poggioli caught his breath.

"What—a million, two hundred and fifty—"

"That's right," hurried Lambert. "Biggest policy ever issued in Miami up to the time he bought it. Now look when the premium's due."

The psychologist followed Mr. Lambert's finger with quickening interest.

"Why, it's tomorrow," he exclaimed.

"Of course it is. Just happened to think of it. My heaven, don't see why it didn't occur to me the minute we found that Brompton Maddelow was mur—"

"Who was the million and a quarter made to?" queried the psychologist.

"His estate—to protect his creditors. When I sold Mr. Maddelow that insurance I told him he was doing the best thing in the world for his business, stabilizing it. My Lord, I didn't dream if he went broke his creditors would kill him to make him solvent again."

"So you think his creditors have done away with him?"

"Of course they have. Every debt against him is worth a hundred cents on the dollar now."

"But Sandley and Lynch—did he owe them anything?"

"No, he didn't. But he sold Lynch a ten per cent interest in this villa for four hundred dollars; later he sold Sandley another ten per cent for two-fifty. He was honest with 'em. He explained there were mortgages against the place and very likely they wouldn't get anything out of it except their room rent up to the time of foreclosure. But now, by murdering him, these rats have paid off all the mortgages and they've got ten per cent interest in holdings worth a cool million."

Mr. Poggioli listened in astonishment to this extraordinary theory.

"Then the vanishing of the speedboat has nothing to do with Mr. Maddelow's disappearance?"

"Why do you say that?"

"Because it would be necessary to Lynch and Sandley's plans that the body should be found. His death would have to be proved to set up the insurance."

Lambert thought a moment, then stretched his theory to fit the conditions.

"They have probably killed him and moored the boat somewhere where it can be found."

At this point the girl behind them caught her breath and gasped:

"Oh, Mr. Poggioli. I—I know what's happened to papa! He did it himself!" And with this Laura Maddelow leaned against the door of the vault and began weeping outright.

The psychologist was shocked.

"Miss Maddelow, why do you say such a thing?"

"Because his policy was about to run out. He had been trying every way lately to get up some money. He had advertised his speedboat for five hundred dollars. Once he thought he had sold it to a Captain Greer on board the *Arequipa*—"

"But he didn't make the sale?"

"I don't think so. Then he saw the time was out on his policy—he—he couldn't make the next premium in—in any way at all, so he—he—" Laura Maddelow began weeping miserably.

The two men looked at each other at this tragic theory.

"He could have done that, Mr. Poggioli," assented Lambert in a gray tone. "Brompton Maddelow had a keen sense of honor; he felt his responsibility toward his creditors. You see, he was a poor man once."

"As a rule," pointed out the psychologist more hopefully, "millionaires recover from any dangerous overscrupulousness by the time they have accumulated their fortunes. I can imagine a wealthy man killing himself if his debts were about to be collected, but not in order to pay his debts."

Mr. Lambert suddenly brightened.

"Look here, I wonder if it's possible. I'll bet it is."

"What is it?" asked the girl.

"Laura, do you know this Captain Greer didn't buy your father's boat?"

"I'm not sure. I heard papa talking to him over the telephone. I understood the captain wouldn't take the boat."

"Good gracious, that explains everything!" cried Lambert. "Your father was a salesman. He never took no for an answer. I'll bet he's down there right now demonstrating his boat to the captain. Here, what's the captain's number?"

The ex-insurance agent started for the telephone.

"He hasn't any number. You call for the *Arequipa* at the docks. But why would papa call to me for help, Lawrence, if he was going to deliver a speedboat?"

"Oh, you didn't hear anything. That was a dream." He put the receiver to his ear. "Operator! Operator! I want the steamship *Arequipa* of the Fruit Lines—now, now, don't argue with me, I want the steamship *Arequipa*—" He put his palm over the transmitter to say, "These simp operators always trying to explain something—"

THE French window opened and Lynch and Sandley entered the library protesting in chorus—

"Look, will you, the Emperor has been trying to double-cross us!"

"What do you think you've found?" asked the girl indignantly.

"Why look at this note! He's paid off a mere personal note of hand—not a mortgage at all—paid it off without saying howdy to anybody!"

Even Mr. Lambert lowered the telephone to stare at the idea of Brompton Maddelow paying off a note.

"That explains why he was yelling for help," suggested Lynch sardonically.

"Why shouldn't he have paid it off?" demanded the girl.

"Because every cent he spent on outside debts weakened our mortgage on the villa," returned Sandley warmly.

"Who's the note made to?" asked Lambert. "Who in the world came here in the middle of the night and collected a note from Brompton Maddelow!"

Lynch put together two pieces of a torn note.

"Tom Snodgrass," he read. "It's for five hundred and sixty dollars."

Poggioli reached for the paper, adjusted the two ends and read the word "paid" scrawled across the face in lead pencil.

"Where did you find this?"

"Out there by the vat. The Emperor evidently paid it, then tore it in two and threw it away."

"That's an odd thing, for a systematic man like him to throw away a canceled note—" Poggioli stood studying the paper. "How did he get five hundred and sixty dollars at three in the morning? Did he have that much money in his pockets?"

"No, nor in his bank either," said Lynch sharply.

Sandley broke into incredulous laughter.

"I've got it, by George! This Captain Greer traded for one of the Emperor's notes and used it to pay for the boat. No wonder the Emperor was mad as a wet hen!" The speaker laughed heartily.

"But he couldn't have done that," objected the girl. "The advertisement says the buyer must pay cash." She walked to a table for a paper. "Here is the ad," she said, coming back, "marked around with a pencil."

Poggioli took the paper and looked at the advertisement curiously. It was two lines describing the *Sea Maid*, forty-six footer, two three hundred H.P. Diesel engines, max. speed 52 M.P.H. Apply private pier Villa Maddelow, terms cash, $500.00.

Poggioli shook his head.

"This is one of the most puzzling features of this case," he said slowly.

"What—the advertisement?"

"No, the pencil mark around the advertisement."

"Why, what's puzzling about that?"

"This is Mr. Maddelow's paper, isn't it, delivered to him here in the villa?"

"Yes it is."

"Then he sat here in his chair, read it and made this mark around his own advertisement?"

"Certainly. What's odd about that?"

"Simply this; the only reason any one marks something in a newspaper is to refer to it quickly. What reason could Mr. Maddelow have had for a quick reference to his own ad?"

"I've got it," said Sandley. "He was expecting Greer to offer him a note for the *Sea Maid* and he wanted to show that his ad said cash."

Poggioli punctured the suggestion with another of his impressive and spontaneous observations—

"But Snodgrass's endorsement is not on the back of the note."

"No-o, but—"

Poggioli interrupted:

"Does anybody here know Tom Snodgrass? Who is he?"

All the listeners stood silent shaking their heads when the telephone bell whirred. Lambert reclapped the receiver to his ear.

"Hello! Hello! Is this Captain Greer of the *Arequipa*? Hello, Captain: Lawrence Lambert speaking at the Villa Maddelow . . . say, is Brompton Maddelow aboard your vessel? . . . Well, did he bring the *Sea Maid* down to demonstrate her to you? . . . don't know whether he did or not . . . But she was down there? Passed your ship going south . . . I see . . . thanks very much . . . Yes, we were getting uneasy about him. By the way, did you happen to notice if he went to some other vessel at the docks? . . . What docks! Why, the docks down at the docks—the Miami docks . . . What? . . . You don't mean it."

Lambert put down the telephone and stared at his listeners.

"The *Sea Maid* passed the *Arequipa* two hundred miles down the coast. They were both going south!"

Miss Maddelow suddenly switched from grief over her father's death to anxiety over his mysterious voyage. The two co-owners were also sharply moved.

"Look here," cried Sandley, "if the Emperor has gone into that game we're sunk!"

"What game? What do you mean?" demanded the girl.

"I guess he got desperate and had to do something," said Lynch.

"But if he gets caught, his creditors will suck everything up like a sponge!"

Laura twisted her fingers together.

"What are you men talking about! What's papa doing?"

THE telephone buzzed again. Lambert leaped to it. He listened a moment, then slapped it back up.

"It's that confounded careless telephone operator. She gave me wireless connection with the *Arequipa* and the bill's six eighty-two."

"You ought to be more careful yourself," reproved Lynch. "You ought to ask if you've got wireless or line connections."

"Me got wireless connections?" cried Lambert sharply. "I didn't get any at all. I was phoning for you people."

"But you called the Emperor up yourself."

"Lawrence—Mr. Lynch, stop quarreling!" cried the daughter in desperation. "What are you men talking about? What do you think papa's doing?"

Gary Maddelow, her brother, entered the library from some search of his own. The girl blurted out to him that their father was on the *Sea Maid* halfway down the coast of Florida and these men wouldn't tell her what her father was after.

Lynch took his courage in his hands.

"Well, Miss Laura, I hate to say it—but we believe your father has—er—turned rum runner."

The girl stared.

"You mean father—Why, you know better than that."

"Then what's he after?" inquired Sandley. "It can't be a pleasure trip."

"Gary, you are not going to stand there and let these men—"

"Listen, sis, if dad has started any such business, you know it was his very last resort."

"You don't believe any such falsehood, I hope!"

"Well, I knew it had been proposed to him."

Laura dropped her hands.

"Gary Maddelow, who in the world proposed such a thing?"

"Why, James," said the brother. "He proposed it to me, too."

"Of all impudence—our man of all work."

"He did it tactfully. I suppose he came at dad the same way."

The two co-proprietors of the villa took up the discussion.

"Look here, how the Emperor got into this business doesn't make any difference. He's in. The question is, how'll we get him out?"

"But look here," put in Lambert. "If Brompton Maddelow goes into this business how do you know he won't make a big success? He's a born organizer. We may be all setting jake the first thing you know."

"Lawrence," cried Miss Maddelow, "do you imagine I'd let father do that for all the money in the world? What can we do to stop him? Tell me that."

Poggioli interposed to ask if the *Sea Maid* had a wireless.

"She did have one, but dad sold it off of her," said Gary.

"Listen here," put in Sandley, "there's just one way I see. Get a plane. Lambert, you telephone the aviation field for a flying boat."

"Who's going to pay for this?" demanded Lambert at once. "If you think you are going to stick me for a flying bill on top of a wireless call—"

"No, no, of course not," pacified Sandley, "and the bill won't be so much either. Air taxi business is slow nowadays. They say the aviators will take you up for the price of their gas."

Lambert picked up the receiver dubiously.

Mr. Poggioli moved over to Gary Maddelow with the torn note.

"Do you know any one by the name of Tom Snodgrass?" he inquired.

"Sure, Tom Snodgrass is our man of all work. We always called him James. Why?"

"Your sister didn't know that."

"Sis," called the young man in surprise, "what do you mean by not knowing James's name was Tom Snodgrass?"

"Why, I did know it. Who said I didn't?"

"Mr. Poggioli, when he showed you this note."

"Oh, the note. You know that Tom Snodgrass isn't James. Papa wouldn't be borrowing five hundred and sixty dollars from the hired man. That's what I meant when I said I didn't know any Tom Snodgrass. I meant I didn't know any other Tom Snodgrass."

At this moment Lynch was shouting:

"Look here, I've got the whole thing figured out! James's note is torn up. Then it's been paid off in some way or other. He had been trying to persuade somebody to go into the rum running business with him. Very well, he got the Emperor. They're partners. The Emperor risked his boat and James risked his note."

"Yes," snarled Sandley, "and they'll both get caught and we'll all lose this villa."

"Everybody hush!" cried Lambert from the telephone. "Is this the flying field?

We want a flying boat—a pretty big flying boat . . . Listen, how many here want to go?"

Came a general clamor and raising of hands.

"Look here, we're not chartering the DO-X," protested Lambert.

There broke out a swift conversation in undertones to determine who should go and who would have the most influence on Mr. Maddelow to persuade him to change his occupation. It turned out that each person thought he was more influential than the others. Just then Lambert put his hand over the mouthpiece of the telephone and called out—

"Listen, how we going to pay for this?"

"What you want to know for?" grumbled Lynch.

"The devil, it isn't me. I already know you can't pay for it. It's the airmen."

"How much is his fee?" asked Sandley.

Lambert made motions for them not to shout so loud; then he answered Sandley's query about the size of the aviator's fee—

"I told him how we were shaped up here and he said he would go for his gas and oil."

"Now that will be the devil of a note," said Lynch, "if we lose this air trip just because we can't furnish the gas and oil."

"Wait," cried Laura Maddelow, flying back to the camouflaged vault. "Wouldn't papa's courtesy card do?"

"Do?" said Lynch. "Good as the Bank of England! Better than it is now. Tell 'em to come on, Lambert. Tell 'em we ride on courtesy cards."

THE girl herself did not share in the general rejoicing over the card. She came up to the psychologist and asked in an apprehensive tone—

"Mr. Poggioli, do you believe papa has—has gone into such an awful business?"

The scientist shook his head.

"I don't think so, Miss Maddelow."

Lynch turned on the investigator.

"You don't think so. Why do you think the *Sea Maid* is on her way to Cuba—or the Bahamas? Is it a pleasure trip?"

"That's odd," admitted Poggioli. "I can form no theory to fit the facts."

"Fit what facts? If a man's going to Cuba, he's going to Cuba, isn't he?"

"I mean," returned the psychologist with dignity, "it does not explain the color left out of the concrete column, or the surplus cement in the mixing vat, or the lead pencil mark around the advertisement."

"What's that got to do with the facts we know?"

"They contradict what you call the facts we know."

"Contradict how?"

"Listen; if a careful man like Mr. Maddelow were leaving home on a hazardous expedition, he would put everything in shipshape. He would have put dye in the concrete, cleaned up the refuse and filed Tom Snodgrass's note in his vault. And you can not imagine a reason for his making a pencil mark around his advertisement. None of these details agrees with your theory that he has turned rum runner."

Here Miss Laura dropped her hands with a gasp.

"Oh I know what's happened," she said weakly, and caught Mr. Poggioli's arm for support.

She was a pretty girl, and the scientist asked very sympathetically what was her idea.

"I—I know papa won't be on that boat when we catch it."

"Why do you think so?"

"He—he'll be gone. He'll pretend he fell overboard. You know, the policy—so it will look like an accident. That's why he was so excited and forgot everything."

Mr. Poggioli attempted to comfort her from a psychological angle.

"You are wrong, Miss Maddelow; the reactions of persons contemplating suicide are extreme orderliness. A suicide never forgets to do anything."

The girl simply shook her head, sobbing.

"I just know papa has drowned himself."

At this point a droning made itself audible in the library and swiftly grew into the roar of an airplane. The group hurried out on the great pier that had been designed for an ocean-going yacht. The flying boat grew rapidly in the sky and a few minutes later took the water and came foaming up to the dock.

The party got aboard; the two motors popped half a dozen times like pistol shots, then started roaring again. The plane moved forward, climbed up on the wavetops, then swung loose from the water and dropped Biscayne Bay slowly beneath her.

As the plane stormed higher, the blue tourmaline sea stitched to the red tapestry of the city by a yellow thread of beach extorted a breath of admiration from every one except the flyer. He began bewailing his lack of trade, explaining to Lambert that the tourists didn't have the money to fly.

On the second seat Lynch and Sandley were astonished at the transparency of the sea. They thought some sharks were mullets until the aviator set them right.

In the rear seat Laura Maddelow was saying to Mr. Poggioli—

"We're doing all this j-just to find out that—that papa is—is—"

"Look here, Miss Laura," advised the psychologist cheerfully, "instead of bewailing your father as dead, you'd better think of something to say to him."

"Something to say—what do you mean?"

"I mean some argument to get him to come back home with you. I think he'll tell us to mind our own affairs."

"Oh, Mr. Poggioli, do you really think papa will be aboard?"

"He couldn't possibly have jumped overboard as you fear."

"Why couldn't he?"

"Because James, the hired man, would have turned around and started back to Miami. If we overtake the boat still going south, your father is bound to be well and alive."

The girl brightened at the theory.

At this point Lynch and Sandley dominated the cabin by shouting and making violent gestures.

"Yonder's the *Sea Maid!* Yonder she is, big as life!"

Both Poggioli and Miss Maddelow peered forward through the small windows. The pilot began laughing.

"Yeh," he shouted back, "and she's a whole lot bigger than life. That's the *Arequipa*—she sailed from Miami yesterday evening."

Sure enough, the distant vessel increased in size, became the ground plan of a ship with its bridge marked across deck, dots for masts and smoke trailing out of circles that represented funnels.

This view of the *Arequipa* produced a vertiginous feeling of height. Miss Maddelow shut her eyes against it. On the forward seat Mr. Lambert became enthusiastic. He shouted to the pilot:

"That gives me an idea! Why not sell real estate from an airplane? A salesman could show his prospect exactly how far his home would be from the golf course."

"Yes," called the aviator, "and if he wanted it closer, all he'd have to do would be to take him higher."

"Say," went on Lambert more seriously, "why not form a company here in Miami to sell real estate from airplanes? I got a slogan for our organization—just popped into my head. Listen to this: 'We Sell Florida From the Sky; not the Sky from Florida'."

"Man, it's a knockout," said the aviator. "Means more and says less than any slogan I ever heard."

THEIR conversation was interrupted by Lynch's shouting to Sandley to look at the white gull below. Then the aviator cried:

"That's no gull. That's a speedboat. Those wings you see are sprays of water. That's bound to be the *Sea Maid*."

"What's he running like that for?" shouted Sandley. "Suppose he's been hitting that pace ever since he left Miami?"

"No, he'd be farther on than he is now," replied Poggioli.

"Then what's he in such a rush about?" demanded Lynch.

"Oh, the Emperor thinks we're a Government plane full of customs men," hazarded Sandley.

Poggioli objected.

"Why would he evade a customs plane? He can't have a stock of liquor aboard now. He's still going South."

"All right, what do you say he's running for?" Lynch demanded tartly of the psychologist.

"I don't know. I can't think of any reason for Mr. Maddelow's running from a plane. It doesn't seem to co-ordinate with anything."

Their remarks were lost in the swoop of the plane to take the water close to the boat. The speedboat itself was hurling aside sheets of spray as it shot across the waves. The motors of the two vessels roared a mighty duet in the empty ocean. Just then Laura Maddelow cried out:

"Look, look! Yonder's James sitting by himself in the cockpit. Oh, papa's drowned! I knew he would be. He's drowned himself."

"No, he's not, Miss Laura," shouted Lynch. "He's in the cabin. He knows it's us and he's ashamed to show himself."

The girl shook her head.

"I'm sure he would be outside. Oh, I know he's dead!"

The plane was now twenty or thirty feet above the water and quite near the *Sea Maid*. An outbreak of shouting burst from the tiny windows of the airplane:

"James! Wait there, James! Where's papa, James? Stop the boat, James; where's the Emperor?"

The pontoons struck the waves and sent a deluge over the flying *Sea Maid*. The man, Tom Snodgrass, cut off his engines. His boat slowed down and he sat staring up at the wide spread of wings with a colorless face. As the door of the airplane opened and the passengers climbed out on to the boat the man of all work exclaimed:

"So that is you-all? Who else you got in there—Mr. Poggioli?"

Sandley turned to the psychologist in amazement.

"By George, the fellow guessed you were inside!"

"James, James, is papa with you?" cried Miss Maddelow.

The face of the man of all work changed.

"M—Miss Laura," he stammered, "I—I shore hate to tell you, but—but your pappy slipped an' fell overboard this mornin' a little before good daylight. We wasn't forty miles out o' Miami."

The news of Brompton Maddelow's death plunged the group into the most diverse reactions. The daughter fainted. The men fell into a quandary whether to return her to Miami on the speedboat or in the plane. Eventually they transferred her to the boat where she regained consciousness, but lay on a couch in the cabin with her eyes closed.

Lynch and Sandley put on expressions of concern, but Poggioli could see they were excitedly happy that their speculation in the villa had ended in such undreamed-of good fortune.

The hired man protested against turning the *Sea Maid* about and going back to Miami. He said the boat belonged to him, that he had given a note which he held against Mr. Maddelow for the vessel. His objections were overruled, indeed they were hardly noticed under the urgent necessity of a millionaire's family. They told him he must come back to Miami and certify to the death of his employer on the insurance claim; after that he could take the boat and do what he pleased with it.

"Why didn't you turn back at once when Mr. Maddelow fell overboard?" inquired Lynch.

"I wanted to get to Nassau and bring back enough stuff to pay for the gas," explained the man of all work. "We went in debt for the gas."

"Mr. Maddelow had a courtesy card. Why didn't he use that?" asked Lynch.

"Why, I suppose he forgot it," said Snodgrass.

"Mr. Maddelow must have been quite excited, wasn't he?" asked Poggioli of the hired man.

"Yes, sir, he was," returned Snodgrass, looking carefully at the psychologist.

Poggioli lolled in the cockpit and considered the ashes of his cigar as the speedboat flung the miles astern. Lynch and Sandley went into the cabin to see about Miss Maddelow.

"By the way, Mr. Snodgrass," pursued the psychologist, "the moment our plane stopped you called to know if I were aboard. That was odd. How came you to think of me?"

"I had the morning paper, sir. I had just got through readin' about you. Then I looked up and there come an airplane, lickety-split, and it just came over me all of a sudden that you was in it after me—"

"Why did you think I would be in it?"

"Because I knew the folks would want to trace up the governor and I knew you was the only man in town who could figger out where he went."

Mr. Poggioli nodded at these correct deductions. It seemed an extraordinary truth for Snodgrass to have hit upon. Mention of the paper set the psychologist off on another tack.

"Speaking of the paper, it was you who marked the *Sea Maid*'s advertisement in the *Herald*, wasn't it?" The investigator drew from his pocket the clipping and handed it to the helmsman.

Snodgrass took it with a slight frown on his leathery face.

"I don't know. I might of. What makes you ask me?"

"It simply puzzled me. I couldn't understand why the ad was marked, but of course you did it because you wanted to purchase the boat. You paid him the note you held against him for it?"

"Yes, I did." The man of all work nodded briefly.

"I'm surprised you got the boat, at that. The ad said cash."

"He made a good thing out of it," explained Snodgrass uneasily. "My note was sixty dollars bigger'n the price he asked in the paper."

"So Maddelow did object to taking the note straight as so much cash?"

"He did till I discounted him the sixty dollars and interest."

"M—huh—" The criminal investigator sat nodding his head. "What strikes me as odd—if Maddelow wanted to go in the rum running business, what made him sell his boat at all?"

The hired man twisted on the cushion in the cockpit.

"Now I can explain that, too. He said he was afraid to risk his boat, and I said, 'I'll take it off'n your han's, an' it's my loss if it gits pinched.' That's what I told him."

"So you had no trouble trading with him?"

"If the governor hadn't wanted to trade, I don't reckon he would of," returned Snodgrass surlily.

THE psychologist sat looking absently at the speeding waves, rearranging the bits of evidence into a more rational design. Finally he said:

"Brompton Maddelow was a heavy man, wasn't he? Weighed about a hundred and eighty pounds?"

Snodgrass looked at his catechist suspiciously.

"Didn't you never see him?"

"No. I was simply making a guess. If you don't care to tell me—"

"Oh, I don't mind tellin' you. That's about right, I reckon. I don't see how you guessed so clost if you never seed him."

"Well, if you must know," said the scientist with a little laugh, "I guessed it from the cement left over in the vat."

The hired man thought a moment.

"Oh, from his tracks in the vat?"

"No, from the amount of cement left in the vat."

"The amount left in? I don't see what that's got to do with it."

"And by the way," interrupted the criminologist, "that last column you and Mr. Maddelow put up—your employer was so excited about this trip he forgot to put any red dye in the mixture. It's just plain yellow. When we get home, Snodgrass, you'll have to tear down that column and mold a new one."

To this the hired man made no reply, but sat wetting his lips with his tongue, staring across the waves with his hand on the wheel.

Mr. Poggioli got up and went into the cabin. Sandley and Lynch were just coming into the cockpit again. The psychologist went to the girl's side, thinking of the simple yet macabre riddle he had solved. He wondered how he would ever tell her. Explain it to her brother, perhaps, and let Gary . . . In the midst of his preoccupation he heard a shout on deck. He turned and ran back. Lynch was holding the tiller and his eyes were starting from his head.

"Mr. Poggioli," he cried, "he slipped and fell overboard!"

"Who did?"

"James."

The psychologist looked astern.

"Where is he now?"

"Why, he's gone. While I was holding the wheel for him, I saw a fin. I called to him to look at it. I said, 'James, look at that shark.' At that very minute he slipped and fell overboard."

"Did you throw him a buoy?"

"Yes, yonder it is now—back yonder where you see those two fins moving about."

Sandley interrupted:

"Mr. Poggioli, how will this affect our proof of Mr. Maddelow's death? If we haven't got James, who saw him go overboard?"

The criminologist made a sick gesture.

"It's easy to prove his death. Maddelow's body is in the last column of the colonnade. He and James had a fight over whether Maddelow would accept his own note of hand for the *Sea Maid*. Of course, Maddelow wanted cash to pay on his life insurance. In the fight Maddelow was killed. Snodgrass dropped his body in the mold and poured concrete over it."

Private Jungle

ON the southbound express out of Tampa, the bride in the seat just ahead of Mr. Henry Poggioli was of the velvety prettiness characteristic of the Spanish strain in Florida women; and so the criminologist had fallen into conversation with the husband.

After they had talked on for some bit, the men telling their names and occupations after the fashion of American travelers, Poggioli was wondering how he could draw the girl into the conversation and hear the quality of her voice, when she looked around and asked with interest:

"And you are a criminologist?"

"Yes, Mrs. Blackmar."

The girl hesitated. "I wonder—I wonder, Mr. Poggioli, you being a criminologist, if you could prove that somebody didn't do what he is accused of?"

A quirk of humor went through Poggioli at the prevailing need of human beings for the service of criminologists. Here was this girl returning from her honeymoon! Aloud he said: "Some one accused of a crime, Mrs. Blackmar?"

"Elora—" warned the husband in an undertone.

A renewed rattling of the rain against the car window gave Mr. Poggioli a chance to veer politely from what appeared to be a delicate matter between husband and wife.

"Does it rain like this all through the wet season in Florida?" he asked.

Mr. Blackmar began explaining that it usually came in squalls like the present, when the girl interrupted with unmistakable earnestness:

"Yes, a crime, Mr. Poggioli, a very dreadful crime—at least the accusation of one."

This headed the conversation once more toward shoals.

Poggioli answered gravely:

"Wouldn't proving a man's innocence be a case for a lawyer rather than a problem for a psychologist, Mrs. Blackmar?"

"This has nothing to do with courts," returned the bride, disturbed. "It's a tale, a rumor that keeps floating around El Jobe-An—why, it happened more than sixty years ago."

The psychologist showed surprise. "Would it be possible today to verify and settle such an old rumor?"

"That's the point," explained the bride earnestly: "a psychologist might do it. You understand how people's minds work; you could show that Grandfather's mind couldn't possibly have worked—"

The young husband interrupted again with some concern: "Which grandfather, Elora?"

"Grandfather Blackmar, of course, Julian; I'm a Blackmar now."

It may have been the bride's emotion, or her dark dramatic eyes, or small eloquent hands; but at any rate, on this rather vague mission, Mr. Poggioli eventually got off the train with the Blackmars at El Jobe-An.

At the way station a gloomy negro driver in an ancient motorcar awaited the couple. Presently this equipage set forth amid an endless level of lean pines and palmettos following a lane of reddish-brown water which represented a public road in this part of Florida during the wet season.

The black man who drove the car kept to the flooded roadbed by a sort of divination. He was oddly silent for a colored man; only once did he speak.

"Mas' Jule, one o' dem Mendezes was at de station jes' befo' yo train come in, an' he lights out dis dorection."

"Yes, that's all right, Goolow." And Julian turned and continued to Poggioli that the rainy season made hunting very good on the high lands, and that the Blackmar estate stood well above the floods.

"What elevation have you above the general level?" inquired Poggioli, who was also making conversation.

"Oh—eight or ten inches or more."

Presently the car came to the junction of another perfectly straight avenue of water amid the endless pines. As the negro turned into this private thoroughfare, he suddenly kicked on his brakes. The white passengers were annoyed at the rough stop. Blackmar rapped out:

"Goolow, what in the devil—"

The black man said in a scared voice: "Dey's a washout, Mas' Jule."

"Washout?" repeated the master incredulously.

He opened the door, stood on the running-board and peered forward.

The dark red water from the deluge moved deliberately along the drainage ditches toward the sea.

"Get in there and wade, Goolow, and see what you can find out."

The black man stepped out into water that was ankle-deep on the roadbed. He splashed toward the culvert—and suddenly, without warning, went under head and ears. He came up blowing and splashing.

"I knowed hit! I knowed hit! Dat low-down Jim R. Mendez floated huh off."

Young Blackmar made a silencing gesture. "You know nothing of the sort. Nobody need have floated it off. The culvert was wooden; it could have washed out or rotted out."

"You cain't tell me, Mas' Jule, what did Jim R. wait at de station fuh twell he see you-all git off'n de train, 'n'en tu'n his flivvah roun' an' come tearin' back dis dorection lak a speedboat—"

"I don't know what he did it for—he wouldn't want to chop a culvert from in front of our car when he knew Elora was in it!"

The negro blinked the water out of his eyes and slapped it out of his wool.

"Somebody boun' tinkah wid dat culve't, Mas' Jule; hit nevah did wash out befo'."

"You cut some logs and float down here; we've got to get this car across some way or other."

Goolow came dripping to the car, fished an ax from under the rear seat, then swam to the other side of the ditch and began chopping down some tall cabbage-palms. Julian Blackmar slowly discarded his own shoes and socks to help his servant. Poggioli briskly followed his host's example. The bride protested against a guest's taking part in the labor, but both men made ready, and presently stepped out into the water. When they had waded out of earshot of the car, Blackmar said in a lowered tone:

"Before Elora, I had to let on that I didn't believe it was Jim R. But if he drove right ahead of us, it *was* him—it couldn't be anybody else."

"What is Jim R. Mendez to your wife?" inquired the psychologist.

"Why, they're first cousins," explained Blackmar, frowning. "Elora was a Mendez before I married her."

Poggioli stood rather at sea. "Would Mendez try to head your car into a ditch of water with his own first cousin in it?"

BLACKMAR nodded gloomily. "More than that, I believe this was aimed directly at Elora."

Poggioli was astonished. "Why do you make such a statement as that?"

The host cleared his throat uneasily. "Well, you see, if Elora has a child, it will inherit the Mendez groves and grazing land. That was the way the old man Jiminez Mendez willed it. The Mendez boys are living on it now, but it will finally go to Elora's children, if she has any."

Poggioli was shocked. "You don't think Jim R. is trying to murder his cousin to prevent her from becoming a mother, do you?"

"Why, of course that's it. That culvert didn't just wash away. The land's too flat. There's hardly any current at all."

In the midst of this conversation old Goolow shouted a warning. The white men looked up, then waded quickly to avoid the crash of a palm top as it fell across the ditch. While they were lost in these green curtains, there sounded a puttering down the road, and a little later Goolow called in an undertone:

"Mas' Jule, yonder come 'at Jim R. now. As he go by, stop him an' look at he breeches."

Poggioli peered out of the leaves. "Why do you want to look at his trousers?"

"To see if dey wet," explained the black in a low tone, "to see if he been out in de water choppin' loose de culve't."

"He might have changed his trousers," suggested the psychologist.

"Huh," grunted the negro; "when Mistuh Jim R. change he breeches, he pulls 'em off, an' when he changes ag'in, he puts 'em on."

The scientist nodded at the single-breeched idea and made a note to observe the newcomer's trousers. The puttering increased, and presently a dilapidated car came plowing through the water, leaving a long "V" of waves behind it. The rusty machine stopped opposite the men, and its driver called out in a hearty nasal voice:

"Hey-oh, sir, you-all stuck somehow? What's the matter?"

Julian Blackmar, halfway across the bole, seemed about to return a scathing answer when Poggioli hastened to explain:

"The culvert's washed out."

"Huh, that's funny," ejaculated Jim R., looking up and down the waterway, "funny it washed out on the very day Jule an' Cousin Lory got back off their weddin'-trip. . . . It shore is quare."

"We thought it very strange, too," returned Blackmar pointedly. "Why should it float off just before we arrived?"

"Naw, I imagine you cain't un'erstan' that," agreed Jim R. sardonically.

It was evident the two men would be in a quarrel the next moment. Poggioli interposed to say they were chopping down palms now to bridge the stream and set the Blackmar car across.

At this Jim R. stepped out of his car into the water, saying:

"By grabs, I don't pass up nobody tryin' to git his car out of trouble. Besides, Jule is kin to me now—cousins by marriage, aint we, Jule!" And with this the yokel suddenly laughed, and a moment later, as suddenly stopped.

THE newcomer fished an ax out of his car and came wading to the palm, to cut off its head and allow its bole to float down to the marooned motor. Poggioli made way for him among the leaves. The fellow pulled off his wet shoes, after the manner of an expert woodsman, then stood poised on the bole in his sock feet and fell to work with dexterous strokes. As the fibrous body notched under his labor, Jim R. found time to glance around and wink seriously and significantly at Poggioli.

The scientist was somewhat puzzled at the gesture; whether it was a denial or an admission of guilt, he did not know. Within a few minutes the trunk parted; Jim R. stepped across the gap and joined Poggioli among the leaves. He winked again, satirically, pulled down the corners of his lips, and nodded across at Blackmar.

"I don't reckon Jule has no idee a-tall who chopped loose that culvert."

"You think it was chopped loose?" inquired Poggioli.

"I shore it was. You know it didn't float away by itse'f. They aint no current here, hardly."

"Who do you think did it?"

"That nigger Goolow, nachelly," retorted Jim R. sharply. "He driv over that culvert this mornin', an' he jest clim' out an' busted that culvert up behint him."

Poggioli appraised the fellow to see if this were a false trail he was laying.

"Why should Goolow do such a thing?"

"Well, two reasons," answered the rustic: "One is them other Blackmars aint going to want a Mendez to step in an' git a wife's share of ol' pirate John Blackmar's holdin's. Another is Jule wants to heir what his wife's got of the Mendez lands. . . . That's why he married her."

POGGIOLI could not tell by the rustic's wooden countenance whether or not he believed what he was saying.

"If Goolow chopped away the culvert, why didn't he drive the car in the ditch when he got back?"

"Because his nerve failed him. Take it the other way, if he didn't know it was gone, what made him stop? You cain't see the culvert through that red water; you cain't tell whether she's thar or not thar."

This reasoning Poggioli was unable to answer, and he wondered if by any possible means Goolow had destroyed the culvert, and at the behest of whom.

The two axmen finished their work, floated the palm-boles down the ditch and established them crosswise. Then they began the ticklish task of rolling the Blackmar car across the ditch. When the machine was finally on the other side, the master of the Blackmar estate began a cold thanking of Jim R. for his services, when the rustic interrupted to say that he would go along with them to their homecoming.

"You know,"—and he nodded his oily black head in open good-fellowship—"I thought some of Lory's fam'ly ort to be here to welcome you-all back."

There seemed no way to order the fellow off after he had been of such service with his ax, so the interloper swung on the running-board, and the car moved forward.

Once in the private thoroughfare the water grew shallower under their wheels, and presently the motor rolled onto a wet sandy road elevated a few inches above the surrounding water. This was the highland of the Blackmar estate. A mile or two farther on lay an ancient house set back behind a scraggly wire-and-board fence that somehow gave an impression of a barbed-wire entanglement before a fort. Behind the house itself arose the densest mass of vegetation Poggioli had ever seen.

The old automobile presently stopped in front of a gate; the cracker swung off the running-board, and with the helpfulness natural to a Florida rustic took one of his cousin's bags out of the car. Everyone got out. Jim R. maneuvered with the bag beside his cousin and started with her for the house. The girl could hardly get away from him without giving offense. Why Jim R. was doing this, Poggioli could not guess; whether it was affection for his cousin, impudence, or an overture to some deviltry, he did not know. By way of passing over his unspoken thoughts, he said:

"That's quite a jungle behind your house."

"Yes; my grandfather, Captain John Blackmar, was a college man, the same as I am. His hobby was botany. He collected all sorts of trees when he went to Cuba in his cattle schooner."

"Yeh," put in Jim R. dryly, "collected trees—and other things."

"His main interest was trees," repeated Julian coldly; then with a change of tone: "You'll love it, Elora; and you, Mr. Poggioli, as a scientific man."

IN the midst of their conversation Jim R. lurched with the suitcase and gave a sharp blow to the bride. The girl, whose nerves must have been at a tension, screamed and staggered away. A sudden horror flashed through Poggioli that Mendez had stabbed the woman, but the next moment he saw the fellow perform some grotesque leaps in the uncut grass.

Julian had rushed to punish the assailant of his wife, when Jim R. made a sudden catlike dive and pinned something in the thick grass. The next moment a dry whirring set up—and the group, horrified, saw Mendez straighten with his fingers gripping the neck of a rattlesnake. The reptile was corded around the cracker's arm as it strained to retract its head through his grip.

Mendez himself bent his arm swiftly toward his mouth; and to the horror of the watchers, bit the vertebræ of the creature just back of its triangular skull. The coils loosed, and Mendez tossed the twitching rattler into the grass, and spat.

Elora screamed; Poggioli blew out a breath of nausea and ejaculated:

"My God, man, how could you do that?"

The rustic turned sharply.

"Why, it was about to strike Cousin Lory. I had to do somep'n!"

Julian put an arm around his wife, who appeared half-fainting, and supported her to the house. Goolow picked up the bag which Jim R. had dropped, and followed his master. Poggioli remained with the cracker in the uncared-for grounds of the Blackmar estate. Mendez appeared at his wits' end.

"Well, I guess I cain't foller her in the house an' see what they got rigged up ag'in' her there."

"Rigged up against her—what do you mean?"

"What I say, of course. Didn't that Goolow chop away the culvert to drown her, and then didn't he tether this rattlesnake where Lory would shore tramp on it as she come past?"

"Tether it?"

"Yes, with a hoss-hair, aroun' its rattles."

"Do you mean you can tether a snake with a horsehair?"

"Shore. I've done it many a time when I didn't have no box."

Poggioli dismissed the technique of snake-catching.

"You really believe that negro is trying to murder Mrs. Blackmar?"

"Oh, he's doin' it fer somebody—maybe Jule hisse'f, to git rid of her and git her proputty."

Poggioli was disgusted. "How can you imagine him so depraved and bloodthirsty?"

"Imagine him!" cried Mendez disdainfully. "Why, he comes from that kind of folks. His granddaddy, ol' pirate John, was the thievin'est, murderin'est ol' devil that ever sailed the sea." He checked his own violence and asked: "Look here, you goin' to be aroun' here for a while, aint you?"

Poggioli said he was.

"All right—will you do me a favor?"

"If it isn't something against Mr. Blackmar. I'm his guest, you know."

"Oh, it won't be against him. It'll be a favor to him, too."

"In that case, what do you want?"

Mendez's eyes narrowed.

"Jes' tell Jule, I'm goin' to be aroun' here: and if anything happens to Cousin Lory, the same thing, only a thousan' times wuss, will happen to him. . . . Jes' tell him that from me."

Poggioli was shocked at the man's intensity. "Now, that's all right, Mr. Mendez; don't work yourself up over this. I can promise you nothing will happen to your cousin."

"Oh, you promise that?"

"Yes, I feel I can promise that."

"Do you mean," inquired Jim R., looking hard at Poggioli, "do you mean yore skin will answer for anything that happens to Cousin Lory?"

An uneasy feeling went over the psychologist. "I mean I am simply giving my best opinion as a psychologist and a student of human nature, that Julian Blackmar is in love with his wife, and will do everything in his power to defend her," he explained precisely.

The rustic turned with a shrug. "Huh, a feller that won't back up his opinion with his hide, aint very shore of what he says. . . . Well, you jes' carry Jule my word; that's all you've got to do with it."

Then without further adieu, he turned and started back to his own car on the public road a mile or two distant.

MR. HENRY POGGIOLI turned and walked slowly toward the ancient house of the Blackmars, rather disturbed at the belligerent chivalry of Jim R. Mendez.

He was glad he had postulated himself out of Jim's reach. As he approached the house, he was surprised to see the girl herself out on the piazza with a basket on her arm. He called to know if she would not better go back and lie down; but she called out that she had heard of her grandfather Blackmar's fruit garden all her life, and for Poggioli to go with her, and they would see it together.

With this the girl picked her way around the wing of the ramshackle two-story house, to the dense tangle of vegetation in the rear. As the two entered the heavy draperies of green, the girl took Poggioli's arm:

"You know, this scares me a little, to go in here."

"I imagine it is a left-over from tales you have heard about it as a child," suggested the psychologist, who was beginning to catch the drift of neighborhood gossip.

This observation seemed to comfort the girl.

"Maybe that is it." She started to ask a question, then thought better of it and kept silent.

IN the garden there was nothing to be frightened at. Its dense, struggling growth was decorated with exotic fruits; red banana plants upholding their scarlet candelabra; an Australian fig with its round globules spewing straight out of its bark; Kaffir oranges from the West African coast. Such dank crowded proliferation charmed the botanist in the guest. As Mrs. Blackmar began filling her basket, she asked in an intimate tone:

"Mr. Poggioli, do you know yet why we wanted you to come here?"

"I think I have an idea, Mrs. Blackmar. . . . It is undefined—"

"We wanted you to look at this estate and house and garden, especially this garden, and tell us what you really think about Julian's grandfather."

"What I think about him?"

"Yes. A lot of people claim to believe that he was a—a freebooter, a very terrible man; do you believe that was possible, if he were so cultivated and scholarly as to make a collection like this garden?"

It was an odd but very earnest interrogation. The psychologist put a question in return:

"Of what weight would my opinion be, Mrs. Blackmar?"

"Oh, you are a criminologist and a psychologist. You know how people's minds work. If you should say that a man of such scientific taste as Grandfather Blackmar could not be a sea rover, it would have very great weight."

"With the people here in the neighborhood?"

"No; that's envy. I mean with me and Julian."

Poggioli perceived the couple really wanted their own confidence buttressed.

"Well, if you must know, Mrs. Blackmar, I think your deductions are exactly right," he comforted. "It would be incompatible for a man to lead a lawless life and at the same time pursue the higher law of botany with such a painstaking collection as this."

Poggioli divined that this sentence was just cloudy enough to sound very profound and comforting to the bride, and sure enough it was. She said earnestly and gratefully:

"Oh, I'm so glad to hear you say that."

The psychologist paused a moment. Then, "What did your grandfather Blackmar really do?" he queried.

"He ran a cattle schooner from Tampa to Cuba; that's all."

"No other ports?"

"No, just Tampa, Key West and Havana. . . . Sometimes he met storms, Julian tells me, and would be gone for a long time, and that's how such evil gossip got started."

Poggioli nodded slowly, and glanced at the Australian fig, the West African orange and a Fiji palm-nut.

"No, I'm sure a man of Captain John Blackmar's scientific attainments couldn't have been engaged in an illicit calling," he repeated.

THIS completely reassured the girl; she began filling her basket again, making graceful reaches a-tiptoe for some Tahitian passion-apples. As Poggioli got them for her, she asked queerly:

"Do you believe in bans?"

"Bans—what do you mean?"

"Why, they say when Grandfather Blackmar died, he cursed any Mendez who ever comes into this garden."

"Why, that's absurd," scoffed the psychologist. "There is no such thing as a curse—not in that sense; you know that."

"Why, yes, of course, I know that."

"So the best thing to do about a curse is to forget all about it."

"I know that. . . . Still—now you'll think this is silly; but awhile ago when we were coming into this jungle, did you have a feeling that—that somebody was here in the dark telling you to stay out?"

"Why, no, of course I didn't!"

"Well—you wouldn't."

"Look here," protested Poggioli earnestly, "now that is nothing but a complex left over from your childhood. When you caught my arm, you were a little girl again, ten or twelve years old. But you are a grown woman now, married, returned from college, and you can't be frightened by old granny tales."

"That's right," agreed Elora gratefully; "that is good sound psychology, isn't it? It was sweet of you to come here with us; it really was."

She finished gathering her fruit and started into the house.

POGGIOLI took the basket and went with his hostess into the decaying manor. They found lunch waiting for them. At the table Julian introduced to Poggioli his Aunt Tabitha, his father's sister, whom he called Aunt Tab. Julian was interested in what Poggioli had thought of his grandfather's garden, and then went on to ask his guest if he did not think his grandfather could have bought these various foreign plants from some arboricultural dealer in Havana.

At this a twinge of amusement went through the psychologist. He saw that Julian was trying to devise some explanation for the garden that would have confined his seagoing grandfather to a strict cattle trade between Havana and Tampa. The ironic fact titilated the guest that within three generations, if the Blackmars prospered financially and socially, the family would be immensely proud of a pirate in their lineage, and would resent it bitterly if any genealogist should suggest that the buccaneer in their family was nothing more than a pacific collector of trees.

Miss Tabitha Blackmar phrased Julian's thought precisely by saying:

"The Mendezes always tried to prove Pappy was a rover, by his trees comin' from so many dif'runt places; but it didn't require trees or anything else to prove the Mendezes were cattle thieves. Ever'body knew that."

"Aunt Tab," interposed the host, "that has nothing to do with Grandfather Blackmar."

"It hasn't!" cried the old woman. "Sence when, I'd like to know? Old Carlos Mendez not only stole cattle; he shipped 'em by Daddy's boat, then claimed he driv aboard more than he had, an' killed Daddy for not payin' him for 'em!"

"Aunt Tab!" cried the groom in a shocked voice. "That's past!"

"Part of it's past and part aint!" snapped the old woman, glancing at Elora.

"Aunt Tab, Elora has just been through a very trying experience," reminded the nephew in controlled anger.

"Jule," flung back the aunt in exasperation, "what would Pappy think if he knowed his grandson would bring a Mendez into this house for its mistress.... A Mendez!"

"Aunt Tabitha!" cried the master in desperation.

The young woman arose with a colorless face.

"I'm not well, Julian.... I feel faint. If you and Mr. Poggioli will excuse me, I'll—go to my room."

The bridegroom arose with her.

"No, stay with our guest," she begged. "I'm all right."

Young Blackmar hesitated, then called Goolow to take a bowl of fruit up for his wife. And the two went up the stairs, the velvety brunette girl followed by the ancient ebony servant bearing a bowl of exotic fruits collected from the garden of a dead corsair.

When they were gone, young Blackmar turned on his relative:

"Aunt Tab, it wasn't necessary for you to mention Elora's grandfather. She is a Blackmar now."

"Well," snapped the old woman angrily, "they all said I wouldn't be able to stay on the place after she come, and I see I cain't. I'll go with the rest of our folks. I won't stay where I'm not wanted, even if it's a Mendez as doesn't want me."

THE young nephew sat silent. The old woman got up, clapped on a hat greenish with age, walked out the back door, followed a path through the jungle her father had planted, and was gone.

A feeling of loneliness and embarrassment penetrated the two men at the table.

"Go to your wife," suggested Poggioli. "I know you are disturbed about her. I think I'll take a walk out into the garden and look at the trees again."

"No, I'll let her rest; but if you don't mind, I will lie down too. . . . The train ride and everything—and I'm accustomed to a nap after lunch."

The psychologist nodded agreement, and then remembered something:

"I don't know whether to mention this or not. I talked to Mendez down yonder in the field."

"And what did he say?"

"Well—he told me to tell you if anything happened to his cousin, he would hold you responsible for it."

BLACKMAR stared. "Anything happen to her—what happen to her?" Poggioli hesitated.

"I don't know whether I ought to mention it or not. . . . He believes you married his cousin to inherit her property."

"Suppose I did, would that cause anything to happen to Elora?"

Poggioli cleared his throat.

"He believes, or pretends to believe, that you—er—plan to put her out of the way."

The bridegroom's face went bleak with anger.

"Don't you see what that means? He has simply credited me with motives like his own. He has tried twice to murder Elora before she has a child; now he suspects that I will murder her."

"But look here," put in Poggioli, "that's illogical. If Jim R. thinks her death would save the property to the Mendezes, it wouldn't make any difference who caused it, you or he. He would see that."

"No, he wouldn't see anything! He probably thinks the one who killed her will get the property! You don't realize the ignorance of these damn' Mendezes. He threw that rattlesnake in her path. He has been a snake-man all his life. Ever since he was a boy, I have—"

"Well, I know nothing of what he thinks; but I believe if anything serious should happen to Mrs. Blackmar, Mendez will make an attempt on your life."

"If anything serious happens to Elora, Jim R. can do what he pleases with my life: it won't be worth anything to me."

With this he went to his room for his own siesta. Poggioli was not accustomed to a noontide sleep, and walked out once more into the jungle. The place fascinated him. The very kinds of trees old Captain John Blackmar had collected bespoke rather the curiosity of an actual voyager than the choosings of a naturalist. The old seafarer's taste had turned to extraordinary trees. In the tangle Poggioli remarked an upas tree, the *Antiaris Toxicaria*, which the rover probably had picked up in Java. Another was a *Peul* which must have come from the African coast, and so on and on. In fact, the whole jungle rattled in the wind, a tacit corroboration of the scandals and crimes laid at old John Blackmar's door.

A breaking of the twigs behind him caused Poggioli to turn with a start of something like superstitious fear. He recalled Elora's saying she felt a sinister presence in the green gloom. Then he did make out a figure through the tangle, and ejaculated:

"Are you still here, Jim R.?"

The rustic said in his dogged voice:

"Yes, I'm here. . . . Are you still here, too?"

Poggioli disregarded the insolence and went around to the fellow.

"What are you doing?"

Jim R. set his heel on something in the moldy earth.

"Garter snake," he said briefly, "hittin' an' spittin'."

The scientist glanced down at the tiny red-banded thing squirming in the mold.

"Why did you come here again?" he inquired antagonistically.

"Why, I come back to ast you what you come here for?" returned Mendez with a hard look.

"I'm here as a guest; and now you?"

The cracker reached in a pocket and drew out a scrap of newspaper.

"Aint this you?" he asked suspiciously.

Poggioli looked at the clipping, and saw his own picture with a brief personal note saying: "CELEBRATED CRIMINOLOGIST VISITS FLORIDA."

"Why, yes, it is," he nodded, wondering at the point of this.

"I thought it was. I got it from the station-agent, who reads papers."

The scientist was perplexed.

"I don't see what my profession has to do with your appearance here. You don't require the services of a criminologist, do you?"

"Naw! I don't want no crime committed!" announced Jim R. hotly. "But by God, I want to know what you're workin' fer Jule Blackmar fer? What kind of a crime is he tryin' to commit, that he has to call in outside he'p!"

Poggioli was amazed. "Do you imagine I assist at a crime?"

Jim R. blinked his eyes. "Well, aint a criminologist a man that a criminal goes to when he wants he'p?"

"Why, of course not. A criminologist is a man who studies to—"

"But look here: a druggist is a man you go to fer drugs; and a dentist is a man you go to—"

The psychologist laughed briefly. "Yes. But a criminologist is a man who prevents crimes; he doesn't abet them. I'm—er—sorry the mistake came up."

"Well, it's all right—it's all right if you're what you say you are."

With this Mendez moved away through the dense growth with curious ease and disappeared in the green gloom.

Mr. Henry Poggioli stood for a long time reflecting on the ignorance and vengefulness of the crackers, and hoping that Jim R. Mendez believed his definition of the word *criminologist*. A hope flitted through Poggioli's mind that Mendez would look the word up in a dictionary and be certain about it, but then he realized that the fellow possessed no such book.

PRESENTLY it struck Poggioli that now was a good time for him to go back to the railroad and continue his journey to Key West. His own services to the Blackmars had really come to an end. All they had wanted was his opinion to establish their confidence in the honesty and uprightness of old Captain John Blackmar, pirate. Well, he had given that, such as it was, and his mission was ended. He looked at his watch, and wondered if Julian Blackmar were awake. He would like to have Goolow take him back to the station.

In the midst of these thoughts, he heard some one crashing his way toward him from the big house. He became alert with a feeling that something had happened to Elora Blackmar, and her animal-like cousin was rushing back to take vengeance on him.

Instead of Jim R., however, he saw the negro Goolow pushing aside the rank growth and looking everywhere for somebody or something.

Poggioli watched him a moment and then spoke: "Do you want me, Goolow?"

The black man's eyes were distended and showed startling whites.

"Yas suh—oh, Lawd, he sent me fuh you quick!"

"Me!" Poggioli moved toward the manor. "What does he want with me?"

"Set up wid Miss Lory!"

"Sit up with her—what for?"

The black man wet grayish lips. "She's daid. . . . Miss Lory's daid."

The white man's heart stopped beating. "You don't mean—she's *dead!*"

The black man nodded in silent horror, and hurried toward the house. Poggioli hastened his stride to a run, with the wildest conjectures as to the catastrophe.

IN an upper chamber of the manor Julian Blackmar stood over the motionless form of his bride, who lay on an ancient four-poster bed. When Poggioli entered, the bridegroom turned and asked in a gray voice:

"Have you seen Jim Mendez around here?"

The psychologist hurried over to the woman, and felt of her hands:

"Has she been shot?"

"Oh, you have seen him?" divined his host.

"Yes, a few minutes ago—half an hour. . . .What—killed her? . . . Is she dead?"

Blackmar made a desperate gesture.

"You see she's dead—poisoned. . . . Some kind of a snake."

Poggioli was seized with revulsion. He bent down and began examining the motionless figure; he felt for the heart; he put his ear to her chest and listened for her breathing.

"You don't mean—he came up into this room—with a serpent!"

Blackmar made a striking motion, and a spasm went across his face. He straightened and strode across to an old chest in the bridal chamber.

"But look here," argued Poggioli, "Mendez couldn't have got up here unperceived. You were asleep in the room below. Goolow, where were you?"

"'Sleep on de steps outside dat do'."

"There you are—asleep on his mistress's steps . . . How could Jim R. have got here unobserved?"

Blackmar drew two pistols out of the chest.

"Where did you see him?" he asked in a monotone.

"Wait! Wait!" begged the psychologist. "Let me examine everything. Don't start a gunfight on bare suspicion!"

"Where did you see him?" repeated Blackmar with a rising voice.

"In the jungle—he came to ask my business."

"What was he doing?"

"He was—" Poggioli caught his breath as the significance of this dawned on him. "He was—killing a snake, a garter snake."

Blackmar nodded: "Just back from her murder."

He started for the door with his pistols. Poggioli thought swiftly.

"Stop! Don't go now! I think your wife is still alive. . . . Her heart—have you camphor—ammonia—strychnine—"

Blackmar looked at him steadily a moment. "You're trying to stop me—set me to work."

"No, I swear, I thought I saw a muscle twitch. . . . For God's sake, man, won't you help me with your own wife?"

The scientist put a knee on the bed, leaned over, placed his palms on the girl's sides, and began artificial respiration.

Blackmar came across to his motionless bride.

"Here, I'll do that. . . . I've studied first aid." He broke off suddenly and said: "Listen, if you're doing this just to keep me from shooting Jim Mendez, I—I'll kill you, Poggioli!" Blackmar made a gesture to Goolow, and the ebony negro shuffled downstairs for the things Poggioli had ordered.

THE psychologist divined that his host did not want any other person to touch the body of his bride, even if she were dead. He stood thinking swiftly over the situation.

"If we only knew what poison it was!"

"Why, a snake—a snake!" cried Blackmar, swinging to and fro above the girl.

"But that's impossible! Mendez couldn't have got in here with a snake. . . . Goolow was on the steps; the windows are too high and narrow, and this is the second story."

Blackmar turned a tortured face to his guest.

"He came up through the chimney. . . . My grandfather, old Captain John, built a tunnel to it from the jungle. Jim R. knew about it. . . . All the Mendezes know."

AT this extraordinary information, Poggioli looked at the big fireplace in the end of the room. Near it, on a table, lay a paring knife and the dish of fruit Goolow had brought up for Mrs. Blackmar. The plan came at once to the scientist to defend himself from Blackmar's anger with the ancient fireplace. He went over to it and began to examine its blackened interior. Its ashes were untracked, its soot appeared untouched. He almost turned to point this out to the tortured man at the bed, but decided to save it until his host was calmer. He continued his investigation to fortify his position that Jim R. Mendez had never climbed through the tunnel, up the chimney into the room. The time might come at any moment when he would need such a demonstration out of a bitter necessity.

Poggioli stooped down and entered the fireplace, then stood up inside the chimney. On the right hand side was set a square of sheet-iron. He worked at this for a moment or two, and succeeded in shoving it to one side. It disclosed a well, a kind of false chimney set with rusting iron rungs. Poggioli stepped into it and began a hazardous descent among a maze of cobwebs. He struck a match in an attempt to determine whether the webs had been recently broken by the passage of a man's body. As he studied the maze of dusty gossamers, the light showed something like a shelf in the side of the false chimney disclosed by the falling out of one or two crumbling bricks; and back in this hole lay a package quite covered with dust. The match flickered out. Poggioli reached into the darkness, took the package and returned to the light that fell into the great fireplace above.

The thing he had found was an old book. In the light he opened it and saw it was a ship's log.

As he did so, he heard a sound from the room. He stepped out of the fireplace and saw Julian Blackmar alternately compressing and releasing the girl's diaphragm at far too swift a tempo.

Poggioli dashed out.

"Stop it! Quit that!" he shouted.

"But she opened her eyes once!" quavered the husband in an agony of excitement.

"Take it slower—slower! Here—let me do it—get away!"

He pushed his host aside, and began a correct timing of the respirations. At that moment Goolow appeared in the door with a great brass basin on his head, and his arms stuck full of bottles.

"Now, what'll we give her?" cried Blackmar, hurrying to the negro.

"What poison was it? What could she have taken?" cried Poggioli.

"Why, a snake—that garter snake!"

"No, damn it, no! The chimney has never been entered. . . . Something else. But what, in heaven's name—" He stared about the room as if he would see the poison. His glance fell on the plate of fruit once more. A sudden possibility flashed over Poggioli.

"Listen!" he cried. "Was your wife familiar with the fruit out of that jungle?"

"No, of course not; this is the first time she was ever here!"

"Did she—could she possibly have eaten the seed of any of that fruit?"

BLACKMAR looked at his guest with a sharp surmise in his face.

"That was her habit—to bite the seeds of fruit. . . . She said they tasted like almonds. Could that have anything to do with it?"

Poggioli motioned to Goolow.

"Mustard—eggs—milk—quick!"

The three men began working with the recovering girl.

"But Poggioli—why?"

"It's the Kaffir oranges. Their seeds are poisonous, but their flesh is good. It never occurred to me she didn't know that."

The men got the emetics down the girl's throat. The ebony Goolow bent over the shining copper basin of hot water, bathing the bride's small feet. Gradually their ivory turned pink with a renewed stirring of her blood. She passed through the usual phases of extreme nausea and hemorrhage. After a long while the sleep of recuperation fell upon her.

Blackmar still sat watching her closely; Goolow had left the room; and the criminologist seized the opportunity to pick up the logbook from the table where he had placed it, and withdrawing to a window, leafed it through. The first entries that caught his eyes were the records of the purchase of a Malay palm from a Señor Moa, a horticulturist in Havana.

Such a proof at such a time, when Elora Blackmar, who had wanted it so, was near death, stung Poggioli with its ironic barb. The pathos of the thing set him so to trembling he could hardly turn through the book. There was mention of the purchase of other rare trees. The log made it clear that old Captain John bought the strange crowded jungle of trees that screened the end of the tunnel.

But there was much more in the log: entries of sails sighted; of ships captured; booty taken; men and women dispatched; and their names and addresses. Old Captain John Blackmar had used a scientific precision in everything he did. With this yellowed log Poggioli could prove that the first of the Blackmars had purchased his trees in peace; but the Mendezes, also, could have proved their contention that their ancient enemy had been a pirate.

Poggioli glanced again across the room toward the bedside. . . . Elora seemed awakening, and her husband entirely preoccupied with her. So the criminologist again leafed rapidly through the log, selected all the exonerating passages he could find, quietly tore them out, then took a match and set fire to the rest of the volume. Then he stepped over to the bedside.

Elora smiled at him weakly. The bridegroom tried to say something, but his voice was so emotion-torn that Poggioli was afraid he would excite the invalid. The scientist began in the cheerful tones one uses toward the sick:

"I found something that will please you very much: The log of the schooner your grandfather Blackmar used to run. I have proof positive that Captain John Blackmar bought every one of his trees from a Señor Moa, in Havana. I found it in the chimney."

THE girl turned her head wonderingly toward the old fireplace.

"He did—*buy* them?"

"Every single one. You can prove it to anybody." Poggioli walked across to the table where he had laid the leaves out of the log.

Pleasure shone like a pale sunbeam in the young wife's pallid face.

"Oh, that's—such a relief." She drew the short breath of the very weak.

"What—what is that—still burning—in the fireplace?"

"Oh, that's where I started a fire. . . . I thought at the time we were going to heat the water up here."

The Shadow

WITH wind and rain whipping at his umbrella, the bank clerk Samuels opened the door of his apartment house and handed Mr. Poggioli inside. He followed after him, opened the inner door, permitting its gush of light to fill the dark street, then closed it again, leaving himself and the psychiatrist still standing in the dark entry.

"Now we ought to see him in a moment," he whispered.

The two men shook the water from their clothes, moved their feet with the slight motions of men settling for a watch.

"You opened this inside door to make a show of going in?" queried Poggioli in a low tone.

"Well, I waited the other night—several minutes . . . Finally I did that and he came."

"I see."

"He may have just happened to get here then."

"Mm-hm," murmured the psychiatrist.

The two men stood listening to the rain thrum the windows and curse the pavement. Finally the clerk began in an undertone of nervous complaint:

"Look here, isn"t there some law against this sort of thing? Can anybody shadow anybody else for no reason at all?"

The psychologist reflected.

"I'm no lawyer. Might bring an action of nuisance, possibly . . . Never heard of such a thing . . . You don't know why he is doing this—can't think of anything you've done?"

"Oh, no."

The psychologist gave a whispered laugh.

"The reason I asked—almost any man can think up something he's done that deserves—oh, almost anything."

The younger man seemed not amused. He remained quiet a moment, then said: "You—you would be in a better position to give me advice if—if you knew what possibly might have caused it?"

"I—imagine so. Of course, I can't tell until I hear what it is. The thing you have in mind may have no connection with this beagle that's trailing—"

The bank clerk interrupted him nervously:

"It—it's a sanitarium."

Mr. Poggioli shifted his gaze from the street to his host.

"A what?"

"Sanitarium."

The psychologist stood for upward of a minute fitting this unexpected bit of information into the shadowy hypotheses he had in mind.

"Is it a—a New York sanitarium?"

"Yes."

"Park Avenue?"

"Fifth."

"Same thing." Poggioli frowned. Finally he broke out, puzzled: "Look here—you're not keeping somebody in a private sanitarium?"

Mr. Samuels was shocked.

"Oh, my Lord, no. There was a—a friend of mine in the sanitarium. . . . We—went out for a taxi-ride to break the monotony."

"This friend—was a woman, of course, Mr. Samuels?"

"If it'd been a man, I'd have sat in his room and talked."

"Certainly. . . . And you've known this lady for a long time."

"How did you come by that?"

"A man doesn't go into a hospital to make new acquaintances, but to see very old ones."

"That's true . . . I've known her ever since we were children."

"I see—children. . . . Then—then she comes from Pennsylvania, the same as you?"

The bank clerk was astonished.

"You guessed that by my accent?"

"Certainly."

"I didn't know I had one."

"Well, nobody does. . . . They think other people have them."

The bank clerk gave a little laugh.

"You must have made a study of it?"

"I have. It's very convenient sometimes to know where a man comes from without asking him. Now and then it is still more convenient to know where he comes from after you've asked him."

The younger man began laughing again, then broke off in the middle of his mirth. After a moment he continued soberly:

"Yes, both of us came from Everbrook, Pennsylvania. I came a year or two before she did."

"H'm—then let me see—what sort of family did this young lady come from—wealthy, middle-class, laborers—"

"Middle-class. . . . Her father was a doctor."

Mr. Poggioli nodded thoughtfully.

"Then in that instance she must be married and wealthy. I should surmise that she married a wealthy man and came to New York to live."

Came a moment's pause; then the bank clerk asked in an odd voice:

"Why do you jump to that conclusion?"

"Money had to come in somehow, Mr. Samuels,' argued the psychologist. "A Fifth Avenue sanitarium is a very expensive thing. It wasn't likely the girl made the money herself, or she wouldn't have been in a sanitarium in the first place. The fact that she went there at all suggests she was married—unhappily married; and a Fifth Avenue sanitarium certifies to a husband of wealth."

The clerk was astonished.

"Well, I declare—that is simple, isn't it? One thing follows the other just as natural as two old shoes—if you happen to think of it."

The psychologist smiled at the naïve compliment.

"Now, let me see: the last thing *you* were saying was, you took this lady, this Mrs.—"

"Hessland—Margaret Hessland."

"—out for a taxi-ride. Then you told me before that the man who is shadowing you—if he had any reason for doing such a thing at all—was doing it because of the sanitarium. That, I'll confess, I don't understand. Why a sanitarium should shadow you—"

Samuels drew a breath.

"Well, it's simple enough when I explain it. We drove out together—but we didn't drive back together."

"Did you send her back by herself?"

"No. . . . I—I drove back without her."

"Why didn't you bring her back with you?"

"I couldn't." Samuels moistened his lips. "She had—disappeared."

"What! She didn't step out of the cab and leave you?"

"No; that wouldn't be disappearing. She disappeared—vanished! It was this way: I found I needed some matches, and stopped the chauffeur and went into a cigar store. I don't suppose I was away three minutes. When I came back outside, cab, girl, and chauffeur were gone."

"And what did you do?"

"I telephoned the sanitarium."

"And what did the authorities there say?"

"Told me to come back at once for an interview."

"You went back?"

"Certainly, and explained what had happened."

"But since you think this—this man who is trailing you is working for the sanitarium, evidently the superintendent didn't believe you?"

"I—suppose not," agreed Samuels gloomily.

"What do you suppose the superintendent does believe?"

"I have no idea at all."

"He couldn't be—well, looking for his patient, could he?"

Samuels lifted a nervous hand.

"I—I don't know. . . . I suppose maybe he is."

"But you have no idea what became of Mrs. Hessland?"

"Not the slightest."

The two men stood quiet, peering out into the dark street.

"Did Mrs. Hessland ask you to come to take her for a drive, or did you suggest it?"

Samuels considered.

"Now that you mention it, I believe she did. . . . Yes, I think she did."

"And who wanted the matches—she or you?"

"Why-y—she did."

"Were you two riding in a new type of cab?"

"Yes."

"Well, look here: when she asked you to get out and get her some matches, didn't you *know* she was going to drive off and leave you?"

The bank clerk turned.

"No. Why should I?"

"Because women enjoy little gadgets like cigarette lighters; she would never have dreamed of sending you after matches unless—"

The bank clerk lifted a hand.

"But, Mr. Poggioli, we are not all of us analytical psychologists; and besides that, it's a lot clearer what she was up to, on looking back at it, than looking forward at it."

Poggioli tapped the floor with his foot impatiently.

"But look here, man, that's the point: you wouldn't have needed to think. You would have handed her the lighter automatically; then if she had asked for matches—if she had asked after that for you to stop the car and get out and buy matches, you couldn't have helped knowing—"

"But I didn't."

"Yes, I see you didn't," agreed the psychologist in a flattened tone. "Look here, there is no earthly use in your trying to confuse me as to the motives behind your actions. In the first place, you couldn't if you wanted to. In the second place, you came to me as your psychiatrist. You are paying me money to get rid of your nervousness and depression. So tell me why you deliberately stepped out of that taxicab, walked into the cigar store and allowed Mrs. Hessland to drive away?"

Samuels began a stammering, then drew a sharp breath:

"Look, look yonder!" he whispered. "There he is!"

Both men fell silent and watched a dim figure on the opposite side of the street. At times the curtain of the rain almost obscured him.

"Now what will he do?" whispered Poggioli, whose heat at the bank clerk was purely professional and vanished the moment another notion entered his head.

"Nothing, just stand at the corner and watch this house."

"Trying to find out where you have—er—concealed Mrs.—er—do you suppose?"

"Damn it, I suppose that's his idea," jerked out the bank clerk.

"But look here, if he is looking for Mrs. Hessland, why doesn't he follow you off somewhere—why does he watch this apartment?"

"Oh, hell! I don't know! I suppose he thinks I've got her in my rooms!"

"You haven't, have you?"

"No! No! Of course not! How long would a bank clerk hold his job with a— Aw, the man's a fool!"

"He must be. . . . Hello, this fellow doesn't seem to be stopping on the other side of the street!"

"He isn't?" The younger man peered out, then drew back a step, stood staring, but finally drew a breath of relief. "Oh, that's all right. He's not the man who's been following me. It was a much bigger man than he is—as big as you are."

Poggioli watched the figure crossing the street toward them, then went back to the point they were discussing:

"You were telling me, I believe, that you stepped out of the taxi to allow Mrs. Hessland to drive away—"

"My God, no, I wasn't telling you anything like that!" ejaculated the bank clerk.

"Not in so many words, perhaps. . . . But why should I probe into that? It has nothing to do with your nervousness, has it?"

"Absolutely nothing," assured the younger man.

The third man had now crossed the street and was climbing the stoop of the apartment house. He stepped into the entrance, blinked, stood a moment letting the water run from his overcoat, and said:

"Will you tell me—is this Number 215? I can't make it out in the dark."

"Yes, it is."

"Does Mr. Oliver Samuels live here?"

The bank clerk looked at the newcomer.

"I'm Oliver Samuels."

"Mr. Samuels, I have a paper here to serve on you. It makes you co-respondent in the case. . . . Lemme see—" The fellow held his paper up toward the dim top light of the entry. " '*Hessland versus Hessland.*' . . . I'll read it to you." And he began unfolding his summons.

The bank clerk stood with a hand on the inner door as if holding himself upright.

"Hessland," he repeated.

"I think it's Hessland. . . . Yes, it's Hessland."

"Why, I don't know where Mrs. Hessland is . . . I haven't the faintest notion."

"Well, you know, sir, I haven't got nothing to do with that. I'm the process-server."

"But listen," pleaded the bank clerk, "I don't know—I really don't. And if I get made co-respondent—what is it, a divorce suit?"

"Why, I suppose so, sir, by you being made a co-respondent."

"I'll lose my job. . . . I'm sure to lose my job in the bank. Listen—couldn't you fail to find me—would that help?"

"But I have found you, sir."

"Suppose you've found fifty, or a—a hundred dollars instead. . . . You understand how this is, Mr. Poggioli—I simply don't know *anything* about the woman, and why should I lose my position for something that will do nobody any good?"

The smallish man smacked his lips.

"Why-y-y . . . no, sir, I fancy not. . . . I know some of the boys who—who have gone out and found—er—money instead o' men; but in the long run, sir, it really don't pay—especially in comp'ny like we are, sir."

The fellow made a notation, gave Samuels a copy of the paper, and turned about once more into the rain.

The bank clerk stood holding the paper, staring into the darkness where the process-server had disappeared. The psychologist studied his companion intently.

"You really didn't expect that fellow, did you?" he asked in a puzzled tone.

Samuels got a breath.

"Why—why, Mr. Poggioli, if—if the roof had fallen in on me—"

The psychiatrist nodded.

"Yes—I see. You really are amazed and shocked."

"I certainly am."

Poggioli pulled slowly at his chin.

"That creates rather a riddle, Samuels: Your actions in the cab with Mrs. Hessland assert one thing, but your shock at being mentioned in divorce proceedings testifies with equal truth to its opposite." The scientist made a little gesture. "Now somehow both those things are true, but I am frank to admit at first glance I don't see it."

Samuels looked at his companion, evidently without seeing or hearing him. He stirred himself out of his consternation, batted his eyes and looked around.

"Well,' he said uncertainly, "I—I don't suppose there is any use watching any longer." He peered into the darkness again. "Suppose we go up to my rooms?"

The psychiatrist gave a nod of acquiescence, and they went through an inner hallway to an automatic elevator. In the little cage Samuels asked suddenly:

"What was it you said to me just then?"

"When?"

"A few moments ago—you were asking—something?"

"Oh, yes, I was puzzled. . . . I'm not so much now."

"Why, what have you found out?"

"I've found out why you invented that story about Mrs. Hessland wanting matches and how she drove off while you were gone to get them."

Samuels looked intently at his companion.

"The story is perfectly true! Why do you *think* I invented it?"

"You and Mrs. Hessland invented it together—to tell at the hospital when you returned to explain her disappearance."

"But she did drive away!"

"I know it; but you both had planned for her to do it. You knew she would go on the moment you went into the cigar stand—that is if you actually went into a cigar stand. I imagine you just stepped out of the cab and let her ride on."

Samuels broke out in an annoyed voice:

"Why do you say that? You know I wouldn't deliberately desert an invalid from a sanitarium on the street!"

Poggioli shrugged patiently.

"You did it because you didn't want to be seen entering the new apartment with her for the first time."

"What apartment?"

"The one you had furnished for her, of course."

Samuels frowned, and moistened his lips.

"Why shouldn't I enter it with her the first time—if there was any such apartment?"

"Oh, that was bank-clerkly caution," hazarded the psychologist dryly. "Anybody is allowed to have an establishment in New York except a bank clerk. You thought after Mrs. Hessland had settled, and a few other friends had called, you might drop in—casually—and avoid the appearance of evil."

The elevator clicked to a halt, and Samuels stood looking at the scientist with a dropped face.

"Well, ye-es, we had planned something like that."

The scientist nodded.

"Those were your plans; but—something went wrong. . . . She never appeared at the apartment you furnished."

"What makes you say that?" asked the bank clerk, almost in terror.

"Why, your shock at being mentioned with her in the divorce papers. That tells me with equal certitude that you don't know where she is now, and you've never been with her at all."

The bank clerk caught the psychologist's arm.

"Mr. Poggioli, if you know that, for God's sake tell me where she went—and what made her go! You don't know the uncertainty, the suspense—waiting day after day, running blind ads in the papers—"

The psychologist opened the elevator door, and the two men moved automatically into the upper hallway.

"Where she went I can't tell you, Mr. Samuels. When she found herself free, she may have decided to make a new start, alone."

"But she loved me! She had been ill-treated, and I loved her!"

"If she really loved you, that would be a reason for a certain type of woman not to live with you illicitly, Mr. Samuels."

"But where is she now? Has she got herself a job somewhere? How can I find her again?"

The psychologist held up his hand and shook it to signify that he could not answer.

"But you've told everything else—why can't you tell that?"

Samuels led the way to his apartment, and unlocked the door.

"Look here," said Poggioli, "I believe there is a little gap in the logic of this disappearance. If she suggested it, why—why should she be the one to disappear?"

Samuels looked at him blankly.

"She suggested it?"

"Yes—didn't she?"

"Why, no. I did, of course."

Poggioli smiled slightly, and shook his head.

"You think that, Samuels, because men always believe they originate such ideas. But you were concerned about her health, about her physical well-being; you were wrought up because she was miserable. . . . You still are. . . . That feeling would never have suggested an elopement. . . . I think it must have come about through her."

The bank clerk was bewildered.

"Why, I know I'm the one who sug—"

"How did you communicate with her?"

"Through notes."

"Well, you probably saved those notes. Working in a bank would cause you to—"

"I did; certainly I would save Margaret's letters."

"Could you find out just who did originate the idea of an elopement?"

"Sit down," invited the host. He went to a closet and returned with a filing-case of letters, drew a chair to a reading-lamp and began going through them with the carefulness of a teller investigating an account. Presently he turned rather blankly to Poggioli.

"This seems to be the first letter mentioning—such a thing."

"So she did write it, after all?"

"Apparently."

"May I see it?"

Samuels hesitated, but finally folded the paper so Poggioli could see only one sentence. It read:

> ... continue like this when we could be together. I don't know what New York may have done to your ideas about things, Oliver, but I feel as if Everbrook were a thousand miles away—

Here the lower fold cut off the sentence.

Poggioli sat frowning blankly at the writing.

"That's extraordinary," he said slowly.

"Why?" enquired the bank clerk.

"A woman—a girl suggesting an elopement, and breaking off to say she doesn't know what New York has done to your ideas about things. . . . You didn't give me a copy of your letter to her, did you, Samuels, by mistake?"

"Oh, no, certainly not. . . . Why do you say that?"

"Because to consider how the idea came into one's head, to break off a suggestion to consider that—a man might think of that, Samuels, but a woman would not."

"Yes, but she did."

"H'm! So it appears. . . . And she disappeared afterward—in the midst of carrying out her plans?"

The bank clerk assented dully.

Poggioli pulled at his chin and nodded slowly as he stared at and through the paper. Finally he turned to his host.

"Let me see two or three more of her letters, noncommittal ones, near the beginning of the correspondence."

Samuels selected a half-dozen and handed them across. Poggioli made a place on the table beside him and spread out the letters. He let his glance brush over them, then shook his head.

"You know, Samuels, it's a difficult task to counterfeit another person's signature; it's still harder to reproduce her general handwriting, and that is the mere mechanical side of it. The mental and spiritual side, for a man to duplicate the thoughts a woman would think and write—that, I am sure, is an impossibility."

The bank clerk strode over to the table and looked at the exhibits.

"Do you mean to say her letter was—" He checked himself to ejaculate: "Why, it was forged, wasn't it?"

"Exactly! I knew some man had dictated this note, when I read it."

"But who forged it?"

"There is only one person in the world who could have any interest in the matter."

"Who's that?"

"Hessland, of course."

Samuels looked at his companion with horror in his eyes.

"You mean her own husband—you think he would deliberately inject the idea of an elopement into—"

"Certainly. That would give him easy grounds for divorce—and avoid the possibility of alimony."

"But how did he get into the correspondence?"

"Why, through the nurses at the hospital. They doubtless read all the notes that passed between you and Mrs. Hessland. . . . He paid them, you know."

"Then—then what has happened to her? Did he follow her to the apartment—and take some sort of revenge?"

"That I can't say. . . . Let me see. . . . What do you know about Hessland? You say he posed as a man of wealth?"

"Yes, Margaret married him under the impression that he was very wealthy."

Poggioli nodded and quirked his lips.

"That doesn't get us very far. There are so many men who pose as wealthy, you couldn't possibly deduce Hessland's type from that. . . . What about the woman herself? Would she incite revenge if she betrayed a husband?"

"I don't know."

"Was she young?"

"Twenty-three—her birthday was the fourteenth of May."

"Pretty?"

The bank clerk drew a breath.

"The most beautiful girl I have ever known."

"Happen to have a photograph of her?"

"Yes, I'll show it to you."

The clerk went back to his closet and brought out a "cabinet" portrait. Poggioli took it, looked at the fluffy lace dress and flowers in the figure's hands. He glanced at the back of the picture.

"This was made by a photographer in Everbrook; it must have been done some time ago?"

"Yes, when she finished high school. . . . It was taken for our Annual."

"She probably doesn't look like this now. Have you anything later?"

"No, I haven't." Samuels took the high school portrait. As he replaced it in its folder, he remembered something. "Yes, I have a recent picture of her, too; but it isn't much good." He handed Poggioli a postcard picture of a very pretty woman.

The psychologist took the cheap photograph, glanced at it; then something seemed to catch his attention, for he gave it a closer look and asked:

"Where did you get this one?"

"Why, she handed it to me when she came out of the sanitarium and got into the taxicab with me. She said she had got a picture made for me, too—" The bank clerk came to a full stop, and ejaculated: "Why, of course—she was fixing to leave me right then—it was her way of telling me goodbye."

As the psychologist continued to study the picture, he shook his head slowly.

"No—no—that's not probable. When she handed you this picture, Mr. Samuels, she must have been in a light mood; she did it casually. Really at the time she must have meant to live with you, as you had planned."

"Why do you say that?"

"Because this picture is plainly no prettier than Mrs. Hessland is herself; it has not even been retouched."

"Well, what's that got to do with it? Why couldn't she have said goodbye with—"

"Because no woman would have given you a farewell picture that was not as pretty as she could have it made. She would want to be remembered at her best, naturally. No; when Mrs. Hessland got into the taxicab with you, she had not the slightest idea of deserting you, Mr. Samuels; this picture is proof positive of that."

The smallish man was puzzled, and annoyed at this hopeful logic which was obviously false.

"But look here, she did leave me, Mr. Poggioli; there's no use your sitting there saying she didn't mean to leave me, when she did!"

Poggioli waved a patient forefinger at his client.

"I didn't say she didn't leave you; I merely said she didn't mean to leave you when she handed you this postcard. . . . What happened in the taxi?"

"Why, nothing!"

"You didn't—make her angry?"

"Why, of course not. I—I drew shut the—No, I didn't make her angry at all, not in the least."

The psychologist frowned.

"H'm. If she left you and did not intend to leave you, then somebody—some third person must have—"

Samuels leaned across the table.

"You are not suggesting that somebody did something to Margaret? How could they, driving through the street in a public taxi, to the apartment I had furnished?"

The psychiatrist waved down this lead to ask carefully:

"She couldn't have got this picture made just for you; did she say what she did with the others?"

"Why, as a matter of fact, she didn't have the pictures made at all, Mr. Poggioli; the sanitarium did that. When they were turned in, she simply kept one out for me."

"The sanitarium? You mean the authorities there in the sanitarium?"

"Yes, of course that was what she meant."

"And did she happen to tell you what the authorities wanted with a picture like this?"

The bank clerk considered.

"Yes," he recalled, "she said she was giving me this to show me how she looked in the sanitarium records."

"Their records?"

"Yes; she said the sanitarium kept a photograph of each patient in their records."

"But she wasn't just entering the sanitarium, was she?"

"Oh, no; she had been there about a year."

"And after a year's residence the authorities suddenly decided they must have a postcard photograph of Mrs. Hessland for their records?"

Samuels looked at his guest.

"That is a queer thing, isn't it?"

"No, it isn't queer at all; it is simply a bald misstatement to throw Mrs. Hessland off the track. . . . They had some reason—"

The bank clerk suddenly sat up. "Look here, you don't suppose they *knew* she was going to run away . . . and with me . . . and they wanted her photograph so the police could trace her!" He broke off, wetting his lips.

"The idea of taking a photograph to trace her when they had her in their hands!" Poggioli pointed out.

"Yes, that is so," agreed the smaller man, breathing a little more easily but still apprehensive.

The scientist sat tapping his lips and studying the photograph. Then he suddenly opened his eyes and ejaculated abruptly:

"Why, my God, making all this mystery out of this, when here the thing is before us!"

"What?"

"Why, this: if the sanitarium didn't want the photograph for their records, and Mrs. Hessland didn't order it, then there is only one thing left for it to be used for!"

"What's that?" asked Samuels blankly.

"Why, a passport, of course! It's passport size, passport finish—"

"Passport!" echoed Mr. Samuels, becoming alarmed on a new tack.

"Certainly. Then the husband must have really had it made. He got a passport for her—Mrs. Hessland has gone abroad."

Samuels' hands fell limply on the table.

"Then she did run away from me after all!"

"No, no, she didn't run away from you—not after giving you that picture for a keepsake."

"But her husband has taken her back—he's gone abroad with her!"

"Good Lord, man, not after he had arranged for you two to elope . . . No man in his position would be so wishy-washy."

"How do you know?"

"Because it takes persistence and nerve and a lack of sentiment to keep up an appearance of wealth on nothing a year. No, Hessland is unprincipled. He had arranged for you to elope with his wife and save himself alimony; then—then something or other popped into his head that seemed even better than that—something or other—" Poggioli beat a nervous tattoo on the desk with his fingers. "Whatever it was, probably—yes, by God, it would be that—it would bring him in money!"

"It was what? What would bring him in money?"

"Why, when he read your letter and found she would go to the apartment alone, he hurried her passport through, and—sold her!"

"What!"

"Certainly, kidnapped her, shanghaied her, sold her! When did you say she disappeared?"

"Day before yesterday!"

"Have you got the papers for that day?"

"Certainly—but Mr. Poggioli, where in the world could he sell—"

"Bring me the sailing lists. . . . What boats sailed at midnight day before yesterday?"

Samuels produced the papers—opened them shakily at the shipping news.

Poggioli skimmed down the list.

"*Megantic . . . Cape Verde . . . Queen of India . . . Uruguay . . . Montevideo* . . . I imagine, I am almost sure, she will be on a South American steamer."

"What makes you say that?"

"Because Europe has plenty of women of its own. . . . By the way, we might save radioing to all of these steamers . . . Where does Hessland live in New York?"

"Park Avenue near Eightieth."

"What's the nearest telegraph to Park and Eightieth?" He picked up the Manhattan telephone-lists, answered his own question, and dialed a number. He sat listening to the buzz for ten or fifteen seconds, then began:

"Western Union, this is William Hessland speaking. . . . I am expecting a wireless. . . . Oh, you've sent it up to me already. . . . Was it from the *Montevideo*? . . . The *Uruguay*? . . . Very well—take this message, will you:

> Captain *Uruguay*, a young woman is aboard your ship in the charge of man or woman who purports to be her medical attendant. She was brought aboard under color of being very ill or insane. Her passport is forged. She is a victim of abduction. Arrest attendant, liberate prisoner. Will have police wire you confirmation of this order.

Sign the name, '*Henry Poggioli.*' Yes, that's correct, operator: the Captain of the *Uruguay*, whoever he is, will know Henry Poggioli."

Samuels leaned across the table with eyes starting from his head.

"My God—sold her—shipped her like an animal! Haven't you made some horrible mistake?"

Poggioli turned and snapped out:

"How could I have made a mistake? If she gave you that photograph, she didn't know she was going away; since it was for a passport, someone else got it for her; if they forged her passport, they kidnapped her; if her husband had her kidnapped, he had her sold. There is no other solution."

Samuels sat staring wordlessly.

Poggioli leaned back, regarding the clerk with a thoughtful half-frown.

"And look here," he proceeded presently, "this couldn't have been Hessland's first offense. The whole thing worked too smoothly. I'll venture he's got a record of divorces from missing wives." He leaned forward on some impulse and picked up the receiver again.

Samuels watched him a moment apathetically; then he roused himself to ask:

"Who are you telephoning now?"

"The police. I'm going to have his record sent over."

He began dialing again; then Samuels stood up with a white face.

"You—you're not asking a policeman to—to come here?"

Poggioli lifted his hand and continued his dialing.

"Sit down, sit down. This may be the final solution of your nervousness, Mr. Samuels."

The bank clerk drew a quick breath.

"My nervousness! What do you mean?"

"You asked me to come here and examine you because you were nervous, didn't you?"

"Why—y-yes—certainly."

"And I have discovered why you are nervous. You spent rather too much money on Mrs. Hessland's apartment—money that didn't really belong to you. . . . That's true, isn't it?"

Samuels wet his lips, swallowed, stared at Poggioli.

"Do—do you suppose the—the bank knows about that? Do you suppose *they* sent out that man to—to follow me around—to shadow me?"

Poggioli sat with receiver to ear.

"The bank employs me to look after the irregularities in its clerical force, Mr. Samuels. . . . I am the man who has been following you around."

THE NEWSPAPER

SENOR XENOPHON QUINTERO SANCHEZ had vanished into thin air. Mr. Henry Poggioli—sometime research man in criminal psychology, but now engaged in the less highbrow task of trying to catch a dope smuggler—and Mr. Slidenberry, inspector of customs, climbed into their taxi on the Miami waterfront rather at odds where to turn next.

These two gentlemen had been cleverly, almost insultingly, hoodwinked by the Venezuelan, Sanchez. In fact, Poggioli himself had been cozened into removing the illegal drugs from the United Fruit Steamer, *Stanhope*, for the profit, criminal use and no doubt ironic amusement of this fellow, Sanchez.

So, highly wrought up, they climbed into their taxicab in the sunshot street of Miami, and Slidenberry rapped out to the chauffeur: "State Fair Grounds—West Miami! Get us there quick!"

Mr. Poggioli, the psychologist, held up a prohibitive and annoyingly superior hand.

"No, no, Sanchez could hardly have gone to the Fair Grounds—"

The chauffeur, a largish youth with a smallish head, hesitated in a twitter of suspense between these contradictory orders. It was dawning on him that his fares were after a criminal, and he hankered to be allowed to take part in their exciting and romantic enterprise; but he did not quite dare to ask their permission.

Slidenberry looked at his companion.

"Why are you so cocksure he hasn't gone to the Fair Grounds? The concessionaires out there will bootleg anything from dope to Gatling guns!"

Poggioli replied absently—

"Simply because the people in Belize, Central America, know nothing about the Florida State Fair."

The inspector wrinkled his forehead.

"What has Central America got to do with Sanchez and his dope?"

"Simply this: Sanchez is a Latin and sailed from Belize. It is part of Latin psychology to follow one logical, completely worked out plan from beginning to end. Since in Belize he couldn't have known of the State Fair, he is not there now."

Slidenberry gave a skeptical smile.

"But if he had been an Anglo-Saxon he would have been at the State Fair?"

"Certainly. Anglo-Saxons are opportunists; Latins are logicians."

The taxicab driver caught his breath at such extraordinary deductions. Slidenberry, however, was impatient at such an academic turn.

"Well, if he is not at the State Fair, where is he? Driver, for heaven's sake, start somewhere!"

The chauffeur hastily cut his car out into the street. Poggioli continued his analysis—

"Well, knowing the character of Dr. Sanchez as I do, and realizing that he was once dictator of a South American state, I would say that he is now in one of the largest and most expensive hotels in Miami."

"Which one?"

"I don't know. Name over a few."

Slidenberry blinked after the fashion of a man thinking.

"The Astair, the Floridan, the Everglades, La Luxuriata, the Ferdinand and Isabella—But look here, don't you suppose he has already sold his dope?"

"You mean delivered," prompted Poggioli. "It was in all probability sold before it left Belize. Whether that confounded money-changer was the final purchaser, whether he was Sanchez's tool who handed back the drugs to his employer when he received them from—er—"

"When he received them from you?" supplied Slidenberry dryly.

"Exactly—from me. That's what I have not as yet determined." Poggioli nodded severely, then leaned toward the chauffeur and snapped, "Didn't I tell you to get us to a drug store with a battery of telephones?"

The taxi man became intensely excited.

"Yes, sir; yes, sir—uh—are you two gentlemen real detectives? I've always wanted to be a detective. I—I believe I got talent. I can always figger out how a detective story is goin' to end—ever' time!"

Poggioli became aware of what the fellow was saying.

"Why, no, we're not detectives; Mr. Slidenberry is a customs inspector and I am a research man in criminal psychology."

"Oh," ejaculated the chauffeur, deeply disappointed. "I beg you-all's pardon, I'm sure." And he addressed himself to his driving.

THE CAB presently halted in front of a drug store. The two principals hurried inside to the cashier, had a dollar changed into nickels and disappeared in the telephone booths. Poggioli looked up his numbers and began dialing. As he worked he could see the taxicab man outside his glass door, peering in at him with wide eyes and plainly straining his ears to overhear the messages of an officer in pursuit of criminals.

Soon the psychologist had the room clerk of the Ferdinand and Isabella on the wire. He began describing the man whom he and Slidenberry were seeking:

"Dr. Sanchez is an old man, heavy set, dark; a somber, rather distinguished face. He is wearing a brand new suit of clothes, new hat, new shoes, everything new—you couldn't help noticing him."

The voice at the other end of the wire was replying tentatively—

"I don't believe we have such a guest, Mr. Poggioli—"

The psychologist dialed another number and began his description again.

Presently, for some reason of his own, the taxi driver gave up peering and eavesdropping outside the booth and was gone. At first Poggioli thought nothing of this, but continued unsuccessfully with his entire list of hotels. Slidenberry came to his booth door, opened it and stood in silent impatience. After a space he asked in a lowered tone, interrupting the psychologist—

"If he is not in one of the big hotels where do we look next?"

Poggioli shook his head with the receiver to his ear.

"If he suspects I am trying to parallel his psychology, he may have taken an illogical step to throw me off."

The customs inspector made an annoyed gesture.

"Forget all that stuff for a minute!" he begged in an undertone. "Tell me what you think of our chauffeur."

Poggioli removed his receiver a little blankly.

"What is there to think of our chauffeur?"

"Why, hadn't you noticed how snoopy he is? I took a look outside just now and he's not in his cab. You don't suppose he's shadowing us, do you? You know, tipping off somebody where we are?"

Poggioli was taken aback at the idea.

"I should think not. It is almost inconceivable that Sanchez should have such an elaborate organization that he would own the very chauffeur in the street—"

"Just step out of that booth and take a look," directed Slidenberry in a low tone. "When I didn't find him in his car, it just struck me maybe he was telephoning too. Well, there you are."

Poggioli was out of his booth now, looking in the direction the inspector indicated. On a long slant they could just see the chauffeur's back in one of the cubicles.

"He'll say," predicted Slidenberry bitingly, "that he's telephoning his wife that he can't be home for dinner."

At that moment the door of the suspected booth was flung open, the chauffeur dashed out and whirled to his employer.

"I've got your man!" he flung out excitedly.

Slidenberry was taken aback at this sudden turn.

"What do you mean—got our man?"

"Why, located him! I been phoning hotels too." He showed a handful of nickels he had not used. "I used the same description you fellows did. He's at the beach hotel, Las Palmas, registered under the name of Ferro."

The customs officer stared, then struck the knob of a booth door in exasperation.

"Dern it, I didn't telephone Las Palmas because that was your hotel, Mr. Poggioli! I didn't dream he would walk right into the place you were stopping at!"

"Neither did I!" ejaculated the scientist. "I assumed subconsciously that he would go to some other hotel. Here, let's get over there."

"Look here," begged the taxi driver as they rushed for the curb, "if I did that much I may do something else. You never can tell. Why won't you fellers take me on full time on this trip—give me a break?"

"Listen," interrupted Slidenberry, "there's nothing else to do. This Dr. Sanchez ran a lot of dope through customs, and we're going to the Hotel Las Palmas and pinch him and it. You've done everything you can do already. I appreciate it. Both of us appreciate it."

"And you won't take me on as a reg'lar detective?"

"Damn it, we can't; we're not detectives. If you want to be a detective why don't you get somewhere where detective work is going on?"

"Well, doggone it," cried the chauffeur wildly, "could you suggest some place like that?"

BY THIS TIME the trio had reached Las Palmas on the beach. All three leaped out and rushed into the lobby. A desk man, who evidently was expecting them, came forward at once with a pass key.

"Mr. Ferro is in 610, Mr. Slidenberry," said the desk man in a lowered tone. "The management would appreciate it if you would get him out with as little publicity as possible."

"That'll be all right," said the chauffeur to the clerk. "I have curtains on my cab, you know, that the youngsters use on necking parties. We can pull them down, and nobody will know who we got inside."

The clerk glanced at the chauffeur, then looked again at Slidenberry.

"I mean, I hope you have a Maxim silencer on your guns if you have to use them. There are the local elevators on your left."

The trio turned to the bank of elevators. Mr. Poggioli entered the cage with a certain annoyed reluctance. On such an expedition as this he invariably forgot the physical danger in the mental problem it posited. Now that the desk man had called the hazard to his mind, it struck him as idiotic to expose an exceptional intellect, such as his own, on a chore which any corner policeman could accomplish.

On the sixth floor of Hotel Las Palmas the psychologist lingered behind his two companions; and when they reached the door of 610 he was several paces to their rear. Slidenberry paused outside the room, turned and silently extended a revolver. Seeing only the chauffeur in reach, he said—

"Here, take this and if anybody fires from the inside when I turn the key, you shoot back!"

The taxi man accepted the post gratefully.

"This may not be using my head in a detective way," he whispered, "but it's part of the work, ain't it?"

"Possibly it is not using your head," corroborated Mr. Poggioli, "but, as you suggest, it is part of the work."

Complete silence followed this observation. Slidenberry lifted his fist and rapped.

"Open the door in the name of the law!" he called.

There was no answer. The customs inspector nodded warningly at the chauffeur, put in his key and turned the bolt. Nothing happened. Slidenberry pushed open the door. He and the taxi driver peered in from the sides of the entrance, then they entered cautiously. After a moment Slidenberry stepped back and growled to Poggioli:

"Damn the luck! We're late; he's sold his dope, blowed his coin on a dame, jumped the hotel and beat it. Here's the whole story right before your eyes."

When Poggioli entered, the bedroom presented a very simple face. It was in disorder; the bed was disarranged; a tray with two glasses and an empty bottle sat on a table; near a dresser on the floor lay a woman's compact; some pieces of torn newspaper were tossed into a corner, and a carafe of ice water had been overturned on a side table.

The taxi driver stood looking around the room with narrowed eyes.

"Love nest," he diagnosed, then glanced at Poggioli to see whether he had made a mistake.

"Well, I suppose this ends our chase," suggested Slidenberry, glumly studying the layout.

"Can't we go on and catch him somewhere else?" asked the taxi man hopefully.

"Why, no, there wouldn't be any use," snapped the customs inspector. "He's evidently got rid of his dope. It's gone. If we pick him up now we won't have a shred of evidence against him except a five-bolivar piece hollowed out, and what does that prove?"

The taxi man was sharply excited at the idea of a hollow five-bolivar piece. This was the kind of thing he had encountered over and over in detective fiction, and it breathed of romance.

"I say, that's great," he praised. "A hollow dollar, what do you know about that! Well, now I suppose it's up to us to collect all this junk here for clews, ain't it?"

He set to work gathering up the bottles, glasses and newspaper in a bundle. Slidenberry glanced at him in distaste.

"What you going to do with that stuff?"

"Why, study 'em, of course," said the chauffeur.

"Oh, nonsense," disparaged the inspector.

Mr. Poggioli moved over to the bed and picked up a hairpin from the rumpled spread. He turned it in his fingers.

"That's odd," he observed slowly. "The woman was a brunette."

"How do you know she was?" asked the chauffeur quickly, giving up his own research for the moment.

"It's a black hairpin," explained the psychologist absently, "you know that blondes wear light pins."

"Why, sure," agreed the taxi driver, "that isn't hard to figger out," and he turned to his own collection to see if it suggested anything to his mind.

Slidenberry went a little deeper into the matter.

"Well, what is there odd about it if she is a brunette?" he asked, slightly out of patience.

"Nothing, except Dr. Sanchez himself is very dark, and if he were casually choosing a woman he'd pick a blonde, so I should say this was not a casual amour as you gentlemen seem to think."

Slidenberry stood frowning in the middle of the floor.

"Will you please tell me what difference it makes what kind of an amour it was, if the fellow's gone?"

MR. POGGIOLI went over to the dresser and picked up the compact. He examined it, sniffed at the powder, scrutinized the lipstick. He held up a hand at the inspector's continued grumbling.

"Gentlemen," he stated, "this has not been a love affair at all. The woman who came here was a business woman, forty or forty-five years of age—a large brunette, dresses very plainly, avoids jewelry and is of a highly ingenious and subtle turn of mind. In fact, judging from this compact, I am sure it was she who hit on the idea of rumpling this room up like a deserted love nest to make it appear that Sanchez had disposed of his opiates and that further search for him would be futile. Incidentally, I will add that this woman is quite wealthy and that she made her money by herself."

To this extended analysis the chauffeur listened with distended eyes and finally gasped in a husky voice—

"My Lord, Mr. Poggioli, do you mean to say you doped all that out from a compact? How in this wide world—"

"Yes, I'd like to be let in on that," put in the inspector skeptically.

"It's very simple," returned the psychologist. "She is a large woman, because her compact is of plain silver. Small women choose flashy toiletries. She is middle aged, because her lipstick has about dried up. Young girls use up a lipstick long before it dries; middle aged women do not. She is wealthy and secretive and subtle, because she purchased a solid gold mirror and put it in a simple silver case. Any woman who buys expensive interiors and hides them in plain covers is not only wealthy, but must have achieved wealth through her own efforts and be cunning rather than straightforward. That's why I knew the appearance of this room was the woman's idea."

The chauffeur was astonished.

"Well I be derned! That's just as plain as A B C now you mention it. I swear, anybody could have seen that." He went back to work on his glasses, bottles and paper with increased determination.

"Then this must not have been a petting party after all?" suggested Slidenberry, impressed by Poggioli's analysis.

"Certainly not. I am quite sure she was the woman to whom the delivery of the dope was made. This compact ought to simplify our problem very much. There can't be many women such as she in Miami."

At this the two listeners combed their minds in their respective ways. The chauffeur stood frowning and at intervals snapping his fingers as various solutions occurred to him and were discarded. Slidenberry mumbled over and over—

"Large brunette business woman, wealthy, cunning—"

"And of course a dealer in illicit goods," prompted Poggioli, "since she was receiving and no doubt buying a considerable amount of narcotics."

Slidenberry suddenly looked up.

"Why, that's—" Then he closed his lips and shook his head. "No, no, it couldn't have been she. She wouldn't stoop—"

"I know who you're talking about," chirped in the taxi man, "but she doesn't deal in illicit goods, does she?"

"Whom are you referring to?" asked Poggioli with interest.

"Why I'm talking about Madame Aguilar, who runs the speakeasy on Esmeralda Boulevard," stated the chauffeur, and he looked at Slidenberry.

The inspector nodded.

"I had Madame Aguilar in mind for the moment. She does fit the description, but I'm sure it isn't she. She has the respect of every business man in Miami and the confidence and the cooperation of the police. I know she wouldn't abuse it by turning a high class speakeasy into a hop joint."

"We might go down there and look into her place," suggested Poggioli.

The other two men agreed reluctantly. The chauffeur began gathering his bottles, pieces of paper and glasses in a bundle. He reached for the compact in Poggioli's hands.

Slidenberry turned to him, annoyed.

"What do you want with that?" he demanded.

The taxi man moistened his lips.

"Why, I—I had a little idea."

"Yes, what was it?"

"I thought I would just hand the compact to Madame Aguilar and tell her I had found it and ask her if it was hers."

Poggioli looked at his man with an odd annoyance.

"Listen," he advised, "if she should say it did belong to her, she wouldn't be the woman who lost it here."

The taxi man's mouth dropped open.

"She wouldn't be the woman?"

"No, the woman who came to this room would never be caught in so infantile a ruse as that."

The chauffeur stared a moment longer, then grew brick-red in the face, made a last fastening to his bag of clews, and the three men started for the elevator and the street level.

IN THE lobby Slidenberry telephoned police headquarters for a squad of plainclothesmen to meet him in Madame Aguilar's speakeasy on Esmeralda Boulevard. He directed them to go in, order their drinks in the usual way but be on watch for a signal from him to raid the place.

The psychologist was distinctly discomfited at such a procedure. For the squad of men to get up and draw pistols rasped his concept of life as an intellectual adventure.

"What will you and your men do when they place everybody under arrest?"

"Why, search the place for narcotics, of course," said Slidenberry in surprise.

The psychologist shook his head slowly.

"You don't want to start the raid until you know exactly where the drugs are hidden," he advised.

The inspector looked at his companion.

"Not search for them until we know where they are? My Lord, man, that's equivalent to keeping out of the water until one learns to swim! Why not search?"

"Because both Sanchez and Madame Aguilar are Venezuelans," replied the psychologist incisively.

"What's that got to do with it?"

"Because the moment men begin a physical search for anything their bodily movements prevent any real mental novelty of search. To run about, peering here and there in every corner, is the most primitive form of search. But, remember, when one reproduces primitive movements, one automatically reproduces the primitive mind-set which accompanies those movements, and therefore one would never find anything hidden with forethought. The only way to hunt for anything is to sit absolutely still and relax."

The chauffeur said in amazement that he had never thought of that, but that he saw it. Slidenberry inquired with considerable satire why so many physical searches turned out very prosperously indeed?

"That's because you were searching for hoards hidden by Anglo-Saxons, men of your own race. Their instinct toward concealment paralleled your own. But if you were searching for something hidden by a Venezuelan, you'd never find it, because the Anglo-Saxon mind and the Latin mind are irrational planes, one to the other."

Slidenberry laughed ironically and asked Poggioli if he could think up an example of something he could not possibly find.

"Certainly, suppose I should dissolve a narcotic and soak it up in a sponge, it would be safe enough from your men."

Slidenberry's mouth dropped open.

"Good Lord, we wouldn't find it like that, would we? I must tell the boys to watch out for wet sponges."

"Don't bother; it won't be in a sponge," assured the scientist.

"How do you know it won't?"

"Because that's an Italian idea. I'm of Italian descent."

The chauffeur shook his head in bewilderment.

"My stars, what a man!"

SANS SOUCI, Madame Aguilar's speakeasy, had the usual simple façade, peephole and two locked doors common to hundreds of thousands of such establishments in America. What distinguished it from the others was an interior characterized by a quiet restfulness and unity of style.

Madame Aguilar had done Sans Souci in painstaking mission style, possibly not so much out of choice as in deference to the prevailing Florida taste for that type of architecture. The interior of Sans Souci suggested a mission church, and the special alcoves around it reminded one of chapels. There were even candles and pictures on the walls of these alcoves and a sheaf of paper spills to touch off the wicks when a guest entered.

The three men had hardly seated themselves at a table when the customs inspector leaned forward and said in an undertone—

"Look yonder by the window; there sits Sanchez!"

The chauffeur became excited at once.

"Why don't you go over and arrest him?" he whispered.

Slidenberry frowned in annoyance.

"Damn it, the trouble nowadays is not in finding bootleggers and dope sellers! Everybody knows who they are and what they're doing; the trick is in getting legal evidence to prove it, and in picking a jury that'll convict them when it's proved. Now, there's that bird, sold his dope, collected his pay and is as free as the air!"

"I swear," sympathized the chauffeur, "I wish to the devil some of these clews would hook up with that old geezer!" He peered down under the table edge at the bundle in his lap, trying to find something in it that would incriminate the smuggler.

Slidenberry touched Poggioli's arm.

"Look here," he whispered nervously, "have you thought out where to look yet? We're going to have to do something. The boys are looking to me for a signal."

"You mean the plainclothesmen? Have they come?"

"Why, yes, that's them—among those tables."

The psychologist fingered his chin.

"Well, it struck me that there is a false note somewhere in the period decorations of those cabinets."

The inspector looked at his companion in bewilderment.

"False note in—Listen, man, my men have got to do something. If they don't Madame Aguilar will get suspicious this isn't a liquor raid and then we'll never find anything at all. Now, unless you know where the stuff is we've got to hunt for it!"

"Wait! Not now," begged the psychologist. "Plague the luck, I almost had my finger on it—"

"On what?"

"The connection between the decorations and a possible hiding place."

"Oh, I see; that's more like it. Now work it out quick. The first thing you know that old devil over by the window will walk out of here and we haven't got anything on him to stop him."

In the midst of this anxiety the chauffeur grabbed Slidenberry's shoulder.

"Say, I got it!"

"Got what?"

"Where the dope is! Mr. Poggioli was right, you can find out more setting on your bottom than you can by getting on your feet!"

"What is it you've found out either way?"

"Why, the dope's in the water," whispered the chauffeur dramatically. "You know, what they serve in glasses. I been watching that yellow haired man in the cabinet yonder. He hasn't eat nothing a-tall. Jest drunk his water and went to sleep!" The taxi man nodded slightly, but urgently, toward one of the booths.

Slidenberry touched Poggioli.

"Is this chap right?"

The psychologist shook his head.

"No, that's an echo of my sponge theory. Say, how did the Spanish priests in this country carry around their fires?"

THE inspector made a gesture of hopelessness and was about to give a signal to the plainclothesmen when a large, rather heavily built brunette woman approached their table. She was almost handsome, but her dark eyes were too impersonal and her lips too thin and resolute.

When she reached the men the chauffeur began a nervous fumbling among his clews. Slidenberry kicked him under the table. The woman paused with a chill polite smile.

"I would appreciate it, Inspector, if you would start your raid and get it over with," she suggested. "Your men make my patrons nervous. And, by the way, I hope in the future to relieve the police of this routine work."

"How's that?" asked Slidenberry amiably.

"Why, I made a little donation to Reverend Harshberger's church on Poinciana Avenue last Sunday. I'll visit the other churches soon." She lifted her jet-black brows with serious implication and passed on among her other guests.

The chauffeur watched her go with wide eyes.

"What did she mean by that?"

Slidenberry was full of repressed wrath.

"You idiot, you came within a squeak of pulling out that damned compact and asking if it was hers!"

"Yeh, don't you think it would have been the think?"

"The thing! It would have advertised to her that this wasn't a liquor raid but a dope search. She thinks we've been egged on to this by the preachers here in Miami. You heard her telling us that she believed she could buy them off too. That would have been the devil of a note for you to pull out that compact and let her know where we got it."

The chauffeur was taken aback.

"Well, I'm just starting in detective work, Mr. Slidenberry."

"M-huh, use your head and be more thorough if you're going to work with one."

"Mr. Slidenberry," chattered the chauffeur, "d-does that mean you've taken me on for keeps?"

"No, it means I haven't kicked you out yet, but I will if you make another break like that."

"Yes, sir," said the chauffeur gratefully; he considered this as something in the nature of a contract to hire.

The inspector turned to the psychologist.

"We've got to do something, Mr. Poggioli. If you haven't got anything figured out, we'll have to start a search."

The psychologist was just opening his lips to ask for a longer reprieve when a waiter with a tray of dishes crossed the dining room to the booth where the man was sleeping.

The scientist leaned forward, watched the waiter intently for a moment and then turned to the customs officer.

"Listen, would indirect proof of the sale of narcotics be satisfactory?"

"Why, certainly, if it's conclusive."

The psychologist made a gesture.

188   Dr. Poggioli: Criminologist

"Then go ahead. It is not the line I had hoped to pursue, but it doesn't admit of a shadow of doubt."

Precisely what signal Slidenberry gave Poggioli did not know, but simultaneously, here and there among the tables, half a dozen men stood up with drawn revolvers. Some one called out that every one was under arrest. A hubbub broke out in the speakeasy. Half a dozen men who had never before been caught in a raid tried to sneak to the door, but were stopped by the officers. Poggioli heard one man saying that he didn't know he was in a speakeasy, that he thought it was an ordinary restaurant.

But the greater part of the crowd were veterans and began laughing and kidding or complaining according to their kidney.

Madame Aguilar came down the aisle to Slidenberry. She asked, with a business-like expression, whether it would be necessary for her to appear personally in court or whether she might simply send the money by her lawyer.

Slidenberry wore the hard, gratified look of an officer making a deserved arrest.

"You'll have to come to headquarters, madame. This isn't a liquor charge."

The woman gave him a quick look.

"Not a liquor charge?"

"No, we are picking you up for selling narcotics."

The woman's face underwent a sudden and rather shocking change.

"You damned stool pigeon," she screamed, "trying to ruin a respectable place! Some other speakeasy paid you to do this!"

Her invective rose to a shriek, and the next moment the woman was at Slidenberry with her nails in his face.

The customs inspector dodged, turned over his chair, then grabbed Madame Aguilar's arms and held them down. She tried to bite. The plainclothesmen rushed to the two, jerked away Madame Aguilar and stood holding her by the arms. The woman continued her oaths and tried to kick.

The crowd collected around the center of turmoil, demanding to know what was the matter. The closer ones began telling those behind them:

"Pinched her for selling dope!"

"Dope, why this ain't a hop joint!"

"I don't believe it!"

A belligerent voice among the customers demanded to know what proof the officers had for such a charge. A plainclothesman snapped back that the proof would be presented in the police court.

"It's a frame-up!" screamed the woman.

Half a dozen voices took it up:

"Sure, it's a frame-up! The madame wouldn't do a thing like that! Come on, everybody, let's break up these prohibition racketeers!"

The crowd surged toward the officers. Slidenberry saw what was coming and shouted for the crowd to stand back and listen to the proof. In the momentary lull he called out hastily that Mr. Poggioli, the world famed expert in criminal psychology, would explain how he knew that Madame Aguilar was dealing in narcotics.

"Ladies and gentlemen, listen to Dr. Poggioli!"

THE scientist oriented himself in the face of this unexpected publicity. He pointed at the man in the booth.

"I think you will all agree this man is doped. Look at him; and, to make this absolutely certain, at the police station, we will use the stomach pump to make sure of what he has swallowed, take blood tests and nerve reactions in his present condition and in his normal condition—"

A trim, bellicose man of legal aspect, who later turned out to be from the office of the attorney-general, asked in a sharp cross-questioning voice why Mr. Poggioli assumed the man had taken the dope in Madame Aguilar's speakeasy.

"Why couldn't he have had his dope on the outside and then walked into the place?" demanded the lawyer.

"That's impossible!" retorted Poggioli with academic brevity. "I had thought of such a possibility, but when I saw the waiter bringing dinner to the doped man, I knew it was impossible for the fellow to have got the drugs anywhere but here."

The crowd stared in perplexity. The man from the State's attorney's office asked in a guarded irony—

"Would you mind explaining the connection between the two, Dr. Poggioli?"

"Certainly I'll explain. To a man under the influence of opiates food is obnoxious. The most he would have ordered is broth. But this is a full dinner. Therefore, he must have taken the opiate after he had ordered his dinner or he never would have ordered the food at all."

There was a silence which was broken by the chauffeur's marveling—

"Now, anybody could have thought of that if it had jest crossed their mind."

This moment of confused and admiring belief felt by all the crowd was shattered by the lawyer.

"What kind of evidence is this you're bringing up against a good woman's reputation? A man orders his dinner and goes to sleep, so a woman—God's last best gift to man—is guilty of peddling the damnable curse of drugs!" He whined to his hearers. "Men of the South! Floridians! Will you stand by and see such an insult put on one of the fair sex? No! You know you won't! Come on!"

The crowd swung forward again when Slidenberry shouted:

"Wait! Wait a minute! My Lord, I didn't know I was ordering an arrest on any such damn fool proof as that. Wait, give me a chance to make an orderly search. If we can't find any dope, that ends it. That's fair, people, that's fair, isn't it?"

The speakeasy patrons tacitly agreed to the fairness of this and fell into an angry buzzing among themselves that Madame Aguilar had been subjected to such treatment. The plainclothesmen scattered through the restaurant looking everywhere for the drugs. The spectators presently began jeering the searchers, calling out:

"Look in the sink!"

"Look in the sugar bowls!"

There was a good deal of laughter at these thrusts. Poggioli went over to Slidenberry.

"There is no possibility of their finding anything. In a polyglot civilization like ours, the law will have to accept psychologic proof or our whole social structure will go to pot."

"I don't care a damn about our social structure," growled Slidenberry, "and not much about the madame; it's that leather-colored old devil by the window that I'm after!"

In the midst of these grumblings a waiter walked across to the booth in which the drugged man slept and snuffed out the two candles burning over the table.

As he did so a sudden revelation burst on Poggioli.

"By George, I've got it!" he cried. "The old Spanish monks used wax tapers to light their devotional candles!"

Every one looked around at the exclamation. Slidenberry was embarrassed.

"What's that got to do with anything?" he inquired.

"Why, simple enough. Madame Aguilar substituted spills for tapers."

"Well, what if she did?"

"She is a woman of enormous attention to detail. She would not have been guilty of such an anachronism without a powerful and practical reason. The only reason she can possibly have is for a use of the spills which she could not accomplish with tapers. Well, spills will hold something; tapers won't. Come on, let's unroll the spills."

AS HE strode toward the booths the crowd followed and the chauffeur called out in amazement—

"Mr. Poggioli, how in the world did you come to think about the spills when you saw the waiter put out the candles?"

At the query the psychologist assumed automatically his old college classroom manner.

"Simple enough, young man; the waiter took time to snuff out the candles even in the midst of all this excitement, so, of course, that made it all clear."

The chauffeur leaned forward and frowned.

"I don't quite see what that had to do—with anything."

Poggioli was surprised.

"Why, it showed the necessity of putting out the candles had been drilled into the waiter until he performed the chore automatically. This suggested that the extinguishing of the candles was of prime importance in Madame Aguilar's business, or why should she have so stressed the act." The psychologist glanced at the crowd. "Of course, the rest of my reasoning is clear to you all."

The chauffeur nodded, half hypnotized by his attempt to follow the thought.

"Yeh—yeh," he agreed, nodding his smallish head on his largish body. "I—I think I see it. Now—"

Somebody in the middle of the restaurant yelled:

"Naw, he don't see it, and I don't either. I don't see how the devil—"

Poggioli shrugged.

"There are always one or two like that."

Then he became sarcastically explicit.

"Now listen," he advised in a complete silence. "Extinguishing the candles was important. Why? Because that allowed them to be relighted for each guest. Relighting was important. Why? Because a spill could be taken from the holder easily and naturally without arousing anybody's suspicion. This was important. Why? Because the upper end of a spill can be touched in a flame, a candle lighted, the spill extinguished before it has burned away half an inch and the remainder of the paper roll can be dropped very naturally and casually on a patron's table. Nobody would possibly suspect that a delivery of illicit—"

A variety of "oh's" and "uh-huh's" and "I see's" trickled over the crowd at the scientist's virtuosity.

A plainclothesman already was at the holders unrolling the spills. Presently a thin powder sifted from one of the rolls.

Slidenberry shouted at the man and made a desperate effort to catch some of the vanishing evidence.

Poggioli waggled a finger.

"Don't bother. There's plenty more left."

"But look here, will we get it all in these spills? S'pose it's all here?"

"Why, no, not likely. I fancy the madame put out what she thought she could use today."

"Then where's the rest?" cried the inspector. "I've got to get the whole—"

"That's another problem," answered the psychologist. "But get these people out, stop these plainclothesmen from jiggling about and we'll sit down and reason out where Madame Aguilar must have secreted the remainder of her hoard."

The plainclothesmen were getting them out just as fast as they could. They were huddling Madame Aguilar, her waiters and her guests toward the door. The lawyer who had so eloquently defended the madame already had got out the door. He knew the officer at the exit and had no trouble getting clear of the speakeasy. The rest of the crowd was herded toward the police van outside.

Slidenberry started another complaint.

"That damned leather-colored smuggler who brought all this in here—not a scratch to prove it actually was him. The madame will deny that was her compact. That hollow bolivar we've got will be laughed out of court. We haven't a Chinaman's chance to pin nothing—"

In the midst of this the chauffeur timidly touched Slidenberry's elbow.

"Uh—er—would you mind looking at this a minute, Mr. Slidenberry?"

"What the hell do you want now?"

"Why these here spills, sir—the ones that had the dope in 'em—some of 'em were torn out of this newspaper I picked up in Las Palmas in the old man's bedroom."

Slidenberry turned and stared.

"They do! How long have you known that?"

"Why ever since I got the first 'un to fit, of course."

"Why in the hell didn't you tell me at once?"

"Why—why—I was trying to make all the spills fit, Mr. Slidenberry. You—you said a detective had ought to be thorough."

A Poggioli Bibliography

T. S. Stribling never wrote a Poggioli novel. The following are the known short stories and novelettes starring Professor Henry Poggioli, Ph.D. There may be more Poggioli stories out there, forgotten or unrecorded. If you come across one, please alert the publisher (at P.O. Box 9315, Norfolk, VA 23505) and the editor (at P.O. Box 313, Williston Park, NY 11596-0313). The editor wishes to thank Richard Moore for his invaluable assistance in compiling this bibliography, and all Poggioli fans should extend a tip of the hat to Joseph Wrzos, who (shortly before this book was to go to press) discovered "The Newspaper," a Poggioli tale not listed in any prior Poggioli or Stribling bibliography.

A. The Three Collections of Poggioli Stories

1. *Clues of the Caribbees, Being Certain Criminal Investigations of Henry Poggioli, Ph.D.* Garden City: Doubleday Doran, 1929; London: William Heinemann, 1930. Reprinted, New York: Dover, 1977.
2. *Best Dr. Poggioli Detective Stories* [ed. E. F. Bleiler]. New York: Dover, 1975.
3. *Dr. Poggioli: Criminologist*, ed. Arthur Vidro. Norfolk: Crippen & Landru, 2004.

B. The Individual Stories

1. "The Refugees." *Adventure*, October 10, 1925. Reprinted in *The New Mammoth Golden Book of Best Detective Stories* (1934); *The Saint Detective Magazine*, June/July 1953 as "Poggioli and the Refugees"; and *Classic Stories of Crime and Detection* (1976), ed. Jacques Barzun and Wendell Hertig Taylor. Collected in *Clues of the Caribbees* (1929).
2. "The Governor of Cap Haitien" [novelette]. *Adventure*, November 10, 1925. Collected in *Clues of the Caribbees* (1929).
3. "Cricket." *Adventure*, December 10, 1925. Collected in *Clues of the Caribbees* (1929).
4. "The Prints of Hantoun." *Adventure*, January 20, 1926. Reprinted in *Sleuths: Twenty-Three Great Detectives of Fiction and Their Best*

Stories (1931 or 1932), ed. Kenneth MacGowan. Collected in *Clues of the Caribbees* (1929).
5. "A Passage to Benares." *Adventure*, February 20, 1926. Reprinted in *The New Mammoth Golden Book of Best Detective Stories* (1934); *Great American Detective Stories* (1945), ed. Anthony Boucher; *The Arbor House Treasury of Mystery and Suspense* (1981), ed. Bill Pronzini, Barry N. Malzberg, and Martin H. Greenberg; and *The Great American Mystery Stories of the Twentieth Century* (1989). Collected in *Clues of the Caribbees* (1929).
6. "A Pearl at Pampatar." *Adventure*, June 1, 1929. Collected in *Dr. Poggioli: Criminologist* (2004).
7. "Shadowed" [novelette]. *Adventure*, October 15, 1930. Collected in *Dr. Poggioli: Criminologist* (2004).
8. "The Resurrection of Chin Lee." *Adventure*, April 15, 1932. Reprinted in *101 Years' Entertainment: The Great Detective Stories* (1941), ed. Ellery Queen. Collected in *Dr. Poggioli: Criminologist* (2004).
9. "Bullets." *Adventure*, May 1, 1932. Reprinted in *Challenge to the Reader* (1938), ed. Ellery Queen; and *Half-a-Hundred: Tales by Great American Writers* (1945), ed. Charles Grayson. Collected in *Dr. Poggioli: Criminologist* (2004).
10. "The Cablegram." *Adventure*, November 1, 1932. Reprinted in *Ellery Queen's Mystery Magazine*, Fall 1941; *Best Stories from Ellery Queen's Mystery Magazine* (1944), ed. Ellery Queen; *Rogues' Gallery* (1945), ed. Ellery Queen; *Contraband: Stories of Smuggling the World Over* (1967), ed. Phyllis R. Fenner; and *Stories Not to Be Missed* (1978; one of a 20-volume set *Masters of Mystery*), ed. Ellery Queen. Collected in *Dr. Poggioli: Criminologist* (2004).
11. "The Pink Colonnade." *Adventure*, February 1, 1933. Collected in *Dr. Poggioli: Criminologist* (2004).
12. "Private Jungle." *Blue Book*, August 1933. Collected in *Dr. Poggioli: Criminologist* (2004).
13. "The Shadow." *Red Book*, February 1934. Reprinted in *Twentieth Century Detective Stories* (1948), ed. Ellery Queen; *Nero Wolfe Mystery Magazine*, June 1954; and *Twelve American Detective Stories* (1997), ed. Edward D. Hoch. Collected in *Dr. Poggioli: Criminologist* (2004).
14. "The Newspaper." *The Big Magazine*, March 1935. Collected in *Dr. Poggioli: Criminologist* (2004).
15. "The Mystery of the Chief of Police." *Ellery Queen's Mystery Magazine*, July 1945. Reprinted in *To the Queen's Taste* (1946), ed. Ellery Queen. Collected in *Best Dr. Poggioli Detective Stories* (1975).
16. "The Mystery of the Sock and the Clock." *Ellery Queen's Mystery Magazine*, January 1946. Collected in *Best Dr. Poggioli Detective Stories* (1975).

17. "The Mystery of the Paper Wad." *Ellery Queen's Mystery Magazine*, July 1946. This story is uncollected.
18. "Count Jalacki Goes Fishing." *Ellery Queen's Mystery Magazine*, September 1946. Reprinted in *The Queen's Awards, 1946* (1946), ed. Ellery Queen. Collected in *Best Dr. Poggioli Detective Stories* (1975).
19. "A Note to Count Jalacki." *Ellery Queen's Mystery Magazine*, October 1946. Collected in *Best Dr. Poggioli Detective Stories* (1975).
20. "The Mystery of the 81st Kilometer Stone." *Ellery Queen's Mystery Magazine*, July 1947. Reprinted in *The Queen's Awards, 1947* (1947), ed. Ellery Queen; and *The Saint Detective Magazine*, September 1959 as "Suggestion of Death." Collected in *Best Dr. Poggioli Detective Stories* (1975).
21. "The Mystery of the Seven Suicides." *Ellery Queen's Mystery Magazine*, April 1948. Collected in *Best Dr. Poggioli Detective Stories* (1975).
22. "A Daylight Adventure." *Ellery Queen's Mystery Magazine*, March 1950. Reprinted in *Ellery Queen's Anthology, Volume V* (1963), ed. Ellery Queen; and *The Oxford Book of American Detective Stories* (1996), ed. Tony Hillerman and Rosemary Herbert. Collected in *Best Dr. Poggioli Detective Stories* (1975).
23. "The Mystery of the Personal Ad." *Ellery Queen's Mystery Magazine*, May 1950. Collected in *Best Dr. Poggioli Detective Stories* (1975).
24. "The Mystery of the Choir Boy." *Ellery Queen's Mystery Magazine*, January 1951. This story is uncollected.
25. "The Mystery of Andorus Enterprises." *Ellery Queen's Mystery Magazine*, September 1951. Collected in *Best Dr. Poggioli Detective Stories* (1975).
26. "The Mystery of the Half-Painted House." *Ellery Queen's Mystery Magazine*, April 1952. Collected in *Best Dr. Poggioli Detective Stories* (1975).
27. "Death Deals Diamonds." *Famous Detective Stories*, November 1952. This story is uncollected.
28. "Figures Don't Die." *Famous Detective Stories*, February 1953. This story is uncollected.
29. "The Warning on the Lawn." *Ellery Queen's Mystery Magazine*, March 1953. Collected in *Best Dr. Poggioli Detective Stories* (1975).
30. "Dead Wrong." *Smashing Detective Stories*, March 1953. This story is uncollected.
31. "The Mystery of the Five Money Orders." *Ellery Queen's Mystery Magazine*, March 1954. This story is uncollected.
32. "Poggioli and the Fugitive." *The Saint Detective Magazine*, December 1954. Collected in *Best Dr. Poggioli Detective Stories* (1975).
33. "The Telephone Fisherman." *Ellery Queen's Mystery Magazine*, January 1955. Collected in *Best Dr. Poggioli Detective Stories* (1975).

34. "Murder at Flowtide." *The Saint Detective Magazine*, March 1955. This story is uncollected.
35. "The Case of the Button." *The Saint Detective Magazine*, September 1955. Collected in *Best Dr. Poggioli Detective Stories* (1975).
36. "Murder in the Hills." *The Saint Detective Magazine*, February 1956. This story is uncollected.
37. "The Man in the Shade." *The Saint Detective Magazine*, April 1957. Collected in *Best Dr. Poggioli Detective Stories* (1975).

Final note: Magazine dates are for American editions. Both *Ellery Queen's Mystery Magazine* and *The Saint Detective Magazine* had British editions; typically the Poggioli stories would see the light of day first in the American edition and later, under a different cover date, in the British edition.

DR. POGGIOLI: CRIMINOLOGIST

Dr. Poggioli: Criminologist by T. S. Stribling, edited by Arthur Vidro, is set in 11-point Times New Roman and printed on 60-pound natural shade acid-free paper. The cover painting is by Barbara Mitchell, and the Lost Classics design is by Deborah Miller. *Dr. Poggioli: Criminologist* was published in October 2004 by Crippen & Landru Publishers, Norfolk, Virginia.

CRIPPEN & LANDRU LOST CLASSICS

Crippen & Landru is proud to publish this series of short story collections by great authors who specialized in traditional mysteries. All first editions, each volume collects "lost" tales from rare pulp, digest, and slick magazines, and each book is edited by a recognized expert in the field.

The Following Books Are in Print

Peter Godfrey, *The Newtonian Egg and Other Cases of Rolf le Roux*, introduction by Ronald Godfrey

Craig Rice, *Murder, Mystery and Malone*, edited by Jeffrey A. Marks

Charles B. Child, *The Sleuth of Baghdad: The Inspector Chafik Stories*

Stuart Palmer, *Hildegarde Withers: Uncollected Riddles*, introduction by Mrs. Stuart Palmer

Christianna Brand, *The Spotted Cat and Other Mysteries From Inspector Cockrill's Casebook*, edited by Tony Medawar

William Campbell Gault, *Marksman and Other Stories*, edited by Bill Pronzini; afterword by Shelley Gault

Gerald Kersh, *Karmesin: The World's Greatest Criminal – Or Most Outrageous Liar*, edited by Paul Duncan

C. Daly King, *The Complete Curious Mr. Tarrant*, introduction by Edward D. Hoch

Helen McCloy, *The Pleasant Assassin and Other Cases of Dr. Basil Willing*, introduction by B.A. Pike

William L. DeAndrea, *Murder – All Kinds*, introduction by Jane Haddam

Anthony Berkeley, *The Avenging Chance and Other Mysteries From Roger Sheringham's Casebook*, edited by Tony Medawar and Arthur Robinson

Joseph Commings, *Banner Deadlines: The Impossible Files of Senator Brooks U. Banner*, edited by Robert Adey

Erle Stanley Gardner, *The Danger Zone and Other Stories*, edited by Bill Pronzini.

T.S. Stribling, *Dr. Poggioli: Criminologist*, edited by Arthur Vidro

The Following Books Are in Preparation

Margaret Millar, *The Couple Next Door: Collected Short Mysteries*, edited by Tom Nolan

Gladys Mitchell, *Sleuth's Alchemy: Cases of Mrs. Bradley and Others*, edited by Nicholas Fuller

Rafael Sabatini, *The Evidence of the Sword*, edited by Jesse Knight

Phillip S. Warne, *Who Was Guilty?: Three Dime Novels*, edited by Marlena Bremseth

Michael Collins, *Slot-Machine Kelly: Early Private-Eye Stories*, introduction by Robert J. Randisi

Julian Symons, *Francis Quarles: Detective*, edited by John Cooper; afterword by Kathleen Symons

Lloyd Biggle, Jr., *The Grandfather Rastin Mysteries*, introduction by Kenneth Biggle

Max Brand, *Masquerade: Nine Crime Stories*, edited by William F. Nolan, Jr.

Hugh Pentecost, *The Battles of Jericho*, introduction by S.T. Karnick

Mignon G. Eberhart, *The E-String Murder*, edited by Rick Cypert and Kirby McCauley.

Erle Stanley Gardner, *The Casebook of Sidney Zoom*, edited by Bill Pronzini

Please check our website for updates: *www.crippenlandru.com*